Linda

Your

and your insights keep me going

Len

Deceived

BY LEN SERAFINO

Deceived

ISBN-13: 978-1720566021
ISBN 10: 172056602X

ALSO BY LEN SERAFINO

Novels

Back to Newark
Keep Breathing
The IOU

Non Fiction

Sales Talk
Baseline to Baseline
-Maximize your tennis
By Robbie McCammon with Len Serafino

Short Stories available,
www.lenserafino.com

For Nancy

BOOK I

1

Blake Stevens decided to take a long overdue shower. He had been grading papers for his Clarksville Regional High School history students since breakfast. Now it was 3:30 in the afternoon on the day after Thanksgiving and he had a six o'clock date later with Claire, the woman he hoped to marry someday. He also wanted to run over to the hospital to see his landlady, Mrs. Cotton, whose COPD was getting worse.

His hot shower done, he had just finished dressing when he noticed a Clarksville police officer in the backyard with a New Jersey State Trooper. The two men were standing next to the detached garage, peering in the garage's side window. The trooper nodded to the officer and the two men walked around to the front of the house.

The weather was miserable that day with freezing rain, wind and even a bit of hail. He had parked his black Camaro in the garage to protect it from the nasty weather that was coming. He didn't think Mrs. Cotton would mind. He had already broken one of her rules by bringing Claire to his upstairs apartment the night before, so breaking one more rule didn't seem to matter. If she found out that Claire spent the night with him, there would be hell to pay. Parking his car in her garage would be a comparatively minor offense.

Blake moved to his living room to see what the men would do next. He couldn't see them, but when his doorbell rang, he knew. What did they want?

He went downstairs and opened the door. Now he recognized the Clarksville officer's face, having seen him around the tiny, southern New Jersey, town. "How can I help you?" He asked.

"I'm Officer Charlie Tanner. This is State Trooper, Tom McDade. May we come in? We want to ask you a few questions."

Blake led them up the stairs and into his tiny kitchen. "What's this about?"

"Did you take a shower today, Mr. Stevens?" McDade asked.

"I just did, why?"

"Won't be anything on his hands," Tanner said.

"I'll take it from here," McDade said, shaking his head at the officer's inexperience in the art of interrogation. "Mr. Stevens, we're investigating an armed robbery and murder in Camden County at the Cherry Hill branch of the Palmyra Bank today. A man was shot and killed. Do you know anything about that?"

"What? No, of course not. What brings you all the way to Clarksville?"

The officer pulled out two photos. Before he showed them to Blake, he said, "I'd like to know your whereabouts today, if you don't mind."

"I've been here all day, except for a trip to the drive through at McDonald's around one o'clock."

The trooper wrote that down. "What did you get at McDonald's?"

Blake laughed. "Is this a joke?"

"Answer the trooper's question, Stevens," Officer Tanner said. Again, McDade gave Tanner a dirty look. Then he looked at Blake and waited.

"What is this about? What's going on here?" Blake asked.

"As I said, we're investigating a serious crime," McDade said. "Now what did you have for lunch today?"

"I had a cheeseburger, fries and an unsweet tea."

McDade nodded and pointed to the trash can. Tanner, taking his cue got up and looked in the trash. He pulled out a bag and the cheeseburger wrapper, plus the French fry container. "Where's your cup, the one with the tea?" he asked.

"Over there, on my desk," Blake answered.

"What did you do today?" McDade asked.

"I graded papers. I'm a history teacher at the high school. As I said, I went out briefly at lunch time to get a bite to eat. I parked the car in the garage when I got back."

"Can anyone verify that?"

Now the alarm sounded for Blake. Until that moment, he was bemused by the officers' inquiries. Suddenly, it occurred to him that, for some reason, these officers were under the impression that he was connected to an armed robbery and a murder. That's why they were looking at his car. "I don't know. As I said, I've been alone here all day."

"How about the people who live on the first floor. Might they have seen you at any time today?"

Since he knew the answer, Officer Tanner spoke up confidently. "The lady who lives downstairs is in the hospital. She lives alone." The trooper gave Tanner another look. There would be nothing further from Charlie Tanner.

The trooper looked carefully at the photos he was holding. "Before I show these to you, would you mind showing me what you were wearing before you showered?"

Blake got up and went into the bedroom. Tanner followed him but didn't say anything. He came out with a black sweatshirt and a pair of jeans with a small tear on the left leg at the knee. "Trooper McDade, I don't know what you're looking for, but you can search my place top to bottom. I haven't been anywhere today, except when I went out for lunch."

"Uh-huh. Now, Mr. Stevens, do you have a Clarksville baseball cap with the letter "C" on it?"

"Yeah, I have three or four of them. Why?"

McDade put the photos down on the table and asked Blake to look at them. Blake was shocked by what he saw. The photos were a bit grainy, but the images were clear enough. The first one he picked up was of a man in his early thirties, about six feet two inches tall, wearing a Clarksville High School ball cap. The man seemed to be looking into the camera, almost as if he was posing. If he didn't know better, Blake would swear he was staring at a photo of his own face. It almost looked like the shot was arranged to make identification easy. The man in the photo looked like Blake, same build, same hair color, but the man in the picture appeared to have slightly longer hair.

The second photo was a picture of a car, a black Chevrolet Camaro, seemingly identical to his. The same man pictured in the first photo appeared to be getting into the front passenger seat. He was wearing jeans and a black pullover shirt.

"Can you explain these photos, Mr. Stevens?" The trooper asked.

Blake stared at the photos. He noticed the date stamp, Friday, November 24th, appeared on each one. "I can't explain it. All I can tell you is I was here all day. You said someone was killed?"

"Yes, a bank customer who tried to stop the robbery. He was just 48 years old, Mr. Stevens, married with three children; a very successful businessman."

"It wasn't me, I don't even own a gun!"

"We have a search warrant for your apartment and the garage," McDade said. "A couple of officers will be here soon to conduct a search. Right now, though, I want you to come with us to the Clarksville Police Department. We have a few more questions."

"I'm not under arrest, am I?" Blake asked.

McDade nodded to Tanner who stood and motioned for Blake to stand. "Mr. Stevens, you are under arrest for suspicion of murder and bank robbery. You have the right to remain silent. Anything you say..." Tanner took pleasure in reading Blake's rights to him. Then he handcuffed him and led him down the stairs and into his patrol car. As they were about to pull away, two other officers pulled into Mrs. Cotton's driveway and got out of their police cruiser. They were there to conduct the search.

In the car, Blake asked if he could make a phone call. "We'll give you a chance to call someone when we get to the station," Tanner said. "You're in deep shit, Stevens."

Blake wondered how they found him. He didn't know anyone in Cherry Hill, except for a few tennis players and staff at the tennis club where he and his friend Parker played occasionally. It seemed that the ball cap was the only thing that would connect whoever did this to Clarksville.

When they got to the police station, Blake was brought to an interrogation room. A tall, thin man with salt and pepper hair, walked into the room and identified himself as Detective Terry Wronko, from the Cherry Hill homicide squad. "Mr. Stevens, we have two photos that appear to be you and we have five eye witnesses, including a security guard, that we're confident can identify you. You can help yourself a great deal by cooperating with us now."

Blake looked at the detective. His eyes were beginning to water now and his throat was tight. "There has to be a mistake, Detective. I was home all day, I swear it. Y'all need to be looking for whoever did this. I mean, somebody had to be driving that car. Have you found him yet?"

"The money you took; you know the bills are all marked, right? Where did you put it?"

"I don't know a thing about this."

Wronko, smiled. "Sooner or later, your partner, whoever was driving your car, is going to spend some of that money. They will be caught. And they'll talk to us, I guarantee you that. I was hoping you would be smart and tell me who your accomplice was. The driver is every bit as guilty as you are. But if your partner talks first, in my experience, he will lay everything he can on you to get a better deal. Now, was it a man or a woman?"

For a moment, Blake started to panic. Would they arrest Claire too? Then he remembered that her whereabouts would be easy to verify. She was volunteering at the church, serving meals to the needy. He took a deep breath and leaned forward toward the detective. "I think I need a lawyer. I'm not saying anything more until I have an attorney present."

The detective nodded. "Suit yourself. He picked up the phone that was seated at the end of the table, handed it to Blake and left the room. Blake pulled out his wallet and searched for the business card Claire's brother-in-law gave him yesterday, during the Clark family's Thanksgiving celebration. Nathan Brower was an attorney with a lucrative law practice in Philadelphia. Blake called his cell and Nathan picked up. "Brower here."

"Nathan, it's Blake. I have a little problem."

"Okay, how can I help?"

"I need a lawyer. I've been arrested for murder and bank robbery."

"What? When did this happen?"

"Apparently, it was some time this morning in Cherry Hill."

"Oh, I heard about that. Why would they arrest you? Are you in Cherry Hill?"

"No, I'm in Clarksville, where I've been all day. This is crazy, Nathan. Can you help me?"

"Let me make a few calls. Don't say anything to anybody, not a word until you see an attorney. I'll call a friend of mine who has a practice in Jersey."

Marie Ventrella Scott was surprised to get a call from Nathan Brower, especially on the day after Thanksgiving. They had been friends in law school, but their paths rarely crossed after they passed the bar exam. Like Nathan, she too had heard about the bank robbery and murder in Cherry Hill. He explained the situation to Marie, how his wife's sister Claire was dating the accused, a guy who had moved to New Jersey from Tennessee about a year ago. Out of friendship as much as professional courtesy, she agreed to check in on Blake Stevens. "I can't commit to taking his case, Nathan. My dance card is already overloaded."

"Understood," Nathan said.

It took Marie Ventrella Scott an hour to drive from her townhouse in Philadelphia's old city neighborhood to Clarksville. She met briefly with the Clarksville police sergeant before being led into the interrogation room where Blake was waiting. She introduced herself to Blake, shaking his hand with a firm grip. Ms. Scott was a petite woman with Italian features and an olive skin tone. A few years short of forty, she wore her dark hair short, which made her look a bit older than she was, a look she deliberately cultivated. She still wore her wedding band in spite of the fact that her husband, a captain in the army, had been killed on his second tour in Iraq five years ago.

She took a seat at the gunmetal gray table and pulled out a file folder. "I've had just enough time for a quick look at the evidence, Mr. Stevens." She pulled out copies of the photos and looked back and forth between them and Blake's face. "I have to say, the man in this photo could be you. The Clarksville police showed them to three different Clarksville residents. All of them said it was you. That, and the ballcap, was how they found you so fast." Marie took another look at the photo and then studied Blake's face again. "Your hair seems a bit shorter, but from their perspective that would just mean you got a haircut or cut it yourself. What can you tell me about this?"

"Nothing, other than it wasn't me," Blake said.

"May I call you Blake?"

"Yes, ma'am, you may. When can I get out of here?"

Marie looked at her watch. "It's almost 7:00 on a Friday night, so I think you may be stuck here, or, more likely, in the Cherry Hill jail, until Monday morning."

Blake sat staring at the table, shaking his head. "I don't believe this."

"Have you had anything to eat?" she asked.

"They asked, but who can eat at a time like this?"

"I need you to be alert and ready to handle the rigors of what lies ahead." She got up and asked if she could have some food for the accused. Ten minutes later a desk cop brought in a hamburger, fries and a Coke, the same meal he had for lunch. Marie walked Blake through his activities, beginning with Thanksgiving Day. She urged him to leave nothing out, not even tiny details. He walked her through the last two days, telling her everything he could remember. Marie smiled when he described his night with Claire, offering a bit more detail than was necessary. She had defended plenty of men and a few women accused of committing capital crimes. This guy just didn't seem to be the type who would do such a thing, but she'd been fooled before.

"Have you ever been to Cherry Hill?"

"Yes, my friend, Parker and I play tennis there at the indoor tennis club."

"When was the last time?"

"Last Saturday."

"Do you have an account with the Palmyra Bank?"

"No."

"Have you ever been in the bank in question?"

"Not to my knowledge."

"What exactly does that mean?"

No, it means no," Blake said. He ate his last bite of hamburger and put the wrapper back in the bag. He finished what was left of his Coke.

Marie reached into her purse and pulled out two cherry flavored Tootsie Roll Pops. She gave one to Blake. "I love these," she said. "I'll be right back."

She went to her car, got in and pulled her cell phone out. She called Nathan and got right to the point. "Does Blake Stevens have any money?" She asked.

"That bad?"

"Nathan, I don't know if your guy did it. He doesn't seem the type, but just for starters they have two pictures of him, one in the bank and one going to a car identical to the one he drives, same make, model and color. When they finish processing whatever they found at the crime scene, who knows what else they're going to find."

"Does he have a credible alibi?"

"Says he was home all day except for a quick stop at McDonald's. Not a soul can corroborate his story though."

Nathan let out a low whistle. "They must have caught him on camera at the McDonald's drive through though."

"You would think so, and of course, I asked about that. The camera's been broken for a week."

Nathan looked at his wife, who was standing nearby. He shook his head and mouthed the words, "Looks bad." He smiled as he listened to a sound from law school days he'd forgotten. "You still sucking on Tootsie Roll Pops?"

"Yeah, sorry. "So, what is this guy's financial situation? As a favor to you, of course, I won't charge him for getting through the arraignment. After that, well, I won't charge my regular rate, but the discount won't be huge."

"Then you'll take his case, busy as you are?" He asked.

"Unless there's something useful he's not telling us, my job will likely be to get him a plea deal."

"Probably best, based on what you told me. I'll break the news to my sister-in-law," Nathan said. "Talk to him about his financial situation, but I don't think it's very good."

"Just what I thought. They'll try to use that as his motive, I'm sure, Marie said."

"Yeah, but a bank? Doesn't make sense."

"Tell me about it. You know what else doesn't make sense?"

"What?" Nathan asked.

"The photos. It was as if he stopped and posed for the camera. No attempt to disguise himself. I mean the guy wore a Clarksville High School cap for goodness sakes."

BOOK II

2

Fifteen Months Earlier

Blake woke up early. He looked over at his bags and again felt the excitement of a new start in a new place. He quickly got ready to hit the road, loading a few last-minute items into the trunk of his black Chevy Camaro. He said goodbye to his Uncle John and Aunt Abigail and hit the road. It wasn't a long ride, less than two hours, but in that short time, he would leave city life in New York, for a small town in southern New Jersey.

As he drove south on the New Jersey Turnpike, he thought about his life before he moved to the New York area. Born and raised in rural Tennessee, it had taken him months to adapt to the frenetic pace of life in Manhattan. He had adapted, but he never fell in love with it. Standing six feet, two inches tall, he preferred to wear jeans, cowboy boots and a Stetson cowboy hat whenever he could. A country boy who had worked on cattle ranches in Tennessee during summer vacations, he felt he had earned the right to dress the part, even in Manhattan.

He found New Yorkers to be a challenge at first. Two weeks after he landed in the city, he got a job as a bartender in an upscale bar and grill, something he had done to earn a few bucks on weekends during his last two years as an undergrad at the University of Tennessee. It took him a while to adjust to what felt like rudeness. The first customer he served had ordered by saying, "Hey, Roy Rogers, two extra dry martinis up, as dry as you can make 'em."

Eventually, he got used to the way New Yorkers talked, their aggressive attitudes, the way they announced, through their words and cadence, that they always knew what they were talking about. He came to realize that many of these men and women were actually very sensitive. They were often surprised to learn that something they said might have caused hurt feelings.

He briefly dated Cameron, a woman he met at the bar, but he knew it would never become serious. For one thing, he wasn't ready for anything serious, not after Nicci disappeared. Cameron had a burning desire to make it to the C-suite. She worked for one of the largest banks in the world. She explained it to Blake on their first date. "I have a killer schedule, one meeting after another. It's a very competitive situation. We all want the same thing," she said. "And then I have to, like, schmooze with my clients at least three nights a week. Last night I had to go to Yankee Stadium. Ever been there?"

"No, I haven't," Blake said.

"Well, you aren't missing anything. The Bronx is a shitty place. Steinbrenner should have moved the team to New Jersey, like the Giants did," she said.

Blake had been amused by Cameron's unrelenting drive to succeed. But, when she pulled out her appointment book at dinner on their third date and said, "If you'd like to do me, you can come to my co-op at 5:45 Tuesday afternoon. I have almost an hour," he dropped her off at her co-op and, politely, wished her well. He really wasn't ready to see anybody.

He did put away his cowboy hat, and learned to dress more like his cosmopolitan customers, but he knew he could never make the Big Apple his home.

He had been able to live in Manhattan because his Uncle John had an apartment there that Blake used for nearly a year while he finished up the work necessary to become a certified teacher in the Garden State. He had been a history teacher in Tennessee before circumstances persuaded him to move on.

By the time he reached his exit on the New Jersey Turnpike that Saturday morning, Blake imagined he had escaped bad luck's gravitational pull, that it had become weaker with every mile. Now, 120 miles south of New York City, he felt like he was finally free of his past, as if he had crossed a point of no return on a one-way journey to good times. He knew it wasn't that simple, but it felt good to believe, if only momentarily, that the past would never haunt him again.

There was a new job waiting for him in Clarksville, a town situated in the southwestern part of the state. Just 50 miles from Philadelphia, Clarksville was in the center of a rural farming area, known for its spinach, potatoes and summer squash. Along with Clarksville, which was the county seat, a few small towns served as focal points for business and social activities. Blake had no desire to return to his home town, Colby Springs, Tennessee, but he longed for the small-town environment he grew up in. From what his Uncle John said, Clarksville was a good choice.

John Major was a powerful New Jersey state senator, planning to run for governor one day. He had to pull some strings for Blake to get him a job teaching US and World History. Blake would also serve as the school's first tennis coach. Clarksville Regional High School had finally added the sport, the last school in the county to do so.

He didn't know a soul in Clarksville, other than the man who interviewed him, the high school principal, Mark Mitchell. He remembered sitting in the principal's modestly appointed office. He noticed that Mr. Mitchell seemed annoyed, about having to hire him and he understood the principal's concerns. "So, you come from a small town," Mr. Mitchell said. "Your references are fine, I suppose. You spent the last year in Manhattan. You did some bartending, I see."

"That's right. New York was fun, but I prefer small town living"

"Why would you choose to come to a remote area in New Jersey, rather than return to your home in Tennessee?" Mr. Mitchell asked. He surveyed the fair skinned, muscular man seated in front of him. He looked uncomfortable wearing a suit. "Are you sure this is what you want to do, and where you want to be?"

"I've thought about that a lot. I want to make a fresh start, move away from the past and start over," Blake said.

"School starts for teachers on Wednesday, September 7th. Will you be available then?"

"Yes sir, I'm ready whenever you need me," Blake said.

The principal shuffled some papers on his desk and glanced at his watch. "Fresh starts always sound promising, but they can be tricky at times, Mr. Stevens. I would hate for you to have a sudden change of heart and leave us mid-term, but I suppose we'll cross that bridge if and when we come to it."

Blake didn't care for the way that sounded, but he had held his tongue, remembering his uncle's advice. Just two days before his interview with the principal, they had been sitting in his uncle's study. "I'm going to be twisting their arms, Blake. I'm the chairman of the Senate's Education Committee and I can make their lives miserable. Whatever you do, don't rub their noses in it." His uncle tapped his arm to be sure he had his nephew's full attention. "Act humble. I'm not sure they even have an opening. They might have to make a spot for you," he said. "I can only push them so far and I'm at the limit now, understand?" Blake understood perfectly. After a lengthy, and not entirely pleasant interview, he was hired.

The long road off the exit led straight into downtown Clarksville, right at Eighth Avenue. He turned left onto Main Street. The rowhouse style buildings were old and made with red brick. Specialty stores, a few law offices, a small luncheonette and a coffee shop sat on one side of the street. The other side was dominated by antique shops. At Main Street and Eighth Avenue, sat the Presbyterian Church, built with a white marble façade and a high spire, reminding visitors this was still a God-fearing town. When Blake saw a general store halfway down the eight short blocks that was Main Street, he felt like he had stepped back in time. It looked and felt much like Colby Springs. As a newly appointed history teacher, he took note that Clarksville, New Jersey was founded in 1795, by Samuel Clark, a signer of the Declaration of Independence and a delegate to the Constitutional Convention. The town was small enough that people knew each other and word of good news, or bad, traveled quickly.

Mark Mitchell had arranged a furnished, one-bedroom apartment rental for Blake on the second floor of a two-story home. The house was located on Fourth Street across from an old granary, long ago abandoned. Blake was relieved to see a Starbucks at the end of his block and what looked to be a nice Mexican restaurant on the other side of the street. When he saw a sign for a bookstore, he was pleased until he realized it was out of business.

As he parked his car, he took a good look at the house. He smiled. This was a home in desperate need of some TLC. The faded white clapboard-sided house needed a paint job. The lawn was little more than patches of crabgrass. He opened the trunk of his Camaro and pulled out his bags. He left his assortment of weights, barbells and a weight bench for later. He would have to lug them up the porch steps and then another flight to his apartment.

He introduced himself to his landlord, who was standing on the sidewalk, watering her shrubs. Considering their sad condition, it looked like this was the first time the plants had been watered all summer. The woman was short and very thin. The smoke from her cigarette was making her eyes water. "Mrs. Cotton, I'm Blake Stevens."

The woman turned off the hose's spigot. "Oh yes, Mark said you would arrive today. Welcome to Clarksville. I'll show you your apartment as soon as you give me the security deposit. That'll be $2,000." The woman absentmindedly pushed a wisp of her thin white hair over her ear.

Blake opened his wallet and pulled out twenty hundred-dollar bills. He counted them as he placed them in Bella Cotton's outstretched hand. The woman thanked him and put the money in her housecoat pocket. "I'll deposit this in the bank Monday morning. Before I forget, when you pay your rent, I prefer cash, please," she said.

"No problem."

"So, you're the new history teacher at the high school. I taught 4th grade in Clarksville for many years," she said.

"Mr. Mitchell mentioned that."

"That was a long time ago," Mrs. Cotton said. She started watering her shrubs again. "I certainly hope you'll take good care of your apartment. If you read your lease, you know I have the right to check it at any time. Any drugs, you're out. If you turn out to be the type who doesn't mind living in filth, out you go. Is that understood?"

"Yes, there won't be any problems."

"No smoking either and no parties of any kind. That's my rule."

"Anything else?" Blake asked. He smiled as she crushed what was left of her cigarette under her slipper.

"That remains to be seen. I want us to get off to a good start." The woman pulled out a pack of cigarettes from her other pocket and lit another one. She grinned to acknowledge she kept two sets of rules. "Here are your keys. This one opens the outer door and the other key will open your apartment door. There's space reserved for storage in the cellar." Blake took the keys. "Thank you, ma'am." He went up the stairs.

It didn't take him long to get settled. As expected, the furniture was worn, but nothing was broken or damaged. The walls were a dingy beige color. The ceiling paint was cracked in some spots. He pulled his cell phone out and took photos of everything. He wasn't taking any chances. He had a feeling that his security deposit was already burning a hole in Bella Cotton's pocket. When he got to the bedroom, he laughed out loud. The room wasn't large, but it was certainly big enough for a double bed. Mrs. Cotton had furnished it with a twin bed, no doubt to discourage any sexual activity.

As soon as he got his things organized, Blake took on the job of getting his weights up to the apartment. After high school, he'd lost interest in body building, but when he moved to New York, he joined a gym and started working out to help him pass the time. He quickly discovered he enjoyed the challenge and started buying his own weights. It was cheaper than a gym membership. In addition to weight training, he had also jogged around Manhattan, at least four days a week, especially in Central Park.

Finally settled in, Blake decided to take a walk and see a little bit of the town. As he was approaching the Mexican restaurant, he realized he was hungry. He went in and had a seat. A server approached. Her name tag said Jonna.

"What can I get ya?" She placed a glass of water, a cup of salsa and a basket of warm chips on the table. She had the blonde hair, blue eyes and long legs that never failed to get Blake's attention.

"Just a burrito, and whatever beer you have on tap would be fine," he said.

"Coming right up, handsome." She walked away, swaying just enough to signal her interest. Blake noticed. Not five minutes later, Jonna was back with his order. "Just passing through?" she asked.

"No, I just moved here this afternoon. I'm going to be teaching at Clarksville Regional High starting on Monday." He stuck his hand out and said, "Blake Stevens."

"Jonna Martinelli, and I went to that high school." She swept her right hand wide from right to left, looking out over the tables and booths. "You can see how far it got me."

Blake noticed she wasn't wearing an engagement, or wedding ring. She looked to be in her early twenties. "What year did you graduate?"

"I think you mean, how old am I, right?" She grinned to show she wasn't angry.

"You got me. How old are you?"

"I'll be 28 tomorrow."

"Is there a party I should know about?" He couldn't believe he said aloud what he was thinking. It really wasn't his style.

"As a matter of fact, a few of my friends are taking me out to dinner as soon as I get out of here."

Blake couldn't think of a thing to say. Jonna hadn't added anything by way of an invitation and he didn't want to start off his stay in Clarksville with a reputation of a guy who was chasing women, or maybe worse, a presumptuous jerk. Jonna smiled and said, "Eat your food before it gets cold."

Fifteen minutes later she brought the check and some flan. "On the house," she said. Then she surprised him by slipping into a chair across from his. "Even though I don't know you, I'd like to invite you to my party, but it's just the girls, you know?"

"Thanks, I appreciate that. Is there a good breakfast place in Clarksville?"

"Uh-huh, there really is. The Waffle Heaven across the street from the hospital."

"Would you like to have breakfast with me tomorrow morning at Waffle Heaven?" Jonna looked at him, clearly worried about something. Blake noticed it and said, "Hey, it's okay. Like you said, you don't know me. Another time maybe."

"It's not that, Blake. I'm divorced and I have two sons, two and four years old. I learned a while ago to get that out on the table right away. No hard feelings if you don't want to take me to breakfast," she said. "It would have to be after church if you still want to."

"No hard feelings. We're just talking about a birthday breakfast. The boys are invited."

Waffle Heaven turned out to be as good as it sounded. At Jonna's insistence, Blake met her and the boys at the restaurant. He was dressed in his jeans and cowboy boots. She looked pretty in her white sundress and sandals, perfect for a sunny Sunday morning. Waffle Heaven offered a large selection of pancakes and Belgian waffles with a choice of toppings. Jonna's little boys kept her busy during breakfast. As she was wiping the older boy's face, Jonna looked toward the restaurant's door. "Oh shit, I can't believe this," she said.

"What's wrong?"

"Derek, my ex, is here." The two-year old was sitting on Blake's lap. "Give me the baby before he sees you."

Blake didn't move. He looked up at the large man headed in their direction. The man's bloodshot eyes suggested that he had spent the night drinking. He walked over to the table and said, "That's my son you got there, buddy. Let me have him." Blake looked over at Jonna and saw a pleading look in her eyes. He handed the baby to her and stood.

He stuck his hand out and said, "Good morning, I'm Blake Stevens."

The four-year-old said, "Hi Daddy," but the man ignored his son.

Derek put his hands on his hips. "Take a hike. If you know what's good for you, you'll leave now, before I kick your ass."

Blake looked him over. The man was powerfully built, but Blake had no doubt that he could take him if it came to that. He had dealt with much tougher looking men in Tennessee's Smokey Mountains. But he knew better than to make a scene in a public place, especially in a restaurant where at least a few of the kids eating breakfast were probably students at Clarksville Regional High School. "I took Jonna and the kids to breakfast this morning. We just met yesterday. Is there a problem?"

The owner of the restaurant walked up to the two men. "Derek, you know the rules here. Any trouble and you're gonna have a problem." He pointed to a table in the corner. "Look over there. Officer Simons is enjoying a nice breakfast with his family. He's already looking this way." The off-duty officer was indeed staring at them, waiting for a sign of trouble.

Derek had come into Waffle Heaven, wanting to make a scene, but he realized now that he had miscalculated. "I got your birthday gift in the truck, Jonna. I'll meet you there."

As soon as Derek was out the door, Jonna turned to Blake and said, "Please stay here until we're gone. You don't want to mess with him. I'm really sorry. I'll call you later."

Blake was itching now to take this guy Derek down, but he did what he was told. He sat down and asked the owner for the check and another cup of coffee. He could feel his muscles twitching, a signal that reminded him of an incident that happened in college when he got embroiled in a fight at a Shoney's restaurant with two men who were harassing a couple of co-eds. For some reason, he just exploded when one of the men brazenly grabbed one of the girl's breasts and started laughing. He jumped up and pummeled the guy. He had never done anything like that before and his own strength surprised him.

Officer Simons stopped by on his way out. He stuck his hand out and said, "Bill Simons, one of Clarksville's four police officers. You handled that well, if you don't mind my saying so."

Blake stood, introduced himself and shook the officer's hand. "I'm the new history teacher at the high school," he said.

"Yeah, I thought I heard your name before. Got here yesterday, right?" Blake nodded. Simons smiled. "How'd you meet Jonna so fast?"

3

Claire Clark woke up early that Sunday morning. The first thing she did was check the ring finger of her left hand. Her shiny engagement ring was securely in place. It had been seven months since she became engaged to Brad Chambers. The thought that in just eleven months, they would be married, made Claire happy.

She checked herself in the mirror, inspecting her pale, white skin. She was a bit unhappy to see a few summer freckles, not that she had many. She combed her shoulder-length black hair, laughing at herself for looking for signs of premature gray. Her mother's hair didn't turn gray until she was fifty. Only 29, Claire knew she had no worries on that score.

As she combed her hair, she thought about how she and Brad reconnected after their schooling had been completed. Brad Chambers was the town's family doctor. Claire smiled, remembering that he had been her boyfriend from the eighth grade through his high school graduation. When Brad went to a college out of state, and then medical school, they drifted apart. Two years younger than Brad, Claire went to college in Boston, earning a degree in secondary education. She became an English teacher at Clarksville Regional High School.

After a residency in Denver, Colorado, Brad came home to practice family medicine. He wasn't home long before they began dating again. In fact, just a week after he returned, they ran into each other at the Clarksville Market. Brad was wearing stylish glasses and had his thin, sandy, blonde hair combed straight back. Only an inch taller than Claire, she thought he looked like a shorter version of the actor, William Hurt. Claire saw Brad reach into one of the freezer compartments for a quart of rocky road ice cream. "You're not setting a good example for your patients, eating ice cream. How about an apple instead?"

He turned and smiled. "I have always loved the sound of your voice. I've missed hearing it, in fact," he said. "How about sharing this with me? I wouldn't want you telling the kids in your English class that I wasn't a good doctor."

"Why, Bradley, are you offering me a bribe?" she asked.

"An invitation to get reacquainted. Think of it that way."

"Who can resist?"

They quickly became a couple again and their families and friends approved. Less than a year later, Brad popped the question. He did it in grand fashion, in front of the entire community during half-time at a championship basketball game at Samuel Clark Auditorium. The school's cheerleaders, with the help of the opposing team's cheer squad, shouted out a special cheer that ended with a marriage proposal. Everyone thought it romantic. But Claire, who graciously accepted, was secretly disappointed. She would have preferred a quiet setting. After all, she thought, it is a special and intimate moment.

After the game, while they were driving to Philadelphia to have dinner and spend the night celebrating their engagement, Brad asked Claire to move in with him. "We can live together now, Claire. No more sneaking around or going to The City of Brotherly Love to get a little privacy."

"I would love to Brad, you know that. But I'm a teacher in a small town. I know it's a very old-fashioned notion, but I feel I need to set a proper example for my students."

"You can't be serious, Claire. Do you actually believe these kids are innocent? After we're married I'll give you a list of the students in your school that have been treated for STDs or had an abortion."

"I'm not naïve. I don't need to see a list. I can usually tell when one of my students is pregnant."

"Honey, all I'm saying is that no one will care if we live together for a while. You remember my friends, Monica and Jason, from Aspen. They moved in together right after their engagement."

"They're not teachers, Brad. I don't want to have an argument with you, especially not today of all days."

"No argument, dear, I guess I'm just a bit frustrated."

Claire decided to take a different tack. "I know in the past, whenever the subject of marriage has come up, you always said you wanted to pay off your student loans first. We won't be able to get married at that rate for another eighteen months. I'm more than willing to wait, if that's what you really want," she said. "But, maybe we could get married this August instead of next, if that would make you happy."

"I thought of that, believe me. But I don't want to enter into a marriage with debt hanging over our heads. We'll wait. It will give me more time to build my practice too."

Claire leaned over and gave him a peck on the cheek. Sometimes, Brad made marriage sound more like a business startup than the romantic adventure Claire always dreamed of. The scientist in him, she thought. "We'll wait," she said.

Claire enjoyed reminiscing, but she really had to get moving. She didn't want to be late for church. She finished putting her makeup on and brushed her hair one more time. Tomorrow she would start her last school year as a single woman. She got ready for church and waited for Brad to arrive. They had seen a movie the night before and made love quickly in of all places the back seat of Brad's Hyundai Sonata, parked behind the church parking lot. Claire had never done that before with anyone. It was uncomfortable for her but satisfying for Brad. She was happy to do that for him.

That afternoon, they would have Sunday dinner with Claire's parents. Afterward, Brad would drive her home, early she hoped, so she could get ready for the first day of school.

When the church services ended, Claire and Brad decided to go for a drive. They would stop by a roadside stand to pick up some locally grown peaches and squash to take to her parents. On their way out of town, they saw something rare for Clarksville. Two police cars were parked in front of the Waffle Heaven, lights flashing. A woman was lying on the ground, bleeding from her mouth. Brad pulled over, grabbed his physician's bag and ran across the street. It was Jonna Martinelli. Then he noticed there was a man he had not seen in town before, standing against the wall. He was holding his left forearm with his bloody right hand, covering a wound.

Claire went to Jonna immediately. "What happened?" she asked.

"Derek hit me. I'm dizzy," Jonna said. "Where are my babies?"

Claire looked at the patrol cars and saw Derek slumped in the backseat of one of them. In the backseat of the other car, sat Jonna's two little boys. "They're safe, Jonna. They're in the patrol car." She reached down and patted Jonna's arm. "I'll call your mom."

The woman struggled, trying to sit up. Claire eased her back down. "Brad is here. Let him have a look at you." They could hear the ambulance approaching. When she turned to call Brad, she saw he was applying a pressure bandage to the man's arm.

"Come here and hold this man's arm for a minute, while I take a look at Jonna," Brad said.

Claire quickly walked over to the wall and took the man's arm. "I'm Claire Clark. The man who was helping you is a doctor. Does it hurt?"

"Not bad, not yet, anyway. I'm Blake Stevens." His arm was beginning to hurt, but Claire's exquisite face offered a very satisfying distraction.

Claire recognized the name. She really looked at him for the first time. She saw a tall and very good-looking man. "Oh my, you're the new history teacher. How did you wind up in the middle of this mess?" She looked over at Brad, who was helping the EMT get Jonna on a stretcher. He gave the EMT instructions and reassured Jonna before they wheeled her to the ambulance. Then he came back to where Claire and Blake were standing.

A police officer approached and said, "Mr. Stevens, we're going to need to take a statement, sir."

"Corky, you can do that at the hospital," Brad said. "Claire and I are going to drive him to the ER. This man needs stitches."

"No thanks," Blake said. "It's right across the street." He pointed. "I can walk."

"We don't mind," Claire said. "We'd be happy to do it."

"Thanks, it's not necessary." Blake turned to the officer. "Can you meet me at the hospital?"

4

Blake met the police officer at the hospital, where he gave a statement. He explained that as he was leaving the restaurant, he saw Derek knock Jonna down. "Then he kicked her. He was about to give her another kick when he saw me. He squared off. I guess he thought he was going to give me what he gave Jonna."

"What happened?" the officer asked.

"I guess I slammed him into the side of his truck. I didn't hit him though. I wanted to, but I didn't," Blake said. "But then he pulled a knife out of his pocket and slashed my arm. I kind of lost it then and hit him hard, his ribs, I think."

"That took guts," the officer said.

"It wasn't the first time I had to tangle with a man holding a knife. It happened a couple of times when I worked in a bar back home. Drunks," Blake said, shaking his head. "Anyway, Officer Simons, the guy I met in the restaurant, showed up and knocked the knife out of Derek's hand. Then he just flipped him around and pushed the side of his face against the truck.

I remember he said something like, 'Derek, you're in big trouble, dude. Don't make it any worse.'"

"How long have you been in town, Mr. Stevens? Did you know Jonna before you got here?" the officer asked.

"Less than 24 hours, actually. I met Jonna yesterday at the Mexican restaurant where she works." The officer wrote everything down. "Did you see Mr. Martinelli hit Jonna?"

Blake thought about it for a moment. "Not exactly, but she was down and her face was bloody. The first thing I saw was when he kicked her."

The emergency room doctor walked into the exam room and said, "Let's have a look at that arm." She inspected it and silently reached for a suture kit. She cleaned the wound, numbed the area and went to work. Fifteen minutes later, Blake had six stiches in his left arm.

"You'll be a celebrity your first day of class," the doctor said. "You'll have a mean looking scar to back it up."

"How's Jonna doing?" he asked.

"The girl you helped? We're going to keep her overnight for observation."

"But she'll be all right?"

The doctor smiled. "From what I've heard, Jonna is a lot tougher than she looks."

"Has to be with that ex of hers around," the police officer said.

"What's going to happen to him?" Blake asked.

"This time, maybe they'll actually put him away for a while. He's looking at two assault and battery charges, including assault with a deadly weapon."

On his way home from the hospital, Blake drove to the grocery store and picked up some items to fill his refrigerator and his pantry shelves. As he was about to climb the steps to his apartment, his landlord, Mrs. Cotton stepped out of her place. "You're not exactly getting off to a great start, are you?"

Blake smiled. "What do you mean?"

"You're not even here a day yet and already you picked up the town hussy and got into a fight with her no good husband."

"Is that what you heard?"

"I hear everything that goes on in this town, Mr. Stevens."

"I'm doing the best I can, Ma'am." He stepped around the woman and walked up to his apartment.

School didn't actually start for students until Wednesday. On Monday morning, Blake was introduced to his department head, Frank Holt, and the rest of the history teachers. Holt was potbellied and middle-aged, his skin pasty looking. He sported long sideburns and a bushy mustache. The department head walked them through changes from the previous school year and explained his expectations. He was a no-nonsense guy. He made it clear that students were there to learn and his teachers were there to teach. While he acknowledged the teacher's union contract, he made it clear that he would not look kindly on frivolous absences by his teachers.

Blake quickly got his bearings and set up his classroom in the B-wing, Room 101. He rummaged through a couple of boxes he'd saved from his last teaching assignment in Colby Springs, Tennessee. He hung portraits of some of his favorite US Presidents on the wall, including Andrew Jackson, JFK, Lyndon Johnson, and George HW Bush. He left an old photo of Robert E. Lee in his desk drawer. He familiarized himself with the student rosters in each of his five classes, none of them honors or advanced placement. One of his new co-workers, a man who planned to retire in two years, let him know that he would have his work cut out for him.

"Advanced placement and honors kids are here to learn something. Kids in the standard classes are just sleepwalking their way through high school." the teacher said. "Rookies always get the sleepwalkers, the ones that'll be washing your car, or serving you dinner at the Olive Garden after they graduate." Blake didn't bother to respond. Maybe the teacher who sidled up to him was bitter. Since he didn't know him yet, he realized the guy could have been just pulling his leg.

He also found time to speak with the athletic director about the tennis team, which amounted to little more than compiling a list of the equipment he would need once tryouts started. The school's principal held a meeting for the entire faculty at lunch time, treating the teachers to pizza. Only one teacher asked Blake about his arm, a woman who had recently returned to the States from Europe. Unsure of what to say, Blake changed the subject.

He spotted Claire the next day as the teachers were walking into the cafeteria for another meeting. When they made eye contact, she gave him a cold "Hello," and quickly walked past him. It was the first time he noticed she was wearing an engagement ring. He assumed she was engaged to Dr. Chambers. When the meeting was over, he made a point of waiting for her in the hall. "Hi, Claire, I don't think I ever got the chance to thank you and Doctor Chambers for your help the other day. I appreciated it."

"You are very welcome," she said. She moved on quickly to catch up with a colleague in the English department. Blake stood there for a few seconds. He had seen plenty of beautiful women in Manhattan. He had studied their faces from behind the bar. Claire had the classic, completely symmetrical face that other beautiful women had. He kept looking in her direction, hoping in vain, she would turn around so he could have one more look.

The next couple of weeks went by quickly. Blake found that he had missed teaching a lot more than he thought. His students, many of whom had heard about the Waffle Heaven incident, asked him about it. He always changed the subject. Most of his students paid attention in class and were doing their homework, not what he had been led to believe. Of course, he set the tone early. On the second day of class, one of the boys sitting in the back of the classroom, started making animal sounds, much to the amusement of his friends. Blake had no trouble figuring out who it was. He didn't say anything. Surreptitiously, he recorded the noise on his cell phone. When the period was over, he told the sophomore to stay in his seat. When the room was empty, he closed the door and walked over to the kid's desk.

"Martin, I want you to hear something." He turned on the recording.

"What's that?" the kid asked.

"That's the sound of you going to detention this afternoon. It's the sound of you explaining your behavior to your parents when I invite them in for a conference."

"How do you know it's me?"

"First of all, your friends all looked at you when you were making these noises. Second, just now, rather than deny it, you asked how I knew it was you. Do we understand each other?"

Martin was a bit confused. He shrugged. Blake stood over him and waited.

Finally, the kid said, "Sorry." Blake tore up the detention slip.

Blake worked hard to coordinate with parents, at least the ones who were interested in making sure their children stayed on top of their schoolwork. Active parents didn't take this lying down. It was not uncommon for interested parents to email, or call a teacher questioning their child's test results or grades. And it wasn't unheard of for a parent to do a child's homework if an important grade was at stake. Parental over-reach didn't occur as much in his classes. Most of his students, if they were college bound, were probably looking at a community college. Not many of the them had the grades they would need for acceptance at a top tier college.

After school, Blake usually kept to himself. He went back to his apartment and made something for dinner. Later, he either worked with weights, or went for a run and then got ready for class the next day. Teacher's pay in New Jersey was better than what he was making in Colby Springs, but it was far from generous, considering the difference in the cost of living. He didn't venture out much. After a few weeks, though, he started to get cabin fever. He was lonelier than he wanted to admit. One Friday night, he didn't feel like cooking. He decided to eat out. Against his better judgment, he went back to the Mexican restaurant where Jonna worked.

The hostess seated him with one of the male servers. When Jonna saw him come in, she cajoled the waiter to let her have Blake's table. "Haven't seen you around, Blake. You've been hiding from me, haven't you? Can't say I blame you."

"I heard your ex entered a guilty plea."

"Uh-huh, in exchange for a lesser charge. He'll probably be out before Christmas, though. Just in time to screw that up for the boys and me."

Blake nodded, not sure of what to say. Jonna looked good, and he had a feeling it wouldn't be hard to convince her to hook up that night. She looked as eager as he felt. "Sorry I haven't called you."

"You should be, leading me on like that, acting the hero and then you pull a David Copperfield act on me."

"I really didn't know what else to do."

"Do you know what to do now?" she asked.

"Order?"

"That's a start."

When he finished eating, Blake decided to linger at the bar for a while. The restaurant was having a slow night, so Jonna spent a good bit of time talking to him. She told him she and her boys lived with her mother. "I wound up marrying Derek, kind of on the rebound," she said.

"Did you have a bad breakup?"

Jonna turned and took a quick look at her tables. She only had two parties and both were in the middle of their meals. "Let's just say I had an unfortunate experience. I was hurting. Derek was kind of wild, a motorcycle guy, partying almost every night, and I was young. We were only dating about four months when he asked me to marry him."

"Were you in love?" Blake asked. He took a sip of a beer he as nursing.

Jonna rolled her eyes and laughed. "Who knows? What is love supposed to be anyway? My father walked out on us when I eleven."

They talked for quite a while, but Jonna did most of the talking. She didn't ask many questions. When she asked Blake why he moved to New Jersey, he kept it simple. "I wanted a change of scenery, I guess." She wasn't the type to probe. The owner came over to the bar and said he was going to close early. It wasn't even ten o'clock.

"You wouldn't want to come to my place for a cup of coffee, would you?" Jonna asked, a sly smile on her face.

Blake was in a bit of a quandary. He was horny enough to be tempted, but he'd heard just enough about Jonna's life to know she'd been hurt a lot. He realized some of that might have been her own doing, but he knew come the next morning, he wouldn't feel good about what he had done. "Some other time, Jonna. It's been a long week and I'm beat."

"Wow, I must be losing it." She quickly wiped a tear that was forming in her eye. "Nobody's ever turned me down before."

Blake stood up and hugged her. He took a step back and said, "Don't underestimate yourself. I like you. I just can't right now."

He left the restaurant and took a walk toward the church. He found another bar. The place was packed, mostly with people in their twenties and thirties. He recognized one of the patrons, a teacher he'd seen in the cafeteria, but hadn't actually met. The guy waved his beer bottle toward him. A live band was playing. They were good, playing a lot of oldies, most of them from the sixties. He drank more beer and felt a nice buzz. Just being around people felt good. Then, just after midnight, a fight broke out between two women, both in their thirties which made him laugh. They had firm grips on each other's hair. The shorter one was trying her best to hit the other woman with a beer bottle. This was a first for Blake. He'd never seen women go at it like this. A bouncer seemed to come out of nowhere to separate the fighters.

Time to head home, Blake thought. He paid his tab and walked back to Mrs. Cotton's place. Tired and a bit high, he suddenly worried about being unprepared for class the next day. Then he remembered it was the weekend. He opened the front door and stepped into the hallway. Before he reached the stairs, he heard Mrs. Cotton's door open. "Did you have a good time tonight night, Mr. Stevens?"

He laughed. He couldn't help it. "Incredible, how was your night, Bella?" It was the first time he used the woman's first name.

"Don't be sassy with me. There are some things that need fixing around here. I'm going to keep you busy this weekend. You'll stay out of trouble that way." She lit a cigarette. "Are you at least handy with a hammer, I hope?'

"Very handy actually, but I don't work for you, Mrs. Cotton, I just rent an apartment from you."

"I'm afraid you're mistaken. The terms of your lease are quite clear, Mr. Stevens. I can evict you without notice. I'm willing to pay for your time if you do a good job. Otherwise, you just may be looking for a new place to hang that silly cowboy hat." Back in a small town with plenty of farms, Blake had taken to wearing his Stetson again.

Blake was too tired to argue. "Tell me what you want done. I'll get started in the morning."

"Fix the porch railing and paint the picket fence," she said, pointing to the front yard. "Rake the leaves and dispose of them. I'll pay you $9.00 an hour." Blake didn't say a word. He went up to his apartment, fell onto his bed and slept soundly until almost one o'clock in the afternoon.

5

Claire Clark's room was in another wing of the school. Since she and Blake ate lunch during different periods, he rarely saw her other than at the monthly faculty meeting. He usually caught a glimpse of her as the teachers filed into the school cafeteria. One windy Friday afternoon in the middle of October he ran into her in the teacher's parking lot, three spaces over from his car.

As he unlocked the car door, he called over to her. "Hi Claire. You going to the game tomorrow afternoon?"

"Haven't decided," she said. "Will you be there?" She opened her car door and waited for a response, ready to get in her car.

Blake took the opportunity to walk over to where she was standing. "That's the plan, if my landlady doesn't have too much work for me. She's a bit of a slave driver."

"Is that right? I know Mrs. Cotton well," she said. She got into her seat and reached for the door handle and held it. "She was my fourth-grade teacher, a wonderful woman."

"Maybe I'll see you and Dr. Chambers at the game," he said. Claire didn't respond. As she drove off, leaving Blake standing there, he thought maybe Claire and the good doctor were a good match, both snobs. He was glad he had refused the ride to the hospital the day Derek sliced his arm. He resolved to ignore her in the future, which he assumed would be fine with her.

Claire drove to her apartment on Third Avenue, a couple of blocks off Main Street. She didn't really know why she was so cold toward Blake Stevens. The man gave off a strange vibe, as if he wasn't quite comfortable in his own skin. She wasn't pleased that Blake's apartment was just a few blocks from hers. They might run into each other shopping on Main Street. The man made her nervous.

She spent that Friday afternoon grading test papers and putting together her lesson plans for the following week. She planned a quiet evening while Brad worked late at the hospital. Claire had been vague in responding to Blake's question about the game because she didn't want to invite inquiries about her plans. She knew she would not be at the game. She and Brad were going to visit his parents, who had retired and now lived in Charlottesville, Virginia. She was looking forward to the five-hour drive together Saturday morning.

But later that night, Brad called to tell her he couldn't leave town. "One of my patients is struggling with a lung infection. I just put him in the ICU."

"Oh Brad, your parents will be so disappointed," Claire said. "Why can't Dr. Puria keep an eye on him? She is a pulmonologist, isn't she?"

"If anything goes wrong, honey, it wouldn't look good to the family if I went away for the weekend."

"Is he that bad?"

"He is. Anyway, I'd spend the entire weekend either on the phone or worrying about him. Wouldn't be much fun. We can go another time. I think I'm in for a long weekend here. Why don't you go to the football game tomorrow?"

"Can you at least do that, go with me?"

"Possibly, but please don't count on it, dear. Why don't you call Victoria and see if she wants to go, just in case I can't make it?" Victoria Gibson was Claire's closest friend. They grew up together and both had become teachers. Victoria wound up teaching middle school kids in the same school district.

Claire was disappointed, but she knew that as a physician's wife, she would one day have to accept disruptions to plans they made. "Okay, maybe I'll do that."

Saturday afternoon was a beautiful October day, with a crisp breeze and temperatures just cool enough to make the perfect fall afternoon. It was ideal football weather. The concession stands were doing a brisk business, selling hot chocolate and hot apple cider made from apples grown nearby. Claire and Victoria were enjoying the game. The unbeaten Clarksville Cougars were having another good day, leading 21-6 at halftime.

During the break, Victoria and Claire each bought cups of cider and a bag of popcorn to share. As they turned from the concession stand to return to their seats, Claire literally bumped into Blake, spilling the hot cider on her favorite sweater. The popcorn went flying too. "Oh, man, I wasn't looking where I was going," Blake said. Only then did he realize it was Claire.

Claire didn't say a word. She grabbed some napkins and started dabbing her sweater, trying to wipe off the cider. Fortunately, it wasn't very hot, so she wasn't burned. "Shouldn't you be painting Mrs. Cotton's porch or something?" she asked, her voice betraying the irritation she was trying to hide.

"I finished it this morning," he said. "I'm really sorry, Claire. I'd be happy to pay to have your sweater cleaned."

"That won't be necessary," Claire said." Victoria was standing by, waiting to be introduced, but Claire just wanted to get away. This man just seemed to court trouble. She walked away and Victoria, followed, glancing back at Blake.

"Who is that gorgeous man in the cowboy hat?" she asked

"That's Blake Stevens. He's the new history teacher, kind of a mystery man and possibly, a jerk."

"Why do you say that? He's a good-looking jerk. Is he from around here?"

"Seriously, Victoria? With that hat?"

"Kind of cool looking to me," Victoria said.

"You mad at me for not introducing you to him?" Claire asked.

"Forever pissed."

"Word around town is he has a girlfriend. You'll never guess who it is," Claire said.

"Tell me."

"Jonna Martinelli." Claire gave her friend a knowing look.

Victoria shook her head. "I have to move back to Clarksville. I'm missing out on way too much." She lived in Franklin, the next town over, where apartments were less expensive.

The Cougars won the game handily, beating the Bridgeton Bulldogs 41-13. As they were leaving the stadium, they saw Blake again. He was walking alone in front of them. Victoria pointed him out to Claire, who immediately slowed down to avoid catching up to him. As if he sensed their presence, he turned his head to take a look at who might be walking behind him. He stopped and waited for them. He was holding a bag of popcorn. He extended the bag to Claire. "I bought this just in case I ran into you. It was the least I could do."

Claire took it and placed it in her carry bag. "Thank you. This is Victoria. She teaches at Whitlock Middle School."

Victoria, who was wearing a green jumper and white knee socks, Clarksville Regional's colors, smiled and shook Blake's hand. "Claire and I are best friends. Welcome to Clarksville. I hope you like our town."

"I do. It seems mostly friendly, I think." He smiled at Victoria. "I guess it's safe to assume that you went to Clarksville too and not that long ago."

"Graduated just last year," she said. "Can you tell?" She laughed.

Blake smiled. "How about that. I had you pegged for a sophomore."

They walked to the parking lot. Blake mentioned that he was parked at the far end of the lot and headed in that direction.

Claire was relieved, but as she watched him take long, confident strides toward his car, she suddenly felt a hint of curiosity about him. It was not a welcome thought.

Victoria was smitten. "You sure you're not interested in him?"

"I have Brad, remember? He's all yours," Claire said.

"If only. The man never took his eyes off of you," Victoria said.

6

On Thanksgiving Day, Blake woke up early. It was a cool, late November morning. The last month had been a busy one, doing odd jobs for Mrs. Cotton and keeping his students engaged in US History. His Uncle John and Aunt Abigail had invited him to spend the day with them, but Blake wanted to go to Clarksville Regional's Thanksgiving Day football game against their arch rivals, Salem Regional High School. He really wanted to fit in. Besides, having played the game when he was in high school, he loved football. Since both teams were undefeated, the game promised to be a good one.

Blake checked his cell for messages. His new buddy, Parker Browne, had sent him a text at one in the morning saying he had run into Jonna at the SilverTop Sports Bar. "She asked for you man," his message read. He got up, went into the bathroom and splashed cold water on his face. He needed to wake up. Parker was a math teacher at the school, constantly on the prowl for women. A year older than Blake, their friendship began over a few margaritas one night after parent-teacher conferences. Parker revealed that his wife left him for another man two years ago. He was still reeling. Three inches short of six feet tall, bespectacled and balding, he rarely got a second look from women. But he was a terrific teacher. Students and teachers liked him and administrators respected his work ethic.

Blake looked in the mirror and decided to shave. He'd been playing around with the idea of a beard, but it was patchy, not to his liking. It was Parker, with his neatly kept beard, who encouraged Blake to give it a try. He lathered his face and made his beard disappear. He checked the temperature and saw it was only 33 degrees. Before he jumped in the shower, he took out a new pair of black jeans and his favorite orange and white flannel, button down shirt. It reminded him of the University of Tennessee, his alma mater.

The game was scheduled for ten o'clock. As soon as he was ready, he called Parker to see if he was still going to the game.

"Hey, what's up, Blakester?"

"Don't call me that, man, I'm begging you," Blake said. "You going to the game?"

Parker looked over at the young woman lying in his bed, still sleeping. "That would be no, not happening."

"You finally picked somebody up?"

"Yeah, I'm in love," Parker said.

"She must be Medicare eligible then, right?" Blake said.

"I'm not even sure she has her driver's license yet, Stevens."

"Not one of your student's though, right?"

Parker laughed. "Can't even joke about a thing like that these days. You sure you don't want to come to my sister's house for dinner? Plenty of room, and she makes enough food to feed the entire senior class."

"Thanks, but you'll need a place at the table for your new love." Parker laughed again and pressed the end call button. Blake wasn't sure what he was going to do for dinner. He had now turned down two invitations. He ate a light breakfast while he watched the Macy's Thanksgiving Day parade. When it was time to leave, it dawned on him that he forgot to ask Parker about Jonna. What was it that Jonna asked him? He had been out to dinner at the Mexican place a couple of times after the night he'd turned down her invitation for coffee. He always sat at her table, though. They chatted, but neither of them said anything that might lead to romance. She sent him a humorous but pointed card a not long ago, but he ignored it One night she called him. Against his better judgment, he had taken the call. She said, "What's wrong? Don't you like me?"

"Nothing's wrong, Jonna. It's like I told you before, I do like you. I'm just not ready for a committed relationship."

"I'm not looking for a commitment either. A little warmth in my life is all I'm asking for."

Against his better judgement he took her out to see a movie. They held hands and when it was over, he dropped her off at her front door. He kissed her lightly on the lips and said goodnight. "You really like to take things slowly, don't you? You're like from another century," Jonna said. "You're not gay, or anything are you?"

Blake laughed. "No, I'm not gay." He hesitated. "This isn't easy for me. We could get together, spend the night, but then what? I'm old fashioned, I guess in one way. I don't believe in sleeping with someone unless, well, I don't know."

"Unless you like them enough so it means something," Jonna said. "At least your honest. That's more than I can say for the other jerks in this town."

A week later she sent him another card that said, "Miss You." He decided it was best to let it go. When he didn't hear from her again, he thought he was in the clear. He hoped she met someone. Now she was asking Parker about him. What had she said? He wanted to call Parker, but correctly guessed that his friend was too busy to talk.

He found a seat at the game, near the top of the stands where a lot of the teachers sat. The stadium was packed with students from both schools. He quickly realized he should have dressed warmer. He was wearing a windbreaker. He wished he had worn his cowboy hat, but recently, he realized that wearing a cowboy hat was a throwback to a time and place he preferred to leave behind. The wind was blowing from behind him, giving him chills. He had been a quarterback on his high school football team and sometimes, he still missed the game. When Salem took an early lead, the Clarksville crowd got quiet. Some people acted like the outcome of this game was every bit as important as the size and quality of their crops that year, if not more so.

Blake scanned the crowd, looking for familiar faces. He saw his department chair; Frank Holt was there sitting with his wife. One of the other history teachers spotted him and waved. She was trying to keep warm, snuggling with her husband, the head of the math department and Parker's boss. It wasn't until just before half-time, with Salem leading 20-13, that he noticed Claire. She was about ten rows in front of him, sitting with Dr. Chambers.

Although he tried not to think about Claire in a romantic way, with her being engaged, he had to admit she was very pretty, easily the best-looking woman in the school, if not the town. He could see why Brad Chambers was so attracted to her. During the half, he wandered down to the concession stands and bought a hot chocolate. He chatted briefly with a couple of teachers and with some of his students. He was hoping to recruit one of them for the tennis team.

"Hello, stranger." He didn't even have to look. It was Jonna. He turned and faced her.

"Hey, Happy Thanksgiving. Where are the boys?"

"Same to you. My mother has them," she said. "That hot chocolate looks so good. I'm freezing."

Blake offered the hot cup to Jonna. "I've only had one sip. It's still hot."

"No thanks." He took her hand and placed the cup in it.

He pointed back to the concession stand. "I'll get another one. Are you having a big Thanksgiving with your mom and the boys?"

"Always do, care to join us?"

They stood in line together chatting. Blake didn't respond to Jonna's invitation. He got another cup of hot chocolate and they moved back to the area under the stands. "I heard you were asking about me last night," he said. Before Jonna could answer, Brad and Claire walked by.

"Hi Brad," Jonna said, her voice showing she was piqued that he was trying to slip by her unnoticed.

"Oh, hello there. How are you Jonna?"

"I'm fine. I never congratulated you on your engagement," Jonna said. Blake shifted his feet, wanting to say something, but not sure what was going on. Jonna's tone was a bit exaggerated, and not entirely sincere. He stuck his hand up and offered a one-shake wave of hello to Dr. Chambers and Claire. The couple ignored it.

"Thank you, Jonna" Claire said. She glanced at Brad, her eyes narrow. Then, turning to Blake, she said, "I hope you two enjoy the game." She tugged Brad's arm and the couple moved on.

"What was that about," Blake asked.

"Brad and I dated for a while when he was in medical school."

"No kidding. What happened?" Blake was still looking at Claire as the couple moved farther away. Jonna noticed but didn't say anything.

"We only went out twice. Seems to be my limit with men, unless I have their baby." She adjusted her newsboy style hat. "Why do I seem to have a one-date limit, Blake? Is it stamped on my body somewhere?"

Blake looked at Jonna, a wry smile on his face. He wasn't about to take the bait. "Sorry."

"At least you apologized. That's more than I got from the good doctor. All I got from him was the money for an abortion." She took a long sip of her hot chocolate. A tear flowed from her right eye. "Shit, I've never told anybody that before. I can't believe I just said that. I'm so stupid."

"Your secret is safe with me, I promise," Blake said. He wiped her tear with his napkin. The game was about to start again. He wanted to get away, but under the circumstances, he knew he couldn't do that. Jonna sensed his discomfort immediately. "You don't have to stay with me. I'm fine."

"I don't mind," He said. "Do you always come to the Thanksgiving game and meet up with old friends? Looks like the whole town is here."

"Please, I came to support my brother. He's one of the assistant coaches." She dropped the paper cup into the trash can. "I guess you have other plans for dinner?"

Blake saw the opening he was hoping for. "Actually, I do. And I was about to leave. Too cold for me anyway." Blake gently squeezed Jonna's hand, wished her a Happy Thanksgiving again, and headed for his car. He wanted to see the rest of the game, but if he stayed, he would have to sit with Jonna now. He felt bad about it, but he knew that wasn't a good idea. At least he was happy to get out of the cold weather. And he felt off balance. He had no idea why, but he felt it.

As he was driving home, he realized what was troubling him. Claire probably thought he and Jonna came to the game together. He wondered why that should bother him. Was it Jonna's reputation? If Mrs. Cotton knew about it, no doubt Claire did too. Did Claire know about her fiancé and Jonna's past?

As he turned the corner onto his street, it occurred to him that he had now turned down three invitations to Thanksgiving dinner. He knew he should have accepted one. Parker's invitation made the most sense. Was it too late to accept? He would be around a large group and have the chance to meet new people. He could occupy his mind and get through the day.

It would be better than last year when his sister, Judy came to New Jersey and spent the long weekend with him and their Uncle John and Aunt Abigail.

Four years older than Blake, she had been going through a divorce and needed to get away. That weekend brought back unwanted memories of the previous Thanksgiving, when Nicci, his fiancé jilted him, leaving him at the altar. They were to be married on the Saturday after the holiday. Everything was set; the church, reception hall and a honeymoon in Paris, where he would get to meet her parents. Nicci Brevard was a bank teller who worked for the local bank where Blake was a customer. From the first moment he saw Nicci, he was captivated. He handed her a check for deposit and couldn't take his eyes off her. He caught a whiff of her perfume when she handed him his receipt. "What perfume is that?" He asked.

"It's French, Nina Ricci. Do you like it?" She smiled and moved her wrist up to his nose so he could get the full effect of the fragrance.

Blake's face had turned red. "Sure do." He turned and walked out of the bank, wondering if anyone noticed him flirting with the bank teller. It was the first time he ever saw her. She must be new in town, he thought. He went back the next day and asked her out.

Everything happened quickly. They dated for just three months before he asked Nicci to marry him. Blake thought she was perfect for him. She was a very private person, reluctant to talk about herself. She told Blake she was born in Romainville, a small town near Paris. Her parents, both American citizens, commuted every day to the City of Light for work. She had a tiny trace of a French accent, which made Blake curious. "Why did you come to America?" he asked her.

"I always knew I would one day. I started out in Dallas, but it was too busy for me. Thought I would try a petite ville for a while." She had a habit of dropping simple French words and phrases into her conversation. Everyone, especially Blake, was charmed by it.

And, it seemed to everyone that she was completely taken with Blake's good looks, his easy manner and his determination to make a difference in the world. They bought a small house together and furnished it. Josef Krause, the bank's chief executive officer, and mayor of Colby Springs, was fond of Nicci. An ordained minister, he offered to perform the wedding ceremony.

After work on the day before Thanksgiving, Blake went out for a drink with some of his co-workers, teachers who wanted to celebrate the short break in the school calendar. When he got home around seven o'clock, he pulled into the driveway, surprised to see there were no lights on in the house. He assumed Nicci's car was in the garage. He was anticipating a night of lovemaking, imagining that Nicci was waiting for him in bed, only a few candles burning to enhance the mood.

When he opened the front door, though, there was an entirely different kind of surprise waiting for him. The place was empty; not a stick of furniture, not a lamp or a chair to sit on. Nor was there a note from Nicci. He called the bank and told Mr. Krause what happened.

"Why, that makes no sense, Blake. Forgive me, but are you sure you're at the correct address?"

Blake stepped outside and looked on the outer wall next to the front door. "Yes, I'm home. Did you speak with Nicci today?"

"No, I'm afraid not. She took the day off to get ready for the wedding. Would you like me to come over there?"

"No, but I'll call you when she gets home." Twenty-four hours later there was still no sign of her.

The police were called and inquiries were made at the Texas address Nicci had given on her bank application. There was no record of Nicci ever living there. The police tried to contact her parents in France, looking for James and Mona Brevard, but that was another dead end. Further investigation indicated there was no record of a Nicci Brevard in, or near, the French capitol. There were no leads. Blake spoke with Nicci's co-workers and her small circle of friends. If anyone knew anything, they weren't saying. He was heartbroken and then angry that the woman he loved so much could have been so cruel. A change of heart was understandable, he supposed, but leaving with no explanation, disappearing without a trace, left him with nothing to help him grasp what had happened. Any lingering doubts he may have had about her being abducted, evaporated when he discovered that she had also made off with $22,000, money that was sitting in their joint bank account. Fortunately for Blake, he had another account with about $7,500.

Embarrassed, mortified really, he decided to leave Colby Springs immediately after the Christmas holidays. He couldn't take it anymore; the constant inquiries from well-meaning friends who asked for updates, pointless rides around the county on weekends, searching vainly for any sign of her. He had to get away. He was growing bitter. His sister, Judy suggested he go to New Jersey and spend time with their Uncle John. Always a supportive man, he welcomed Blake and agreed to help him get through his ordeal.

When Judy visited last Thanksgiving, they talked about the possibility of his return to Tennessee. Judy was going on about having to go through the stacks of papers left by their parents. "Blake, Mama died almost four years ago, and I still can't bring myself to open a single box and start going through their papers."

"Next time I come home, I'll help you go through everything," Blake said.

"Will you do that? Will you ever come back to Colby Springs my brother?"

"Not if I can help it."

Judy laughed, but she worried about him. "You'll come home someday, I know that."

He parked his car in front of Mrs. Cotton's house. Although there was a driveway and a detached two car garage, Mrs. Cotton made it clear it was for her use only. As he climbed the steps to the front porch, he admired his handiwork. The place looked a lot better than the day he moved into it. The elderly woman never paid him for his work and never mentioned her original offer of nine dollars an hour either. He stood on the porch for a moment, fumbling with his keys. The wind made him shiver. Suddenly, the loneliness hit him full force. Another Thanksgiving. He no longer cared why Nicci left him, but the scars of abandonment still haunted him. He hated the feeling and yet, he knew that many people who lived alone fought their way through the holidays year after year.

He wasn't sure what he had in his tiny freezer, but he knew there wasn't even a frozen turkey dinner waiting for him. Bad planning; the stores and the restaurants in town were closed. For a moment, he considered driving into Philadelphia for dinner, but he doubted that would make him feel any better. At least he was proud of himself for turning down Jonna's invitation. The woman had experienced enough hurt in her life. He wasn't about to add to it just so he didn't have to eat alone.

He opened the outer door and walked in. Just as he put his foot on the first step up to his apartment, Mrs. Cotton opened her door. "Dinner is at two o'clock, Mr. Stevens. If you don't have other plans, I'll expect you then."

Blake was stunned. He looked at the woman. She was wearing an apron over navy blue slacks and a blouse. With dress shoes, earrings and a bit of makeup, she looked completely different. After almost three months living in her house, it was the first time he could even imagine that she'd ever been a teacher. Until that moment, the only thing he ever saw her wear was a housecoat and plain white sneakers. He nodded and said, "Okay, thanks." He didn't think that committed him exactly. To his mind, he was simply acknowledging her invitation.

As soon as he got settled, he opened his refrigerator door to see what his options were. He had a half-dozen eggs, nearly a full quart of milk and not much more. He checked the pantry and saw several cereal boxes and a few cans of green beans. Then he noticed a box of chocolate cake mix he had forgotten. His Aunt Abigail had given it to him as part of what she called a bachelor survival kit. He laughed because he knew even a store-bought cake mix was a challenge for him. He picked up the box and went to the kitchen stove. He searched around and found he had one suitable pan. At least he could have a nice dessert. After he put the cake in the oven, he sat on his couch, watching the early NFL game. It was 12:30 when he heard his cellphone vibrate. It was a text from Jonna. "We made a huge comeback and won 34 -20. Thought you would want to know." He was about to answer, just to say thanks, but he thought better of it. I'll send it later, he thought. There was no point in getting involved in a long round of texts, which he assumed was exactly what Jonna was angling for.

He stretched out on his couch and started to doze. Luckily, the timer went off before he fell into a deep sleep. The cake was done. He took it out of the oven and set it on the counter. Sleep came easily then and he probably would have slept away the afternoon, had it not been for someone slamming the front entrance door downstairs. The noise startled him. He jumped up, opened the door to his apartment and looked down the steps to see who it was. The hallway was empty. Did he dream it? The aroma of Thanksgiving dinner filled the hallway.

He checked his phone and saw it was five minutes after two. He laughed. Mrs. Cotton probably wanted to get his attention. Obviously, the old woman wanted company. He could probably add the slammed door to the repair list. He washed his face and hands, placed his cake on one of the two dinner plates he owned and went down to Bella Cotton's apartment. "Come in, Mr. Stevens," she said.

"I decided to accept your invitation to dinner." He handed her the cake, embarrassed that it was naked.

The old woman took it and said thank you. "I'll sprinkle it with powdered sugar later."

It was the first time Blake had seen her apartment. So far, none of the jobs she gave him involved her living quarters. The place was well kept, but the walls were a tired gray, probably an eggshell white at one time. It felt as if he'd stepped into a time warp, as if he was appearing in a 1950's sitcom, like the reruns he used to watch as a child. A good bit of the furniture was surely genuine antiques, he thought. Her small dining room table was set for two. He was glad he made the effort. No doubt, Mrs. Cotton was lonely too. "You have family nearby, Mrs. Cotton?"

"No, I have a sister who lives in Vermont, but she rarely travels. I don't travel much anymore either," she said. She pointed to a bottle of white wine and said, "Would you pour us a glass please?" He picked up the bottle and poured. He was worried now, thinking it could be a very long afternoon trying to make conversation with this woman.

"I understand you were a teacher too," he said, knowing it but looking for something to say, it slipped out anyway.

"I was, for 42 years. I taught fourth grade to most of the people in this town. You're probably wondering why no one invited me to Thanksgiving dinner."

"Not really. People get busy this time of year."

"Did you receive any invitations?" she asked.

"No." He lied.

"Would you mind saying a prayer of Thanksgiving before we start?"

Blake hesitated. Her new demeanor had him off balance. "I'm sorry Mrs. Cotton, but I have to ask. You've been riding me pretty hard since I got here. Why are you being so nice to me today?"

"I suggest you enjoy the respite, Mr. Stevens. It's quite possible I will begin riding you hard again tomorrow morning. Can you say a prayer, or don't you know any?" The woman had a slight smile on her face.

Blake said a brief prayer. Mrs. Cotton took his plate and filled it with turkey, stuffing, cranberry sauce, potatoes, green beans and yellow squash. The woman had prepared a traditional meal that could easily have served six.

After dinner, Blake got up to clean the table, but Mrs. Cotton wouldn't hear of it. "You're my guest. Anyway, I have nothing but time on my hands. If you would like to leave immediately after dessert, I won't be offended."

Blake suddenly had a hunch about her. Mrs. Cotton looked tired. He continued to clear the table. "You did the cooking. It's my job to clean up. I'll fill your wine glass and you can come sit in the kitchen and watch me work. If you'd rather sit in the living room, I won't be offended."

Mrs. Cotton was surprised, but she did as she was told. "Another thing, Mrs. Cotton. If I'm good enough to sit at your table, I'm good enough for you to call me Blake."

"Thank you, Blake. I will do that. I prefer to be called Mrs. Cotton. I hope you understand." He laughed and nodded his head. When the dishes were done, and put away at Mrs.

Cotton's direction, they went back to the dining room for dessert. Mrs. Cotton made a pumpkin pie earlier that day to be served with whipped cream. She placed Blake's cake on the table, garnished now with powdered sugar. She also had a pot of coffee ready.

As Blake was about to sit down, he saw an envelope with his name on it next to his coffee cup. He knew exactly what it was. He had worked at least 40 hours doing various projects for Mrs. Cotton. He had already decided not to accept payment from the old woman, mostly for the pleasure of saying no thank you to someone who never seemed to have a kind word for him. After sharing Thanksgiving dinner with her, he realized he may have misjudged her. Certainly, he didn't want the money, but now he needed a kind way to refuse. "Is that what I think it is?" he asked after they each sipped a bit of coffee.

"I don't know. What do you think it is, Blake?" Mrs. Cotton lit a cigarette.

"Mrs. Cotton, I think it's the money you offered to pay me for my handyman work."

"That is correct." The woman took a slice of chocolate cake and placed it on her plate.

"Well, I can't accept it just now. I have more work to do around here. You'll probably want it back if I break something."

"I see," she said. "Perhaps you have a point."

"Good. This whole apartment needs a paint job. I think I'll use this money to buy brushes and paint."

"Don't be presumptuous, young man. I did not invite you for dinner so you could insult my living quarters."

"I apologize," Blake said. "You have a lovely home, actually." He looked at the walls, his gaze exaggerated. "What color would you prefer?"

"You're incorrigible, do you know that? Exactly as I thought you were the day I met you." She took a drag and inhaled. "Eggshell blue would be lovely."

7

Blake Stevens grew up in a happy family. Ernest Stevens, after graduating with honors from the University of Tennessee, was hired by a community hospital in Johnson City, Tennessee as an assistant hospital administrator. That's where he met Patricia Julian, a nurse at the hospital. They dated for only nine months before deciding to marry. Patricia, who was pregnant, lost the baby just one week after the wedding. The couple were disappointed, but they were in love and the marriage thrived. They were simple people with simple tastes. As was customary in those days, they lived in housing provided by the hospital. When Judith was six and Blake two, the Stevens family moved to Colby Springs, Tennessee, not far from Knoxville, where Patricia Stevens had grown up. They bought a modest four-bedroom home and settled into the community. Mr. Stevens accepted a job at one of Knoxville's larger hospitals.

Both busy people, they made time for their children. Blake was a good student in school. Not the type who would ever make Honor Society, but he did well enough to gain entrance into the University of Tennessee, which pleased his parents.

Colby Springs was a great place to live, especially for kids. The town had a cozy downtown, four blocks long and a mix of small housing developments and farms. One of Blake's best friends during his childhood was a boy named Daulton, who lived on a cattle farm. During the summer, Blake and Daulton would find a few other boys and spend hours playing baseball in the fields. When the afternoons grew hot, they jumped into the farm's large pond. One day, on a dare, Blake tried to swim across the pond, which was about half the length of a football field. He was twenty-five yards from the bank when he developed a severe leg cramp. In trouble, he yelled for help. The other boys stood along the bank, paralyzed, but Daulton jumped in and swam out to Blake and rescued him. Not wanting to get into trouble, the boys swore each other to secrecy.

By the time they got to high school, Daulton had become a terrific baseball player, pitching the team to a championship his senior year. He was signed by the Pittsburgh Pirates after high school, but a promising career ended when he developed elbow pain that surgeons couldn't fix. He joined the Marines after that and was killed trying to rescue two fellow Marines in Iraq. Blake spoke at Daulton's funeral. Fighting back tears, he finally told the story of the day his friend saved his life.

Blake was an excellent athlete, which pleased his father. He had taught his son to play tennis when he was twelve years old. Within a year, he couldn't keep up with his son. But what really delighted the whole family was Blake's prowess on the football field. He led his high school team to the state championship game in his senior year. He ran for 110 yards in the game and threw two touchdown passes. In spite of his effort, his team lost. He was offered football scholarships by two smaller colleges in the south but turned them down. He wanted to attend the University of Tennessee. Although he was a very good football player, he was not good enough to play in the Southeastern Conference. He decided to go out for the tennis team, naively hoping to walk on without a tennis scholarship. He wound up playing club level tennis instead, which he enjoyed.

Blake didn't date much in high school but made up for it in college. There, he dated a lot of women, including an Asian girl he was crazy about and later, an African American girl named Sasha. His parents were less than enthusiastic about the Asian girl and positively apoplectic over the black girl he brought home for dinner one Sunday.

While Mrs. Stevens did the dishes with the young woman's help, Mr. Stevens invited his son to help him with something in the garage. Mr. Stevens didn't mince words. "What are you thinking son? This is wrong and you must end this relationship."

"Y'all don't like her?" Blake asked, pretending innocence. "Why not?"

"You know perfectly well, why not. Sasha is a nice girl, but she's black and no one in this town will even begin to understand your strange behavior."

Blake picked up one of his old tennis rackets that was sitting on a workbench and fiddled with the strings. "By no one, you mean the people you and Mom associate with." He put the racket down and stuck his hands in his pockets. "The old South is dead, Dad."

"You're being naïve, son. Is it deliberate?"

"I'm not naïve. Anyway, it's not serious if that's what you're worried about."

Mr. Stevens stroke his chin. "Really? The girl looks at you as if it's quite serious."

"Are you sure you're not imagining that, Dad?"

"Your mother noticed it and said so when you two went into the kitchen."

"Well, I'm not in love with her Dad, so don't worry."

Mr. Stevens nodded, relieved, but wary. "Since we're out here, would you kindly help me put these boxes on that shelf?" They lifted the boxes, heavy with books onto the shelf. "Your mother will be grateful. Now maybe we can get both cars in the garage."

"Happy to help," Blake said. He turned to go back into the house, but his father caught his arm.

"Just a minute, son. Let's just assume this girl really does love you. Is it fair to her to keep seeing her if you know she isn't the right one for you?"

"Are you trying to tell me you're worried about her?"

"In a sense, I am. Someday you'll understand. Take my advice, Blake. For everyone's sake, let her go."

The young woman broke up with Blake on the ride back to the campus. She grasped the problem quickly. One dinner with the Stevens family was enough. "Your parents will never accept me. What were you thinking, bringing me to meet them?" Blake didn't date anyone more than twice after that. He liked Sasha more than he had let on to his father.

After he graduated and began teaching at his old high school in Colby Springs, he dated frequently, but never seriously until he met Nicci. Their whirlwind courtship surprised everyone in the Stevens family. Nicci seemed likeable, was eager to please and certainly appeared to be in love with Blake. She was almost six feet tall, had a perfect figure and wore sunglasses even on cloudy days.

After their second date Blake asked Nicci, "What made you choose our little town?"

"I don't know if I'll stay here. I just saw a job posting on line for a bank teller. That's what I was doing in Dallas. I did some research and decided what the heck, you know?"

"Well, maybe you'll learn to love it here," he said.

"I like you. That's a start," Nicci said.

He was drawn to her carefree lifestyle. Her apartment was tiny. The only furniture she had was a bed, a Futon chair and ottoman and a TV. Blake thought her exotic. He had never met a girl from France. Nicci told him she had spent a lot of time in Paris

The relationship moved along rapidly. The first time they made love, he saw the tattoo on the small of her back that said, *rempli de surprises*. "What does it mean?" He asked her.

"Full of surprises," she said. "It describes me well, don't you think?"

They became a popular couple in a town that had recently become something of a hotspot for young professionals, eager to find the elusive work-life balance that trendy publications were touting. If Nicci tended to be vague about her life before Colby Springs, no one noticed. She had interesting tales about her time in France, impressing everyone in their circle.

Blake proposed to Nicci in front of their friends one Saturday night at the Denny's off the Interstate. Nicci's response was a bit subdued and Blake noticed. She accepted his proposal and everyone at the table cheered. On the way home he asked, "Are you sure Nicci? I mean I probably put you on the spot in front of our friends."

Nicci leaned into him and they kissed. "I'm very sure Blake, I promise."

A year later, having spent time in Manhattan, Blake would wince at the thought of choosing such a casual dining spot to ask such an important question. Regardless, Nicci had quickly said yes. Less than a week later, she suggested they live together. It didn't take long to find a home they felt they could afford. They moved what little furniture Nicci had and combined it with what Blake had in his apartment. At Nicci's insistence, they also spent a small fortune on furniture, including a king-sized bed, bureau and dresser, a dining room suite and a widescreen TV. Everything was charged to Blake's credit card.

It wasn't until she disappeared that it occurred to Blake how trusting he had been, how little he really knew about Nicci. That she may have fabricated a good part of her history became clear when he asked the school's French teacher to make inquiries about her. The teacher had a friend who lived in Paris. The woman checked out Romainville and discovered there were at least a half-dozen residents named Brevard in the area. It would have taken a great deal more time and effort to properly research Nicci's background.

Friends implored him to look into her story about living in Dallas as well, but he refused. He was embarrassed as it was. He saw no need to add to his humiliation. He moved to New York, swearing never to return to Colby Springs.

8

Thanksgiving at the Clark home was considerably more festive than the quiet afternoon Blake spent with Mrs. Cotton. The house was decorated to reflect the approaching holidays and everyone was in good spirits. Relatives were visiting from northern New Jersey and Claire's friend Victoria was there with a man she met through Claire and Brad. Charles Remolina was a surgeon, twelve years older than Victoria and recently divorced.

Over dinner, there was of course, some chatter about the wedding that would take place in just nine months. Claire looked radiant, thoroughly enjoying the attention. Her parents, Terrence and Elizabeth, were delighted with their daughter's choice. Over spiked eggnog after dessert, the two doctors regaled the party with medical tales of heroic actions and near misses that could easily have ended in calamity.

Brad preferred to talk about his ability to diagnose difficult cases, retelling one of his favorites about recognizing pheochromocytoma, a rare tumor on the adrenal gland that can be life threatening. "This patient came to me after seeing umpteen specialists for high blood pressure. Nothing seemed to work, until I ran some lab tests. I was sure I nailed it and then I confirmed it with a CT scan." He smiled and took a sip of his drink.

His friend, Dr. Remolina, preferred to talk about cases that frightened him in the operating room. His candor charmed the Clark's guests and impressed Victoria. Eventually the conversation drifted to the football game that morning. Brad said, "I noticed the new history teacher from Dixieland didn't stay for the second half."

"How do you know that?" Claire asked.

"I don't know it for certain, but when the second half started, he wasn't there, unless he sat somewhere else."

"I didn't notice." Claire said. "Brad performed triage on him after the stabbing incident, I told you about," she said to Charles and Victoria.

"I remember. Blake Stevens? Now that man's a hunk," Victoria said. Having only recently met Dr. Remolina, she felt comfortable expressing such an opinion.

"Apparently Jonna Martinelli thinks so," Claire said.

"What do you think, dear?" Brad asked, looking squarely into Claire's eyes.

"He's good looking in some mysterious way. I think he's a weird duck though. I mean imagine living in an apartment above Mrs. Cotton's."

"He probably left at half time to throw a few passes to Jonna," Brad said.

Mrs. Clark had been standing nearby listening to the young people banter. "Isn't Jonna the girl with two little boys and that awful ex-husband?"

"Right, long blonde hair, tall and on the thin side," Brad said.

"Very descriptive, Brad," Claire said.

Mrs. Clark went on. "That's what I thought. Your father and I noticed her talking to one of the coaches when the game was over. She was hugging him."

"That's her brother," Victoria said.

"Jonna was sitting not far from us. I don't think she was there with a date," Mrs. Clark added.

Claire picked up a bitesize creampuff and bit into it. She was surprised to hear that Blake and Jonna didn't go to the game as a couple, unless, perhaps, they did, squabbled at some point and parted company. She looked at Brad and said, "Was Jonna ever one of your patients?"

Brad had been about to take a creampuff from the tray. He stopped and said, "Heavens no. Whatever gave you that idea?" He picked up the creampuff again and took a bite.

"She acted as if she knew you," Claire said.

"We went out a couple of times when I was on a break from internship, I think."

"Define going out, Brad," Victoria said, a mischievous smile on her face.

Dr. Remolina, eager to assist his friend and colleague, said, "My dear Victoria, are you trying to get us uninvited to what promises to be a splendid wedding?" Everyone laughed.

Claire finished what was left of her creampuff and waited. Brad finished his creampuff and smiled. "Actually, it was nothing. If I'm not mistaken, it wasn't even a date, although Jonna, poor girl, may have thought so. I don't remember much about her."

Victoria sensing a bit of tension in the room now, said, "I wonder why our mystery man didn't stick around for the second half?"

"Maybe Mrs. Cotton gave him a to-do list. Claire told me Mrs. C keeps him busy fixing up that old house," Brad said. He turned to Dr. Remolina. "Everybody in this town had that old woman in the fourth grade and nobody liked her."

"That's unkind and it's not true," Claire said. "Everyone loved her."

Brad put his hands together, wringing them slightly. "It seems my lovely fiancé is determined to be cross with me today. Perhaps I should have taken the on-call assignment at the hospital."

Dr. Remolina laughed and put his arm around his colleague. "I think I'll have one of those creampuffs for the road."

That evening, Claire made it up to Brad, spending the night with him in his condo for the first time. She assured him it was not a breakthrough. Rather, it was a one-time event. They made love and she was especially tender with him. Yet, she was troubled by his obvious discomfort when Jonna's name came up. And she was not at all happy with the familiar way that Jonna had addressed Brad at the football field.

Over breakfast on Friday morning, she broached the subject again. "Is there anything about you and Jonna I should know?"

"That's an odd question, Claire. Absolutely not." He dabbed the corner of his mouth with his napkin. "I know Victoria is a playful soul, but she was out of line last night. And the way she went on about that Blake character was unkind to Charles."

"I'm sure she didn't mean anything by it. Does Charles really like her?"

"I think he does. Do you think she's genuinely interested in him?"

Claire was careful. If she said what she really thought, that Victoria was probably more interested in Charles's bank account, she was sure Brad would relay that to his friend. Regardless of Victoria's desire for the good life, it was still possible that she could fall in love with the man. It was simply too soon to say. "I think she believes the relationship has possibilities."

Blake had a busy morning the day after Thanksgiving. It was a year to the day before his arrest. As he was leaving Mrs. Cotton's place after their Thanksgiving dinner, she had handed him the envelope she had tried to give him earlier and asked him to buy paint. "If you were serious about giving my home a paint job, I'd be ever so grateful. I will pay you for your time of course and you aren't allowed to say no, understood?"

"What if you need the money for the casinos in Atlantic City?" he asked.

"Don't be ridiculous, I can't stand foolishness and gambling is a very foolish thing to do." The woman's tone sounded more like what Blake was used to hearing.

"There's money hidden all over this place isn't there?"

Mrs. Cotton smiled. "There's money, but you'll never find it."

Late that morning he took a ride to Millville, where the Home Depot was and bought enough paint to redo the walls and ceilings in Mrs. Cotton's apartment. He bought brushes, tape and plenty of plastic drop cloth to cover her hardwood floors and furniture. He didn't have enough cash to cover it, so he used his credit card for the rest.

On his way out the door, pushing a cart filled with paint, he saw a familiar face walking in. He couldn't quite place her, which annoyed him. She was worth remembering. She was pretty. The woman's auburn hair and mischievous green eyes got his attention.

"Must be my lucky day," the woman said.

"You win the lottery?" he asked.

"Not yet, but I'm working on it. It's nice to see you again, Blake. You were all Claire and I talked about yesterday."

He pointed his finger toward her. "Ah, Victoria, right?" Now he knew why he didn't really notice her before. Victoria was very pretty, but to his mind, Claire was perfection. The two women were together when he met Victoria the first time.

"That's me. What are you painting?"

"My landlady's apartment. What are you doing here?"

"I need to replace the air filters in my apartment. I'm such a bore."

"Somehow, I doubt that you're ever boring, Victoria. But it is possible that you are occasionally bored. Yesterday, for example. If my name came up in conversation at your table, I'll bet Y'all were very bored." Blake hoped his voice had just the right note of humor.

"Well, Bradley mentioned that you were MIA for the second half of yesterday's game, which led to juicy speculation about your whereabouts and deeds."

"I see. You folks must have been quite bored." He looked at her and shook his head. Then, he turned away and pushed the loaded cart to his Camaro.

Victoria was stunned. She couldn't believe that Blake would walk off, with an attitude. What had she said? She just teased him a little. She picked up her phone and started walking toward the aisle that had the filters. "You will never guess who I just ran into at Home Depot."

"Whoever it was, you don't sound happy about it." Claire was on her way home from Brad's place.

"I'm not. Your friend, Blake Stevens, was here. We chatted a little and then, out of nowhere, he walks off in a huff. Didn't say goodbye, just turned his back to me and left."

Claire was aware that Victoria was prone to saying things that could offend people who didn't know her well. "I wouldn't call him a friend, Victoria, but what, exactly, did you say to him?"

"I told him we missed him at the game, that Bradley noticed he was gone after halftime. I teased him a little about what he might be doing with Jonna instead of watching the game, that's all."

"Doesn't sound like much, but he doesn't really know you. Maybe he thought we were gossiping about him."

"He was so rude, Claire. I know you have to work with him and I don't want to make it uncomfortable for you."

"Don't worry about it, please. I rarely see him at school. You know, I thought he was quite rude the day he refused to let Brad drive him to the hospital, but he was just stabbed by a crazy man, so I felt maybe he wasn't thinking clearly." Claire turned into her driveway. She took the key out of the ignition. "As I said yesterday, there's something odd about him. There was no reason for him to be rude to you."

9

Claire Clark grew up in world of privilege. Her father, Terrance, held a full professorship, at the University of Pennsylvania, teaching philosophy. He worked hard to look the part, with the Pince-nez reading glasses and the tweed jacket with elbow patches. His home library was filled with the works of the great philosophers. Elizabeth Clark was a historian, who wrote scholarly articles and was very active in the New Jersey chapter of the Daughters of the American Revolution. Although Mrs. Clark's forefathers were not among the American Revolution's leaders, at least one of them fought gallantly during the war.

She was a meticulous woman in her choice of words and dress. Always a lady, Mrs. Clark never left the house, not even to get a quart of milk, without wearing makeup and jewelry. She always wore a skirt, or dress, and low heel pumps. She was also meticulous in the way she raised her two daughters, Deanna and Claire.

One afternoon, after a lecture, she got home just in time to hear Claire, then just 16, place a call to a boy she liked in her algebra class. She stood quietly in the mud room waiting for the call to end. Then she addressed her younger daughter. "My apologies, dear, but I couldn't help overhearing your phone call. I cannot stress enough that a lady never calls a young man. We do not chase a man, ever. If he is a gentleman, interested in you and the pleasure of your company, he will call you. Otherwise, he is not worth your time."

Claire answered her mother, saying, "Mom, that may have been the way you did things in your day, but my generation believes in equality between men and women. There is no reason I shouldn't call a boy I like, or vice versa."

Mrs. Clark nodded her head. "I'm all for equality Claire, but I certainly hope that leaves room for a woman to act like a lady. You'll find that no matter what the trends are, being a lady, will not only keep you out of trouble, it will open doors for you that you will want opened. Understood?"

"Yes, mother," Claire said. It was the easiest way to end such conversations and there were many of them.

As children, Claire and her older sister Deanna sensed they were special. While their parents never suggested such a thing, the fact was they lived in one of the nicest homes in Clarksville. That the town was called Clarksville certainly wasn't lost on them. The Clark residence, built late in the eighteenth century by Samuel Clark, was one of Clarksville's first homes, built by Samuel Clark.

Their parents set high expectations and reminded them frequently of their responsibilities to live up to the Clark name. After all, Terrance like to point out, Samuel Clark founded Clarksville. From kindergarten on, teachers would point out to the class that a descendant of the town's founder was among them. The boys and girls she went to school with teased her about it, of course, but Claire chose to ignore them. She hated it when teachers mentioned her family history. By the time she was a junior in high school and about to study US history, she approached her teacher and asked her not to bring it up when they studied the Declaration of Independence. The woman answered her saying, "Why would I bring that up, Claire? You didn't sign it, did you?"

At least once, their social standing kept them out of trouble, thanks to a kindly police officer. One hot summer afternoon, Deanna and Claire decided to walk downtown with some friends. This was when Deanna was 16 and Claire was just 14 years old. There was an empty lot with only an abandoned fruit and vegetable stand a block from the center of town. As they were walking past the lot, one of the boys suggested they go behind the stand's back wall. "I want to show you something," he said. He pulled out a marijuana cigarette and a lighter. He lit up and said, "I dare everybody to take a hit."

"You're crazy," Claire said. "Put that thing out." But one of the other boys in the group took it and inhaled. He passed it to Deanna.

She looked at her sister and asked, "Promise you won't tell daddy?" Claire was too frightened to respond. She couldn't believe her sister would actually smoke marijuana. Deanna took a hit and handed it back to the boy.

He took a quick drag and offered it to Claire. That's when they noticed the patrol car. The boy dropped it and squashed it under his sneaker, twisting back and forth, hoping he could bury it in the dirt. The officer got out of the patrol car and walked over to the group. He knew exactly what they were doing. He told the boys to wait for him next to the patrol car. Then he turned to the Clark sisters. "You know your father and mother would be devastated to learn you were smoking marijuana, right?

"Yes sir," Deanna said. Claire started to cry.

"If I ever see either one of you doing anything like this again, I will arrest you. I don't care who your parents are. Am I making myself clear?" The girls nodded. "Go home and remember what I said."

The girls spent many weekend afternoons with their mother in Philadelphia's historic district. Long after they tired of the sightseeing tours of Independence Hall and the Betsy Ross house, they accompanied Mrs. Clark to lectures. The Clark's older daughter loved learning about the nation's history. Claire, on the other hand, was more interested in literature, especially the writings of Philadelphians like James Michener, Walt Whitman and Edgar Allen Poe. Even Mark Twain had a Philadelphia connection. But what both girls enjoyed most about these trips was having high tea at the famous Belleview Stratford Hotel. The tea and scones with Devonshire cream and finger sandwiches, served in such elegant surroundings, delighted them.

In spite of frequent arguments with her mother on the merits of proper behavior and protocol, Claire was like her mother in one way. She dressed conservatively, even in high school. Yet, she had a young woman's curiosity too. She had a boyfriend, Joshua Tallaca, a young man who was smart enough to be accepted by Temple University for academic performance alone. The son of a successful farmer, he was also the school's star basketball player. Mrs. Clark thought he was a nice boy, but certainly not someone Claire should consider for marriage.

One night during the Easter break of her senior year, Mrs. Clark met her daughter at the front door after Claire and Joshua said good night. "Not that I'm worried, dear, but I assume you know that Joshua isn't headed for the White House someday."

Claire walked past her mother in that insolent way young people can do. Not bothering to turn around, she said, "He already lives in a white house mother, a big one on Bridgeton Road."

Mrs. Clark took a few quick steps and took her daughter's shoulder firmly. "You know exactly what I'm talking about. You were doing some rather heavy petting in his car, right in our driveway, Claire. Are you truly shameless?"

"Mother, how dare you spy on me. I know what I'm doing. I'm not a fool."

"No Claire, you are nobody's fool, but you are human. Just be careful. He isn't someone you should give yourself too."

She wasn't in love with Joshua, but in spite of her mother's warnings, she ended her virginity on prom night at the cemetery, where so many other young men and women had sex for the first time. Her mother was right. She was human and she got carried away, abetted by a pint of whiskey she and Joshua shared. While she enjoyed the sex and grasped its promise, she knew instinctively that it wasn't to be wasted on casual encounters.

But one month later, when Claire didn't get her period, she soon realized that casual though her first sexual experience was, its impact on her future was anything but casual. When Claire tearfully told her mother she was late, Mrs. Clark took her to an obstetrician in Northern VA, driving her daughter there for the appointment. The Clarks momentarily considered abortion, but notwithstanding the convenient solution it offered, both were morally opposed.

Claire struggled with her parents. She insisted on keeping the baby, but, they wore her down, pointing out the difficulties in trying to raise a child as a single mother. Certainly, Claire had no desire to marry Joshua, assuming he would agree to it. In any event, his background posed a problem for the Clarks. "Tallica," Mr. Clark said, "As I understand it, the Tallica clan is native American Indian, right?"

"Please don't patronize me daddy," Claire answered. "Obviously, you know that. You know the genetic makeup of everybody in the county."

Mr. Clark deliberately reached for his pipe, filled it with tobacco and lit it. He had to busy his hands, otherwise, he might strike his daughter, something he had never done.

"Quite right, Claire. Their tribe comes from the Raritan River area, as I recall." That Tallica's ancestors were already here centuries before the Clark tribe arrived, didn't impress Mr. Clark. His older daughter, Deanna, was already married to a Jew. He had high hopes that Claire would find a young man with patrician blood lines to match his own. A Native American, whose parents were scratching out a living as farmers wouldn't do.

Claire went away to a home for unwed mothers in Virginia. The cover story was that she decided to do a year in the Peace Corps before heading off to college. Neither young Joshua Tallica, or his parents, were ever informed of the pregnancy. A private adoption was arranged through Mr. Clark's very discreet attorney. The father of the child was never revealed.

When it was time for college, Claire chose Boston University over Swarthmore as much as anything because her mother wanted her to go to Swarthmore. While she attended college, she had sex with just one man, a graduate student she admired and for the first time in her life, felt something like love. When she listened to her friends talk about sex, she felt they missed the whole point. With the right man, she believed sex was a deep expression of love, a gift from God that made life's trials not only bearable, but hopeful.

Until her senior year, she insisted she was going to live in Massachusetts, which drove her mother crazy. But then, in the spring of that year, Mrs. Clark was diagnosed with breast cancer. After she recovered from the ordeal of surgery and chemotherapy, it changed Mrs. Clark's outlook some. She was clearly more empathetic toward the problems of others and less certain that she always knew what was best for the people around her. Claire was terrified by the prospect of losing her mother. She relented and returned to Clarksville after graduation.

It was during one of Mrs. Clark's chemotherapy treatments that Claire learned that her mother wasn't always quite so puritanical. She confessed to her daughter that during the 1960s she had been a hippie. One summer, after her junior year in college, she took a cross country bus ride with a radical group determined to put an end to the Vietnam War. She smiled and said, leaning close to Claire, "I had a love affair, torrid you might say, with the protest group's leader. He was a marvelous speaker; he was very motivating. His eloquence really moved us," she said. "It was over by the time we arrived in San Francisco. I flew home from there."

"Does Dad know about that?" Claire asked.

"Heavens no. We were dating at the time. He never understood why I chose that bus trip over the demonstrations that were going on in Washington," she said. "Your father has always been a bluenose. It's his strength and his weakness." Claire felt she understood her mother better after that, and they grew closer. Like so many women, her mother became what she thought her husband wanted her to be.

Claire earned her degree with high honors in secondary education focused on English. She had no trouble finding a job at Clarksville Regional High School. She dated a few men, including a partner at her brother-in-law's law firm, but never became serious with anyone until she ran into Brad Chambers again.

10

When Blake got back from Home Depot, he knocked on Mrs. Cotton's door and waited. Mrs. Cotton asked, "Who is it?"

"It's Blake, I have your paint."

Mrs. Cotton opened her door and looked at all the paint cans, brushes, rollers and coverings. "Oh my. How much do I owe you for all that?"

"Nothing. Can you believe it? I had exactly the right amount of cash to cover everything."

"Don't lie to me. I have no tolerance for liars," Mrs. Cotton said. She had a stern look on her face

Blake could see the old woman was quite serious. "You owe me $39 dollars."

Mrs. Cotton was back in one of her housecoats. Her hair wasn't done. "Wait here please. I'll get my purse. I assume you knocked on my door to collect your money. I wish you had simply said so."

"Mrs. Cotton, I was hoping I could store the paint and all this equipment in your back bedroom. That's why I knocked on your door."

"Why didn't you say that instead of asking me for money?"

"I didn't ask for money. Can I store the paint?" He shoved his hands in his pockets.

"May I store the paint. You mean may I, Mr. Stevens."

"So, its Mr. Stevens again. I think I've been demoted."

"I'm sure it's not the first time," Mrs. Cotton said. She looked at all the cans of paint, the brushes the rollers, the roller pan and the drop cloths again. "Well, I suppose you'd better put these things in that back bedroom."

"I can start work today if you want."

"Don't be ridiculous. It's Thanksgiving weekend. You can start next Saturday. I want the kitchen, the dining room and the living room done before Christmas. Can you manage that?"

"I think so."

"Don't make a mess in that bedroom. Be neat." As he was carrying paint cans into the bedroom, he heard her say something from the kitchen. "When you finish, I'll have a turkey sandwich waiting for you." Blake smiled. He was beginning to figure out Bella Cotton.

He was pleased not to have to work that weekend. He was itching to get on a tennis court. Parker, a very good player, had a membership at an indoor tennis club an hour's drive away in Cherry Hill. He called his buddy.

"Yeah, I can play. I'll pick you up," Parker said.

On the ride to the club, Parker told Blake about his romp the night before Thanksgiving, but he was circumspect when it came to details. "We went to a dance club not far from the tennis club. We danced until almost midnight. I had a real sweat going."

"I'll bet that turned her on," Blake said.

"She's an excellent dancer, better than my ex." Parker liked to dance as much as he liked tennis. He and his ex-wife had been ballroom dancers. "Anyway, we got along great. Went back to my place and really got it on."

"And?"

"And I really like this girl. Her name is Penny. She's three inches shorter than me, which isn't easy to find these days. She wears her hair short, the way I like it."

"You meant to say, shorter than I am, not shorter than me," Blake said, enjoying the moment.

"Damn it Blakester, Mrs. Cotton is getting to you."

"I guess so. What else can you tell me about your new girlfriend?"

"She's from Orlando, used to work at Disney World." Blake realized that Parker really did like Penny. He wasn't going to offer any of the graphic details some guys offered about women they slept with when it was only a casual encounter.

"When are you going to see her again?"

"Saw her last night and we're going out again tonight. She wouldn't have Thanksgiving with my family. She thought it was too soon. Why don't you call Jonna and we'll all go out, get a bite and go dancing again?"

"Jonna's looking for a relationship. I'm not ready for that."

"When I saw her at the bar the other night, she asked about you. Wanted to know if you were involved with anyone."

What did you say?"

"I said I didn't know. Are you?"

"I'm working on my landlady."

Parker laughed. "She pretty much looked the same when she was teaching fourth grade as she does now. Jonna wanted me to call you to see if you would come over to the bar."

"Really? I saw her at the game on Thanksgiving. She didn't mention it."

"You might be better off steering clear of that girl. You know we went to high school together, right? She was a few years behind me. Anyway, when she asked me to call you, I said it would be better if she called you. As I recall her exact words were, 'Thanks a lot, asshole.' Or something like that."

The men split two spirited sets, each winning 6-4. They limited the third set to a tiebreaker, which Blake managed to win 7-4. The workout made Blake feel good, and, more importantly, he was pleased that his game was improving. He hadn't played much tennis during the last five years, but since moving to Clarksville, he and Parker were playing at least three times a month. When spring came, they would probably play more. He was also looking forward to coaching the high school tennis team. It was a new sport at the school, so he knew he would have to be patient, but he was confident that he could build a good team if he stayed at the school for a few years.

How long would he stay? Clarksville was a very small town. While he always liked small town living, he felt the people in Clarksville were standoffish, not like the welcoming souls he knew so well in the south. His encounter with Victoria was a case in point. He detested gossip and learned early in life not to do it. One summer afternoon when he was in middle school, he came home from the swimming hole and said, "Mama, did you know the Kendrick's are getting a divorce?"

"Who told you that? She asked.

"One of the kids I was swimming with."

His mother put down her magazine, got up from her chair and walked over to him. "We don't gossip in this house, ever. You're grounded this weekend." She was genuinely angry with him.

Knowing that people he barely knew were gossiping about him, made him uncomfortable. That Claire may have participated in the talk bothered him more than he wanted to admit. He knew he had to stay in Clarksville for a couple of years to build his teaching resume, but beyond that, he wasn't sure what he wanted.

The time between Thanksgiving and Christmas flew by. Blake's sister Judy, invited him to spend the holidays in Colby Springs, but he quickly declined. "Judy, I don't want to come back to Colby Springs until I'm sure I can handle it," he said. Memories of Nicci still haunted him at times.

He was making progress, but he wasn't ready to go home, not yet. In fact, some nights, when he couldn't sleep, even after all these months, he would still think about ways to find Nicci. He mentioned that to Judy.

"Whatever would you do if you found her, my brother? Lord, I hope you're not still in love with her, are you?"

"No, no. I just want answers," he said.

"I want to send her to prison, Blake."

As Christmas approached, he worked hard with his students to get them ready for the end of semester exams. He knew their scores would be closely scrutinized by his department head, Frank Holt and the school's principal. He sensed there was some resentment over the way he'd been hired. At least one local prospect had been turned down because there were no openings, only to learn that someone had been hired after all. Blake worked his students hard. Now it was up to them.

Every Christmas, each department held a Christmas party the night after the students got out of school. Some departments combined to make a bigger party. This year the English, math and history departments were getting together at the town firehall to celebrate. Spouses and significant others usually attended these parties, to enjoy a few drinks and dance.

Blake had decided not to attend. He didn't feel welcome, but Parker, who was still seeing Penny, insisted. "If you want people to like you, Blake, they have to get to know you," he said. The party was held on Thursday, just four days before Christmas. Blake didn't have a date, of course, but Parker and Penny offered to fix him up with one of her friends who was visiting from Florida. Reluctantly, he agreed. The woman's name was Becky. She was shy, not one to make conversation. They danced a few times, but spent more time watching Parker and Penny put on a show. Blake and Becky both knew from hello, that in a matter of weeks, they would barely remember meeting.

Blake saw Claire and Brad a couple of times, once on the way into the hall and once at the buffet table. They were never in close enough proximity to actually exchange pleasantries, until later in the evening when Blake was leaving the restroom. Coming in his direction was Claire. He stopped and said, "It's safe. Neither one of us is carrying anything hot."

She didn't even break her stride. As she passed by, though, she said, "No popcorn either, I see." As usual, Blake was struck by how pretty she looked. And, brief as their exchange was, Blake felt something. Claire had a special quality he found impossible to ignore. He had met women before that excited his imagination, but he never felt his insides pulse as if he had just taken a potent drug, until he met Claire. It bothered him that she could do that to him. They had gotten off on the wrong foot and nothing had changed since they met in front of Waffle Heaven almost four months ago. Was she aware of her effect on him? He hoped not.

Lost in an uncomfortable thought, he nearly ploughed into Brad Chambers. "Whoa there, boy. Slow down on the margaritas," Brad said.

Blake laughed. "Are you telling me I missed the margaritas?" He hadn't planned it, but he saw an opportunity, late though it may be, to make amends with the doctor. After all, the man had attended to his immediate needs outside Waffle Heaven the day Derek sliced his arm.

"How are you doing?" Brad asked.

"I'm fine. Let me take a moment to thank you for helping me that day. I should have done that a long time ago."

"Forget it. Glad I could help. I understand that maniac might be released soon. If you don't mind a little bit of advice, stay away from him. I've known him since we were kids. Always in trouble and always very angry."

Claire came back and joined them. Before she could say a word, Brad stuck his hand out and said, "Well, Blake, no more margaritas for you. Doctor's orders." With that the couple walked away. And Blake wished he hadn't apologized.

Less than a week before Christmas, Blake decided to accept an invitation to spend his holiday vacation with Uncle John and Aunt Abigail. It had snowed on Christmas Eve which made it hard for Blake to get to northern New Jersey. Driving was treacherous, but he arrived in time for dinner. He had planned on leaving two days earlier, but he ran out of paint half-way through his work on Mrs. Cotton's kitchen and had to wait a few days for Home Depot to get a shipment in. Mrs. Cotton was upset because her sister would be visiting her for the first time in many years. He promised he would finish the job before he left, so he waited until the paint arrived and managed to apply the final coat of paint late on the twenty-third.

Uncle John and Aunt Abigail pressed him to stay with them for at least a few days. Judy had planned to join them too, but she canceled at the last minute when a man she recently started dating invited her to spend the week in San Francisco. His uncle sweetened the offer by insisting that Blake should use their Manhattan apartment for a few days, including New Year's Eve.

Blake invited Parker and Penny to visit him. They were very excited about it and spent a couple of days in the city. Blake didn't see much of them, but he didn't mind. He managed to go with Parker and Penny to watch the ball come down heralding the New Year. As he stood in the crowd at Times Square with his friends, he felt lonely. Just before he went to sleep that night, he vowed that the year ahead would be one of renewal. He would finally put the past behind him and let go of what might have been. He realized now that even if Nicci had gone through with their wedding, it was likely that she would have run eventually. The best thing he could do was move on with his life. He vowed to do that moments before he slept.

He returned to Clarksville on the second day of the New Year. It was snowing and once again, driving conditions were hazardous. He stopped at the supermarket and picked up a few grocery items before heading home. He was dreading going back to his apartment because he knew it would be cold. It would take a while for the heat to kick in and remove the chill. But when he opened his door he found the apartment was warm. Mrs. Cotton must have stopped by and turned up the thermostat.

He had work to do because he still had some exams to grade. He was pleased with what he had seen so far. While the scores weren't particularly high, his students did better than expected. After lunch, he decided to go downstairs and check on Mrs. Cotton. Her sister was probably gone. He decided to unpack first. Then his phone rang.

"Did you hear?" It was Parker.

"What?"

"That dirtball that cut your arm is in critical condition. They don't expect him to make it."

"Derek?"

"Yeah, him. Your old girlfriend nailed him with a frying pan while we were ringing in the New Year," Parker said.

Jonna Martinelli had finally had enough. Her ex-husband had been released just two days before Christmas. He kept his distance for nearly a whole week, avoiding alcohol and spending most of his time at his mother's house.

His mother was so pleased. Certain her son had changed, that she decided it was safe to tell him what Jonna did while he was out looking for work. "Your ex came by this afternoon." Mrs. Martinelli was sitting next to the tree, drinking a glass of wine.

"What did that bitch want?" Derek asked.

"Well, you're not going to like it, but she returned the presents you bought the boys for Christmas. She left them on the front porch with a note. They weren't even opened."

Derek had been eying the wine bottle on the coffee table. He'd been looking for an excuse to have some. "What are you talking about, Ma?" She did what?"

"Now don't get worked up. She said she didn't want the boys to be confused, or some silly nonsense. Anyway, the presents are right here under the tree."

He grabbed the half-filled bottle and drank it in one long swallow. He went to the kitchen and found some rye. He drank that too. The first thing Derek had done when he was released from the county jail was borrow money from his mother so he could give his boys something for Christmas. Mrs. Martinelli had wrapped each gift. Worried that Jonna and Derek would have an argument, she insisted on delivering them to the boys.

He was furious. He swore and grabbed his keys. "Don't go over there Derek," Mrs. Martinelli said, "they'll put you away again, son. Tomorrow you and I can go there together and give the boys their presents."

"Fuck that," Derek said. He picked up the gifts and headed out the door.

Mrs. Martinelli, who was not fond of Jonna, was worried about her grandsons, but decided not to call Jonna to warn her. She might call the cops.

Derek took the presents over to Jonna's and rang the bell. Jonna had company, one of the waiters at the Mexican restaurant. When the doorbell rang, she was in the middle of moving sausage and peppers from the frying pan into a bowl. She asked her friend to answer the door. When the guy saw the look on Derek's face he brushed past him and left, forgetting his jacket and leaving Jonna to fend for herself. Surprised to see him, she tried being nice to him at first, offering him some of her sausages. But, fueled by anger and alcohol, he ignored her. She let him give the presents to the boys who were crying now, afraid of him. He blamed her for that too.

It was when he decided the boys should spend the night with him that she panicked. "I'm taking my kids to stay at my mother's house tonight. You can go ahead and be a whore for your fag boyfriend." He picked the boys up, one in each arm and headed for the door. The boys, wearing only pajamas, were not dressed for cold weather. They started crying for their mother.

Jonna chased Derek down the hall. "You're not going anywhere with them. You're drunk and there's a restraining order. Did you forget?" She reached for the boys. He put the older one down and took a swing at her, landing a glancing blow on her right cheek. The boys were screaming now. Jonna picked up the older boy and ran to the kitchen. "I'm calling the cops," she said. He followed her and hit her again, harder this time. Her head hit the edge of the kitchen table, causing a gash. He picked up his older son and said, "Shut up both of you. I'm taking you to see your grandma."

Bleeding profusely, she grabbed the first thing she saw, the cast iron frying pan. The handle was still hot, but fearful for her sons, she didn't notice. Furious that she was still forced to deal with this man, frightened for herself and her sons, she hit him hard on the back of his head, knocking him down. The boys fell too and ran to their bedroom. She stood over Derek and waited, ready to hit him again. He didn't move. Jonna's mother came home from work and found her daughter sitting in the hallway, the frying pan in one hand and a bloody dish-towel in the other, holding her head where the gash was. She called the EMT squad. They stuck Derek in an ambulance and then went to work on Jonna's injuries. The emergency room doctor put three stiches in the right side of her head and treated her for first and second degree burns on her right hand.

Derek wasn't as lucky. She had hit him with enormous force and he still had not regained consciousness. The doctors were doubtful about his prospects.

Blake could hardly believe what Parker was telling him.

"How's Jonna doing?" He asked.

"I heard she took a shot to the head, too, when he knocked her down. I think she's back at work today though, if you're in the mood for Mexican food," Parker said.

"Thanks, Parker. You're always thinking. Is she really back to work already?"

"Money's tight and she wasn't hurt that bad, I guess."

"Are they going to charge her with anything?"

"I doubt it. She told the cops she hit him in self-defense."

Early the next evening, after getting the last of the mid-term grades recorded, Blake looked out the window and saw it had stopped snowing. About six inches of snow covered the ground. He had checked earlier with Mrs. Cotton, but the woman told him through the door that she wasn't feeling well. Now he was hungry and not in the mood to cook. He found himself wondering about Jonna and what she had been through. Would it be a mistake to look in on her at the restaurant? Would she misinterpret his intentions?

He put his coat, hat and gloves on and went downstairs. He knocked again on Mrs. Cotton's door. "Can I get you anything?" he asked.

"No, nothing, thank you." Her voice sounded weak. Blake wished Mrs. Cotton's sister was still visiting.

He didn't see Jonna right away at the restaurant. The place wasn't very busy. A short, middle-aged man, approached. "Nice to see you Mr. Stevens. Sit anywhere you like."

Blake looked at the man, wondering how he knew his name. "My daughter, Payton, is in your class."

Blake took a good look around, hoping to see Jonna. She came walking out of the kitchen a large band aid still attached to the right side of her head. She smiled when she saw him. She pointed to one of her tables. "You come by to check on me, or are you one of those guys who likes dangerous women?"

"One dangerous woman is enough in a man's life. I came to see how you are and maybe eat a couple of tacos."

"Just my luck, beat out by another dangerous woman. Who is she?"

"She was my fiancé,' Blake said. He suddenly realized that was the first time he had ever said a word about Nicci to anyone who wasn't family except for Parker. Parker's response had been interesting. After he heard the story all he said was, "That's what I should have done to my ex."

"So, commitment is something you can do?" She was laughing, a good sign.

Blake shook his head. He took a seat and said, "This place is dead, so let me buy you dinner and I'll tell you the whole story."

Over dinner, Blake told Jonna everything, including how devastated he had been. It almost seemed comical as he told it, but a new feeling emerged. "Running away was cowardly, wasn't it?"

"What did you run away from exactly?" Jonna asked. "She was gone. There was nothing to run away from. Maybe you just wanted a fresh start. You're entitled to that." In that moment, they actually became friends. "You're all right, Stevens." She picked up the plates, walked over to him and kissed his cheek.

When she came back to the table, they talked about Derek. "My head still hurts," Jonna said.

"Are you in any legal trouble?" Blake asked.

"My lawyer doesn't think they'll file charges, no matter what happens. I just don't want him to bother us ever again."

"From what I hear, that's unlikely."

"Who knows? Now that I've scrambled his brain, he'll probably just be worse."

Two days later, Derek Martinelli died.

Students returned to school a week later. Blake had turned in his grades, confident that his superiors would be satisfied with his work. He was wrong. After school, Mark Mitchell, the Principal, called him into his office. "Your students didn't do as well as we hoped in the fall semester finals."

"Really? I thought they scored pretty well. If I'm not mistaken, they're above the nationwide average for students taking standard classes," Blake said.

"That's true, but we strive for significantly better outcomes here, even among the students who may not strive for academic excellence." Mitchell, who shaved his head and wore black wayfarer glasses, stood and walked over to the window. He watched a few teachers walking to their cars.

"So, was I at least close to your expectations?"

Mitchell turned to face Blake. "The other history teachers all got better results." Blake started to protest, but Mitchell anticipated him. "Obviously, they all had at least one honors or advanced placement class. What I'm saying is, if you want to be here next year, you'll have to do better in the spring semester."

"Overall, my kids averaged three points above the national midpoint on the exam. Only seven out of 126 failed. I want to know now, how many points over the national average my kids need to be for you to be satisfied."

Mitchell stroked his chin and fiddled with his pen. "It doesn't work that way, Blake. Let's see how the numbers look in June. If you need any help, Frank Holt has assured me he's available to assist you."

Blake could see it would be pointless to argue. Mitchell was obviously out to get him. The guy wanted something on the record to justify what he planned to do. Blake had kept to himself, never causing any problems. He had not been absent, even one time, a far cry from what other teachers did. He knew for a fact that Parker had been out six times during the first semester. Maybe it wasn't just that his uncle had pressured the school system to hire him. In such a small town, any number of things could derail a new guy. Maybe the fact that he came from the south was an issue. Who knew what drove people's attitudes?

He was not a quitter, though. He would work hard to improve his students' performance. What he wouldn't do, would never do, was take it out on his students. They had to want to improve. It was his job to help them see why. He always tried to make his classes interesting, relating historic events to present day circumstances. He would just have to try harder. He was pretty sure that unless his students performed like the kids taking honors and advanced placement classes, however unfair it might be, he would be fired.

Two days later, there was still no sign of Mrs. Cotton. He telephoned her a couple of times, only to be told to go away. She was resting. Then, on Saturday morning, he tried again, but this time, she didn't answer. He walked down to her apartment and knocked hard on the door. Still no response. He thought about breaking in, but knew she had a heavy-duty deadbolt lock on her door. She would be angry if he broke in and found her sitting at her kitchen table sipping tea. He knew there were times when she became quiet and didn't want company. But this didn't feel like one of those times. He called 911 and waited.

The EMT crew tried calling her, too. When she didn't pick up, they had no trouble breaking in. They found her in bed, semi-conscious. They took her to the hospital where she was treated for dehydration. Her regular doctor had retired a year ago. Dr. Brad Chambers picked up her case. He diagnosed her with the flu. Later, he would add that she was suffering from emphysema.

Blake followed the ambulance to the hospital. Dr. Chambers met him in Mrs. Cotton's room, surprised to see him there. "It seems I run into you everywhere," he said. "What brings you to the hospital? Were you loitering in the halls and happened to notice your landlady?"

Blake looked Brad over, giving it an extra beat. The man was smiling, but it was really a sneer. "I found her. I don't think she has family who lives nearby." Then, just to let Brad know he wasn't just some hick from small town Tennessee, he asked, "Were you out chasing ambulances? Is that how you became Mrs. Cotton's doctor?"

"Touché!" Brad was surprised. Was he underestimating this guy?

Blake sat next to Mrs. Cotton's bed, wishing he had brought something to read. He was bored to death. Having read the labels on her IV bags, counted the tiles in the ceiling and on the floor, he was falling asleep. Then two visitors stopped by, both former co-workers at the elementary school where Mrs. Cotton worked for so many years.

He took the opportunity to get something to eat. He didn't want the old woman to wake up alone in her room, wondering how she got there. On his way to the cafeteria, he saw Claire get into the elevator. She was carrying a vase filled with flowers. She didn't see him. He ate a garden salad and went back up to Mrs. Cotton's room. Claire was sitting there, holding the woman's hand. Mrs. Cotton was awake now.

"Well, there you are. It took you long enough, I must say." Mrs. Cotton said.

"What do you mean? I've been here since you arrived."

"Ha! A likely story. You were probably busy ransacking my apartment. Did you find what you were looking for?"

Blake had come to really like Mrs. Cotton. "No, you were right, I haven't found the money yet. Where did you hide it? It would save me the trouble of ripping up your floor boards."

Mrs. Cotton extended her hand and Blake took it. "Claire told me you rescued me. Have you met her?"

"We work together at the high school, Mrs. Cotton," Claire said. She looked at Blake and smiled at him, perhaps for the first time since they met.

"Of course, forgive me. I'm not myself yet," Mrs. Cotton said.

"I didn't rescue you, but I want you to know I did try to rescue your front door. The EMT guys broke it anyway. I'll fix it when I get home."

"And charge me a pretty penny for it, I'm sure."

"What difference does it make? You don't actually pay me anyway," Blake said, winking at her.

Mrs. Cotton shook her head. "Such an impertinent young man. Mr. Stevens, do you know I was Claire's fourth grade teacher?"

"From what I hear, you were everybody's fourth grade teacher. Lately, I've been wondering if you were mine and I just forgot."

"She was the best teacher I ever had," Claire said.

Mrs. Cotton announced she needed another nap. "Fix my door and call my sister Edna, okay?" she said to Blake.

"I'll take care of it Bella."

"Bella?" She turned to Claire. "As I said, he is impertinent." She turned back to Blake. "Lucky for you, I'm confined to this bed. As soon as I get out, I'm going to have you evicted."

Claire and Blake chatted in the elevator heading to the hospital's lobby. "She really likes you. Mrs. Cotton has become rather reclusive over the last five years. The way you talk to each other reminds me of the way she used to be. I'm impressed."

"Don't be. I have that effect on everybody I meet, except you."

"You seem to have a knack for ruining a nice moment, do you know that?"

Just then, as they walked out of the elevator, Brad Chambers approached. "Hello darling. I see you've run into the man of the hour."

"Speaking of people who ruin moments…nice to see you again, Claire," Blake said. "She's all yours, Doc."

11

Claire visited Bella Cotton two more times before the woman was discharged from the hospital. She made it a point to visit when she knew Blake wouldn't be there. She drove past Mrs. Cotton's home to make sure his car was there. He had again been rude to Brad. She sat with her former teacher for about thirty minutes each time she visited. Mrs. Cotton was interested in what Claire thought of today's student body and whether a teacher's lot had changed much over the years.

"Well, there is more paperwork," Claire said.

"Are you happy with your students? They must be very different now with cell phones and computers, all that technology," Mrs. Cotton said.

"I don't know that they're different," Claire said, "but I will say we need to keep them entertained more now. Their attention spans are shorter. We show a lot more videos, documentaries and even movies as part of the course work."

On her second visit, Claire's curiosity got the better of her. "You seem to like your tenant, Mr. Stevens."

"Oh, I do. He's very helpful. He's been practically remodeling my apartment for me. I try to pay him, but he always has an excuse, tells me I'll need the money for some new project."

"I find he's hard to get to know. He's only made one friend at work, a math teacher."

"Oh yes, Parker. He comes over and helps sometimes. They play tennis in Cherry Hill now and then." Mrs. Cotton motioned for Claire to hand her the glass of water that was sitting on her overbed table. Claire got up and filled it. She thanked Claire and said, "I think something dreadful must have happened to Mr. Stevens. That must be why he moved here, all the way from Tennessee."

The women talked about Blake's run in with Derek Martinelli and the man's subsequent death at the hands of his ex-wife. "I was not pleased when Mr. Stevens got involved with Jonna. That child was bound for a hard life. I could see that even when she entered my classroom as a ten-year-old. Talk about dreadful. That poor girl has made some unfortunate choices."

"They don't see each other anymore?"

"I doubt it. I'm not sure they ever did, actually. Mrs. Rosenthal would have told me. She is quite the gossip, never misses a thing. I'm just as bad, I suppose. I always listen. Gives an old woman something to think about besides how close I am to the dirt nap."

"I don't think you're ready for that. Brad seems to think you'll be fine," Claire said.

"Bradley is a good doctor," Mrs. Cotton said. She took another sip of water and looked at Claire, not sure how to say what she was thinking. "He was always a smarty pants, even as a youngster. Always raising his hand and terribly disappointed when I didn't call on him."

Claire smiled. "Yes, he is a good doctor. I guess he's always been driven, always very competitive. Still is, I suppose."

A nurse stuck her head in the door and announced, "It's snowing again, just flurries, right now."

Grateful for the interruption, the women turned their attention to the window where they could see large flakes falling. Changing the subject, Mrs. Cotton said, "As I recall, Claire, you were quite the athlete in school. You played basketball and softball, didn't you?"

"I did. The only thing I do now is the Stairmaster and a bit of weight training with a trainer."

"Stay active dear. You'll never regret it. Perhaps you should take up tennis."

Mrs. Cotton was released from the hospital a few days later. Blake drove her home. She was pleased to see that he had finished work on her apartment and was now painting the hallway. When she paid him for the additional paint and supplies he purchased while she was hospitalized, he told her, "Pretty soon we're going to have to take a break. Tennis tryouts will start in another month."

"I think you might miss painting my walls," Mrs. Cotton said. "There's nothing like a fresh start, is there?"

Blake smiled. "Maybe so, but pretty soon I won't have time for it."

"I'm sure my lungs will appreciate the respite from the smell of paint," Mrs. Cotton said.

"Good point." He stopped work on the hallway and promised he would pick it up again in the summer.

In March, as soon as the weather was above 40 degrees in the afternoon, Blake held tryouts for the tennis team. He was pleasantly surprised to have ten boys and nine girls attend the tryout sessions. Although he didn't tell them, he knew that every player who attended tryouts regularly, would make the team. He held practice Monday through Thursday, after school.

Starting in mid-April, they played one match a week. As expected, they lost most of them. When both the boys' and girls' teams won their first match, it gave Blake a real boost. He had never coached before.

One morning in early May, during his planning period, Mark Mitchell called him into his office. "I've noticed that you are fully engaged in tennis, as you should be. You are the coach, after all. I wonder, have you considered finding a volunteer, someone who can handle practices?"

"No, not this year. Next year, if we have enough kids to form a junior varsity team, I'll probably do that."

"I see. You realize, of course, that in your situation, next year for you depends on your students' academic performance this year. Are you confident that your students are shaping up?"

Until that moment, Blake had faithfully followed his Uncle's advice. He had held his tongue. He never made waves. Now he was angry. He was working hard with his students. He meticulously planned every lesson. He coached students who needed extra help. Although he felt he was being set up, that the first semester grades would, under other circumstances, have been deemed acceptable, he played it straight. For some reason the school's principal didn't want him around. He was setting him up to fail and he wasn't even being subtle about it.

He didn't raise his voice. Southerners are taught to be civil at all times. "Mark, if you don't want me here, I wish you would just say it. I'll finish out the year and move on. It isn't necessary for you to issue threats."

Mitchell pulled his glasses off. He closed his laptop and stood. He walked around to where Blake was standing. "I'm tough on every new teacher. Nobody told you that? Some teachers, not many, I'm happy to say, try to do just enough to get by for their first four years. They get tenure and phone it in for twenty-five years after that. I'm trying to build something special here. Don't expect me to apologize for that. If you can't take the heat, you really don't belong here."

"That's not it at all, Mark. I feel like I'm being singled out because of the way I got this job. I think you resented having to hire me."

Mitchell nodded his head. "Sit down Blake." Both men sat down, sitting side by side. "Resentment is an overstatement. But I think you should know that four middle school teachers wanted to come here, two of them excellent teachers." He paused to let his words sink in. "I received several applications from recent graduates. I had to turn them all down because I had no opening in the department. To make room for you, I had to transfer a history teacher to geography. She wasn't happy about it, which explains perhaps, why some of our staff have been cool toward you. So, don't complain to me because I set high expectations. Just do a better job and we'll see what happens."

"You're asking me to achieve exceptional scores, which I could accept if I had at least one honors class."

"It's not a perfect world, Blake. I'm asking you to do your best, nothing more than I ask of every teacher in this school."

Claire and Brad's wedding plans were running smoothly. The church, the reception menu, dresses, flowers, music and photographer were all set. Invitations were printed and ready to be sent. The only thing the couple hadn't decided on was a honeymoon. Claire wanted to keep it simple, spend a week in New England, a favorite area since her college years. Brad wanted to do something more in line with his status as an up and coming internist. He had recently been featured in two magazines as part of a new breed of doctors who were returning to their rural roots to practice much needed primary care.

They were sitting in the town's only movie theatre one night, waiting for the feature to start when Brad proposed going to Europe for three weeks. Since the wedding was set for the last Saturday in August, Claire would have to miss the first two weeks of school.

"No Brad, I can't do that," she explained. "In some ways that first week is the most important of all. Honey, that's when I establish the entire foundation of my relationship with my students. I set expectations, I get to know each child. Can't we go to Europe next summer?"

Brad's answer shocked her. "Why not just wait until next July to get married? It seems our entire lives are going to revolve around your school year and your relationship with your students."

"Honestly, Brad, would you leave a patient who needed you?"

"You're not serious, Claire. I think you can see the difference between a matter of life and death and kids, most of them reluctantly taking English to begin with."

Claire suggested they were both tired, feeling the stress that planning a wedding was bound to cause. "Perhaps we should discuss this later," she said. They watched the movie in silence, not looking once in each other's direction.

The next day over coffee, she discussed it with Victoria, who was still seeing Dr. Remolina. "Have I misjudged him after all this time?"

"You're marrying a doctor, Claire. They think they discovered the planets and invented chocolate. What did you expect?"

"I expect him to respect my work as much as I do his." Claire said.

Victoria broke an almond biscotti in half and handed a piece to Claire. "I'm sure he does. I know you love him and I certainly like Brad, but he has always been, well, a prima donna. You know that, right?"

"I've never really seen that side of him."

"You're a Clark. Your ancestors founded this town and the Chambers family wasn't far behind."

"What does that mean, Victoria?"

Victoria held her hands up. "Nothing. I'm just talking as usual. Let's go shopping." They got into Claire's Toyota and headed to Atlantic City where they could choose from scores of retail outlets. They both bought shoes and Victoria bought an expensive dress, paid for with a credit card given to her by Dr. Remolina. She showed the card to Claire and said, "I have to say Charles knows how to treat a woman."

On the way home, they drove in silence for a long time, until Victoria said, "What's wrong Claire?"

"You think Brad and I are snobs."

"Are you crazy? We've been friends since the second grade. I think no such thing, not about you. Brad, I'm not as sure about, but he's a good catch."

Claire laughed. "Nobody in our generation actually talks about a husband as a good catch, Victoria."

"Fine, he's a good man then, but he can be pretentious. I'm only telling you this because I believe I'm the only one who can."

"Are you saying people don't like him?"

"Not at all. You're blowing this way out of proportion, Claire."

"Do you really think so?"

"Absolutely." Victoria wasn't happy with herself for upsetting Claire. She had said what she felt she could say. Dr. Chambers was not well liked and never had been. For some reason, Claire couldn't see that. Victoria consoled herself with the thought that she tried.

12

Although no one would ever acknowledge it, certainly not the school's principal or the school board, what happened on an unseasonably cool Monday near the end of May, guaranteed that Blake would be rehired for the next year. It had been a routine school day one week before the Memorial Day weekend. Blake was just beginning to review with his classes what he taught during the second semester. The students looked bored, which concerned him. It was the last week of the tennis season, so he decided to cut practice short that day and return to his classroom. That would give him an opportunity to put together a few ideas that might make the review more interesting.

As he walked through the hall, he decided to stop in the teacher's lounge to grab a Coke from the vending machine. He opened the door and all hell broke loose. Five minutes before he arrived, a senior, who had no business being in the building that late, walked into the teacher's lounge to confront his English teacher, a Mrs. June Kendall. The woman was short and stout, about 45 years old. The student was a big kid, a football player whose grades were just good enough to make him eligible to play football. Once the season ended, he stopped trying, assuming his teachers would give him passing grades and be done with him. But Mrs. Kendall wouldn't go along. She had told him earlier that day that he needed an excellent exam score to graduate. Otherwise, he would have to attend summer school.

The young man hated her for pushing him so hard. He hated her nearly as much for her indifference to his football prowess, which was considerable. If he failed English, his grade point average would dip below the 2.0 minimum he needed to qualify for a football scholarship. Failing English would be a disaster and going to summer school would eliminate his chances of finding a much-needed summer job.

When Blake walked into the lounge, he saw the student towering over the woman waving what looked like a World War II bayonet at her. The woman's blouse was ripped open and there appeared to be a thin scratch running from her bra down to the top of her pants. Out of the corner of his eye he saw another woman standing against a far wall, trying to reason with the kid. He was becoming more agitated and was shouting obscenities.

Blake didn't hesitate. He ran across the room and slapped the kid hard in the face, stunning him. He grabbed the student's right wrist and slammed it hard against the wall, knocking the bayonet out of his hands. When the kid scrambled after it, Blake had no choice. He bent down and put his arm around the boy's neck, yanked him back and slammed his body to the floor. He got on top of him then and pinned the boy's wrists to the floor. He said, "It's over. Don't make me hurt you."

The kid immediately recognized and respected Blake's strength. His muscles went slack and he started to cry. Blake looked up and realized for the first time that the other woman in the room was Claire. "Pick up that weapon and toss it outside," he said. She started to move toward it just as the door to the lounge opened again. It was the school security officer, a sheriff's department employee. Blake stood up and the officer took over.

Claire and Mrs. Kendall were crying softly now. Mrs. Kendall said, "Thank you. I've seen you around, but I don't even know your name. Thank you so much, you're so brave."

"His name is Blake Stevens. He teaches history here," Claire said. "He coaches the tennis team too," she added, which for some reason, made all three of them laugh, releasing some of the tension.

Fifteen minutes later, two Clarksville Police officers arrived. One of them took the student away in handcuffs. The other one, Bill Simons, the officer who had been sitting in the Waffle Heaven when the incident with Derek occurred, stayed to take statements.

"You sure teaching is your calling, Mr. Stevens? Where's your Superman cape?" Officer Simons asked.

Blake didn't answer him right away. He was rubbing his left elbow. It had hit the floor when he took the young man down. The officer turned to June Kendall. "Can you tell us what happened?"

Mrs. Kendall was still shaking. "This man saved our lives," she said, gesturing toward Blake.

"I think he wants to know what happened with Connor," Claire said. Now Blake remembered who the student was. He had seen him around, but it was a big school. Connor Watts was indeed a star player, on the offensive line and as a defensive end.

"I told him he was failing. He must have followed me in here. Ms. Clark and I were chatting when he walked in. The first thing he said is, 'You gotta pass me, Mrs. Kendall, or I'm -please excuse my language, fucked.' I want to say it exactly the way he did."

"Then what happened?"

"I said you don't belong in the teacher's lounge, Connor. Leave immediately, or you will be in deep trouble." It finally occurred to Mrs. Kendall that her bra was on full display. She tried to put the two ends of what was left of her blouse together, but it didn't help much. Blake was wearing a hooded sweatshirt. He unzipped it and handed it to her.

"Thank you," she said. "It wasn't a sexual assault, officer. When he refused to leave, I tried to walk out of the room, but he grabbed me, very rough like. We kind of wrestled. I wasn't about to let him put his hands on me. When you see him again, you'll notice a scratch on his face. I did that. That's when he pulled out that machete, or whatever it was."

"How did you get the scratch? Was it the knife?"

"No, I don't think so. It was his fingernails when he grabbed me."

"Did he threaten you verbally?" Officer Simons asked.

"He said he was going to slit my throat if I didn't give him a decent passing grade. I think he was hopped up on something."

"Why do you say that?"

"His eyes. They were wild. Anyway, I've seen plenty of kids come to school on something. It's always in their eyes, if you know what I mean."

"Okay, then what?" Officer Simons asked. By this time, Claire had moved closer to Blake. They were looking at each other as if they were meeting for the first time. Something was in their eyes too.

"That's when Mr. Stevens got here. He punched or kicked Connor and knocked that thing out of his hand. Then he wrestled him to the floor."

Officer Simons looked at Blake. "I didn't punch him, I slapped him, pretty hard I guess."

"Tell it to me in your own words."

Blake explained what happened. Then he listened while Claire answered the same question. The officer asked a few more questions and then the interview was over. When they stepped outside, the hallway was crowded. There was a local TV reporter who covered the area for a Philadelphia affiliate and a local print journalist along with two of the school's football coaches. Word had traveled fast.

Certainly, the word was already out that Blake was a hero. Mr. Kendall, June's husband, grabbed his hand and shook it. The few teachers who had been working late in their classrooms shook his hand and patted him on the back. Mark Mitchell also shook his hand and smiled. "We owe you an enormous debt of gratitude, Blake. We're going to honor you at our graduation ceremonies next month. You can bet on that."

The media wanted to interview him, but he refused. This wasn't a time to take credit for something. He couldn't help thinking about Connor Watts. The kid was in more trouble than he could possibly understand.

An older man came up to Blake when the media people finally started packing their gear. "My name is Terrence Clark. I serve on the county school board. My daughter tells me you saved her life." He stuck his hand out and Blake shook it.

"I don't know about that. I'm not sure he would have actually used the weapon. I hope not."

"Don't be so modest, young man. Even if my daughter overstated things a bit, your heroism sets an example for everyone in this community."

The hallway was nearly empty now. Blake looked for Claire, but she wasn't there. "I'm glad Claire is all right. You should know that she tried hard to calm Connor down. She was very brave."

"She didn't mention it," Mr. Clark said.

Blake nodded. "She deserves as much credit as anybody. I'm sure she distracted Connor. He never even saw me coming."

"Very kind of you to say so."

Dr. Chambers was walking from one exam room to another when one of the nurses stopped him and mentioned that there had been an incident at Clarksville High. "One of the teachers, I think his name is Stevens, disarmed some student. I don't believe she was interviewed, but I saw Claire was on television. I think she was in the room or something."

Brad called Claire immediately. She assured him she was safe, telling him it was scary, but over now. No harm done, she said. She let him know she'd be having dinner with her parents at six o'clock. They insisted, she told him. That evening, Brad went to the home of Claire's parents as soon as his last patient of the day left his office, just after 7:00 p.m. The lingering aroma of fried chicken was still in the air, but it was too late to join them for dinner.

Mr. Clark handed him a martini and said, "We're celebrating Claire's narrow escape."

"Oh, was she seriously in danger?" Brad asked. "I haven't seen the news yet."

With Claire and Mrs. Clark standing in the Clark's library alongside Brad, Mr. Clark repeated what was on the news. Then he added," "Mr. Stevens was kind enough to tell me that Claire was very brave too, distracting the boy long enough to allow Stevens to disarm the miscreant."

Brad looked at Claire. "So, you and Stevens are both heroes. How nice."

"He was amazing," Claire said, her eyes glistening. "He didn't hesitate for a second. And I think what impressed me the most was his restraint."

Brad pulled the toothpick from his martini and put the olive in his mouth. He wasn't happy about the look he noticed in Claire's eyes, a look he was sure she had never given him. "Thank goodness for Blake Stevens, protector of women, a mysterious stranger from afar turned hero."

"Thank goodness indeed, Bradley. We could have been having an entirely different conversation had he not been there," Mrs. Clark said. "I'm sure you are grateful, my dear."

"Yes, of course. Claire and I should take him and Jonna out to dinner sometime to thank him." Brad enjoyed the reference to Jonna, a reminder to Claire of the other man's taste in women.

Claire looked at Brad and said," "I'm exhausted. I'm going home." She was disheartened by Brad's pettiness. His jealousy was ridiculous. Or was it? She felt now that she had misjudged Blake Stevens. She had heard him tell a reporter that his concern was for Connor Watts, that the real story was about what would drive a high school student to such self-destructive behavior. Obviously, he had no interest in basking in the limelight.

"I'll follow you home," Brad said.

"I really am exhausted. I just want to take a shower and go to bed. Finish your drink with dad."

13

When Blake got to his apartment that night, Mrs. Cotton was waiting for him. She asked him to come in and visit a while. He walked in and found Parker and Mike Wollman, another teacher he had recently become friendly with. He was surprised to see his department head, Frank Holt, too. On her dining room table was a cake. "I taught everyone in this room, except Blake. Nice to know when I call, they still come," Mrs. Cotton said.

She had allowed Parker to bring a six pack so each of the men could have a beer. "Take a beer, a piece of cake and go on upstairs. Don't make too much noise, or I'll call the police. I taught all of them too, you know." Blake and Parker tried to persuade her to join them, but she wouldn't hear of it.

There was a lot of good natured joking around. The men enjoyed teasing Blake about picking on a high school boy, but they were sincere in their praise. Frank Holt took Blake aside before he left and told him not to worry about next year. "There is no way they won't rehire you now," he said.

The next day at school, Claire came looking for him. She walked into his classroom early that morning, before classes started. "Good morning, Blake. I never got the chance to properly thank you. You were truly amazing."

"I'm glad you and June weren't hurt. I heard this morning that they're going to charge Connor as an adult," Blake said. He was getting his laptop set up on his desk in preparation for the day. "Seems a shame, but I suppose they have to set an example."

"If he had actually stabbed one of us, I'm sure there wouldn't be dissenters on that score," Claire said.

"True." Blake paused, wanting to word what he was going to say just right. "Listen, I feel as though we got off on the wrong foot, starting with the day we met outside Waffle Heaven. I just want to say I'm sorry about that."

"Completely forgotten," Claire said. "It would be nice to run into you, though, when one of us isn't being attacked, or throwing hot cider at each other."

"Lucky for you you're marrying a doctor," Blake said.

"Lucky, that must be it," Claire said, surprising herself. "How is Mrs. Cotton doing?"

"Lonely, I think." Blake told her what Mrs. Cotton did the night before. "It was cool, and I don't think she minded having a little company."

"I should pay her a visit," Claire said. The first bell rang. Claire gave Blake a quick hug. He didn't mind at all.

Mark Mitchell kept his promise on graduation day. It was unseasonably warm, more like the middle of July, rather than the last week of June. He had invited the town's chief of police to take part in the ceremony. The chief was all too happy to be in front of so many people, including the mayor, to award Blake with a plaque for bravery. When Blake accepted the award, the chief asked him to say a few words. As Blake approached the lectern, dressed in a white shirt and tie, the chief whispered to him, "Make it short. It's brutal out here."

Blake nodded and stepped up to the microphone. "Thank you all for doing this. I'm honored. And I hope we all appreciate what June Kendall and Claire Clark did to keep the situation from becoming a complete tragedy. While I hope you will be inspired by our story, we should also remember a student made a terrible mistake, an expensive one that will change his life's trajectory. As graduates, moving on to take your rightful place in the world as adults, please remember that the decisions we make have consequences."

Claire was sitting on the platform with the other teachers behind Blake. Listening to his words, she hoped he was right. She sat there looking at the bare ring finger on her left hand. The night before graduation she had returned her engagement ring to Brad. It wasn't an easy decision. She hated hurting him, but she had seen in him some traits that worried her. She hoped she made the right decision.

After their initial conversation about their honeymoon plans, she and Brad had argued about it twice. He refused to compromise. He insisted they travel to London. She was being unreasonable, he told her. Things really changed for her though, the night he came to her parents' home after the incident at school. He showed little concern for what she had been through, as if in the absence of any physical injuries, everything was fine. That she had endured a traumatic emotional experience, didn't seem to faze him. She could see Victoria's point clearly now. How could she have been so blind, she wondered? When she told Victoria that she was going to break her engagement to Brad, Victoria said, "If you have any doubts, do it. Brad isn't going anywhere. If you change your mind, he'll come running."

"What makes you say that?" she asked.

"You're still the catch of the county; a beautiful blueblood who can trace her ancestry back to the Mayflower."

Claire rolled her eyes. "I wish you wouldn't say things like that."

After the graduation ceremony, Blake got some good news. Mark Mitchell approached him in the cafeteria, where the staff was enjoying some cake and fruit punch. He said, "Your students' final exam test scores improved by four points over the first semester. I see no reason why you shouldn't return next year. In fact, we'd love to have you back. Do you think you could handle a couple of honors classes?"

Blake shook Mitchell's hand and thanked him. He promised to earn his keep, his way of acknowledging something he hadn't been willing to acknowledge before. His Uncle John's intercession, while good for him, had been hard on Mark Mitchell.

He got even more good news on the high school's tennis court the next day. It was the first day of summer vacation. He and Parker had already agreed to start a little side business doing home repairs and house painting. There were a lot of older homes in Clarksville. More than a few of them needed work. They had really made the outside of Mrs. Cotton's house look good, even planting some fresh shrubs at their own expense to enhance its appeal. They agreed to take a week off before they started looking for work.

During a break between sets Parker remembered something he meant to tell Blake. "Guess who isn't getting married after all?"

"You and Penny?" The couple had moved in together two weeks ago.

"Actually, my friend, we are talking about getting married." Parker picked up a towel and wiped the sweat from his forehead. "I heard Claire broke it off with Dr. Chambers."

Blake was sitting on the bench taking a long drink. "She's out of my league."

"No kidding. I know that, but does she? You should give her a call."

"Let's play tennis, Bozo."

Independence Day was always celebrated in a big way in Clarksville. The town had been the site of a little known, but significant battle against the British. The Continental Army, made up mostly of local farmers, held off the Brits in bloody fighting for days on the fields to the northwest of the town, giving Washington's Army time to regroup and prepare for bigger battles to come.

Immediately after the war, land near the battlefield was designated for the remains of the patriots who died during the battle. Many of the men and women who died in the wars that followed were also buried there. Every year, on the morning of the Fourth of July, promptly at 7:00 a.m., the town's churches got together and held a prayer service at the cemetery to kick off a day filled with celebratory events. Beginning at ten o'clock that morning, downtown streets were closed to allow for a festival where merchants and handicraft vendors displayed their wares. Shoppers filled the street, buying pottery and handcrafted jewelry done by local artists and assorted woodcraft items. Food trucks and kiddie rides were also prominent. The temperature rose to 101 degrees that day, which kept the emergency medical squad busy.

Blake and Parker played tennis early that morning and then worked until almost noon. They finally finished painting Blake's apartment. The interior of Mrs. Cotton's entire home was now freshly painted.

As they were cleaning paint brushes, they talked about their plans for the day. "You going to the town square later?" Parker asked. "Penny and I are going."

"It's gonna be too hot. But since I don't have air conditioning, I might go downtown and look for a bar, maybe cool off a little."

"Penny's friend, Becky, is visiting from Florida again. Why don't you come with us? You might like her this time."

"Has she ever said she liked me?" Blake asked.

"Not in so many words." They laughed the way good friends do.

"Always trying to do me favors. You want somebody to take her off your hands, right?"

"Gotta admit, that would be nice too."

"Wish I could help you, pal," Blake said. Before he left his apartment, Blake stopped in to ask Mrs. Cotton if she wanted to go with him to see the fireworks that night. Every year, the town held an enormous fireworks show put on by the famous Zambelli family. People came from as far away as Trenton and New Brunswick to see the brilliant, colorful displays light the evening sky.

She laughed and said, "I'm too old for that nonsense. Anyway, by eight o'clock I'm tuckered out."

"When was the last time you saw them?" Blake asked.

"I stopped about ten years ago. Used to go every year with my husband until he died. Then I went with another widow, Mrs. Travisano. When she died, I stopped going."

Blake had his pocket knife out and was absentmindedly cleaning paint from his nails. "Well, it's been a while. Why don't you watch them with me?" Mrs. Cotton opened her refrigerator and took out some iced tea. She asked Blake if he wanted a glass, but he declined.

"You asking me for a date, Mr. Stevens?" she asked. "I would appreciate it if you would clean your nails in the privacy of your own apartment, standing over a sink I hope."

"Sorry, I hear these fireworks are unbelievable."

"Oh, they are." She took a sip of tea. "I made love to my husband for the first time on the Fourth of July at the cemetery in 1962. I was 21 years old." She smiled at the memory of her youth. "Happened while the fireworks were going off. It was beautiful. And I don't think we were the only ones in the cemetery that night."

"I thought maybe that was a more recent tradition," Blake said. He put his knife away.

"That's the problem with every generation. They all think they invented everything that's ever happened. My mother made love to my father in that cemetery in 1941, not long before he went off to fight in the war. He never came home, so I never knew him." She shrugged. "He's buried in that cemetery."

That afternoon, Blake went to the town square and took a walk down Main Street. The sun was working overtime to deepen his tan. Wearing dark sunglasses, and a white polo shirt, he looked like a man who stepped out of an Esquire Magazine ad. Although he didn't say it to Parker, he was hoping to run into Claire. He was perusing the tables filled with mostly homemade crafts or specialty foods made by local farmers, when he saw her standing in front of a jewelry booth chatting with the woman behind the table. He walked over to her and picked up a wide, brass bracelet that was adorned with turquoise, lapis and red oyster shell. "Should I buy it?"

"It's definitely you," Claire said.

"How much?" he asked the owner.

"Thirty-four dollars."

"I'll give you thirty-two-fifty."

Claire and the owner laughed. "It's a deal," the woman said.

Blake made a show of looking into his wallet. "Can you lend me $32?"

Claire didn't miss a beat. "I'm sure she'll take a credit card."

Blake pulled out two twenties and handed them to the woman.

"It's $34.77 with the tax," the woman said.

Blake put his new bracelet on, knowing immediately that he would never wear it again. He was showing off a bit, which wasn't his style. He had never behaved this way with a woman he liked, but Claire excited him and she scared him a little. They started walking down the street, both sweating in the heat. Claire was wearing a light peach colored sun dress and sandals. The heat was becoming unbearable. "Have you had lunch yet?" he asked.

"I haven't."

"Let's get out of this sauna and grab some lunch." He lightly touched her arm and guided her toward a restaurant called Hammer and Nails, a converted hardware store. When they sat down, Claire pointed out a couple of large black and white reproduction photos on the wall. One was a picture of the original storefront and the other was a photo of a man named Toby Clark. "The man in the photo was my great grandfather. He opened a hardware store here in 1917."

For the first time since they met, Claire and Blake had a real conversation. They talked about their history, Blake telling her what it was like living in a small town in Tennessee, his education, his family and his decision to leave Colby Springs for New Jersey. He was finally able to talk about Nicci's desertion, keeping the lingering rancor he felt from his tone of voice. He even joked about it a little. He said, "If I ever get married, I'm going to make sure I use my wife's credit card. If she runs off with the sofa, I don't want to have to keep making the payments."

Claire talked about growing up in a small town named after an ancestor who founded the town. "People seem to think that our family is somehow responsible for the entire town's well-being," she said. "At times, especially when I was in high school, I felt this pressure, like I had to set a good example."

"You don't feel that way now?"

"Sometimes I do. Lately I've been wondering if that was the real reason I picked Brad. His family goes back almost as far as mine does."

"When a relationship goes bad, I think most of us question our judgment. It's easy to blame ourselves. We forget that we fell in love honestly."

"Or blindly," Claire said.

"It's always blind, or at least through cataracts. Most of us fall in love long before we really know the person we fell for. Then we spend years trying to mold each other in a way that will make the relationship work," Blake said.

"That isn't a very romantic thought."

"I don't know," Blake said. "If true love isn't tested, how do we know it's true?"

"You have a point, I suppose. Did that bracelet you bought come with a pool of wisdom?"

Blake reached for her hands, looked into her eyes and said "I don't have a drop of blue blood in me, Claire, but I feel like we are about to see how much that matters."

She smiled warmly and squeezed his fingers. "I would really like that." They spent the rest of the day together, walking through town, hiding under canopies to get out of the sun while they listened to musicians play. They ran into Claire's friends and neighbors and chatted with several of them. Blake could feel a couple of them checking him out, perhaps wondering what he was up to. It made him a bit uncomfortable. That night they had a simple dinner standing in front of a food truck. Claire never felt so free. Before she met Blake, she would have felt completely out of place eating a hot dog on the street, fearful of being judged.

For dessert, they walked over to a truck selling soft ice cream. There they ran into Jonna with her two boys. Standing next to her was a man named Zeke Flowers. He owned a small construction company. Jonna smiled and said, "Hi, Blake. Have you met Zeke Flowers yet? He's a builder." She said hello to Claire with a wave.

Blake said hello to Jonna's boys and shook the man's hand. "We've probably seen each other at Home Depot. I've been doing some work on my landlady's house, mostly paint."

"Mrs. Cotton, right? Haven't seen much of her lately." Zeke turned his head toward Claire. "My daughter has you for English next year."

"For goodness sake, Zeke, I can't believe Madison is going to high school already." The two couples chatted for a while. Eventually the women started talking to each other while the men talked about construction work. Zeke asked Blake if he was interested in doing some work painting the interior of three houses he was building. The men agreed to discuss it when the houses were ready in early August.

Jonna was a bit nervous talking to Claire. She had been a few years behind Claire in school. She envied Claire's popularity and good looks. She bent down and wiped some of the ice cream from her younger boy's face. "I heard you broke your engagement to Dr. Chambers," Jonna said.

"I did, last month," Claire said.

"I hope it wasn't because of what I told Blake."

"What did you tell him?" Claire asked, casting a glance at Blake who was still chatting with Zeke.

Jonna froze. "Oh shit, I did it again. Never mind. Pay no attention to me." She changed the subject, going on about how she hoped things might work out with Zeke. They had been dating for two months and already it was getting serious. He was divorced and had joint custody of his two daughters.

Their ice cream cones finished, the two couples said their goodbyes. Zeke promised to call Blake when the houses were ready. The fireworks show would start in about an hour at the high school football field. Blake asked Claire if she wanted to watch them together.

"I would, but I always sit with my parents and my sister Deanna's family. It might be a bit uncomfortable to have you join us so soon after my breakup with Brad."

"I understand. I would like to see the fireworks. People have been talking about them ever since I moved here."

"Oh yes, by all means you should watch them, Blake. Could you sit with Parker?"

Blake knew that wasn't a good option for him, but he didn't want to tell Claire why. That Penny's friend, Becky, would be there. "I asked Mrs. Cotton if she wanted to come and see them, but she said she'd be too tired by eight o'clock."

"That was sweet of you, to even ask. You're an interesting man, Mr. Stevens."

They walked back down Main Street together. They came to a corner where they would go in opposite directions toward their homes. They stood for a moment, neither of them sure of what to do. Blake took Claire's hand and held it. He was again taken aback by his own physical reaction to her touch. The chemistry was obvious. He wondered if she felt it too.

Claire looked into Blake's eyes. "Can I ask you a question?"

Blake nodded. "Of course."

"What did Jonna tell you about Brad?"

"What do you mean?"

"She said something odd earlier about my breakup with Brad. She hoped it wasn't because of what she told you about him."

Suddenly, Blake was wary. He knew exactly what Jonna was referring to, but he had promised her he wouldn't tell anyone. And he hadn't, not even to his friend Parker. It was possible too that he misinterpreted Jonna's comment. Assuming Brad actually gave her the money for an abortion, it didn't necessarily follow that Brad had gotten her pregnant. Regardless, he didn't want to be the one to tell that story to Claire even if it was true.

Yet, he didn't want to lie to Claire. He knew what it was like to be lied to. How many lies had Nicci told him? The way Blake saw it, running out on him, taking everything, he owned, save his clothes, was the ultimate betrayal; a lie, not in words, but worse, in her actions. He decided to buy a little time. "I don't remember Jonna telling me anything about Brad. Did she offer any details?"

"No, but she seemed upset with herself for bringing up the subject."

The couple stood quietly, neither wanting the day to end. "I really have to run," Claire said. "The fireworks should have started already." Just then the first burst lit up the sky. She pointed to it. "So pretty," she said.

The display was to Blake's back. He didn't turn to look. Instead, he looked at Claire and said, "I've never seen anyone so beautiful before." Then he bent down slightly to kiss her, but Claire pulled back.

"It's too soon for that Blake. I'm sorry."

14

"What did you and Claire do last night?" Parker asked. Blake had just mentioned he ran into Claire and how he had spent the day with her on the Fourth.

"They probably did it in the cemetery late last night," Mike Wollman said.

"Nah, too many pebbles. Irritates the skin," Parker said.

Blake didn't answer them. They were finishing up a small paint job for the owners of a two-man accounting firm. He picked up a can of paint and dabbed the brush enough to put the last bit of paint on the office's front door. Parker and Mike exchanged knowing glances, smirking as they went back to work.

Blake and Claire had their first actual date on the Saturday after Independence Day. He took her to Philadelphia to see a concert held at the Philadelphia Art Museum. She loved it and when they got home, he kissed her goodnight for the first time. He had given the kiss a good deal of thought during the day and throughout the concert. His first instinct was to wait for her to initiate the kiss, not wanting to be turned down again. But on the ride home, it occurred to him that he should trust his instincts. If Claire said no again, he was willing to wait. When the moment came, outside her apartment, he took her in his arms, pulled her to him and kissed her. Blake really liked Claire, but he didn't realize how much he liked her until their lips met. He had never felt anything like it before; certainly not with Nicci, a woman he had shed tears over. His body responded and he knew Claire would be aware of it, but he held her close and let the kiss linger.

"Oh, my," Claire said. "I can't invite you in for coffee, Blake. I know what will happen and I want us to go slow. Do you understand?"

"I do." He brushed a strand of her hair away from her face. "I'm going to kiss you again." This time their lips parted and the energy flowed between them, momentarily sweeping away their surroundings. They stood kissing for another five minutes until Claire said, "I'm weakening, Blake. Help me, please."

Blake stepped back, needing to catch his breath too. "Goodnight Claire. I'll call you tomorrow."

From then on, they were inseparable. They spent the rest of the summer seeing movies, going to the Jersey shore, and trying new restaurants in Philadelphia. A month into their relationship, they knew they couldn't hold off any longer. Blake jokingly suggested the cemetery, but Claire said, "Absolutely not." Her tone surprised Blake.

"I was kidding," he said.

"Well, please don't kid about that," she said. "I do have a very romantic idea. I've never been to the Waldorf Astoria Hotel in Manhattan."

"You'll love it."

They drove up the New Jersey Turnpike, through the Lincoln Tunnel and into the city on a Saturday afternoon. They were both very excited. The plan was to have dinner first, but by the time they got to the hotel, neither of them could bear to wait any longer. Blake even carried their luggage up to the mini suite to avoid the inevitable delay of waiting for a bellman to bring the bags to their room. Once inside the room, they began to kiss, gently at first, but the pace picked up and soon they were eagerly undressing, simultaneously removing their own clothing as they tried to undress each other. As soon as they were naked, Blake swept Claire into his arms and carried her to the bed. Comically, she insisted they roll the comforter down first because, she explained, she couldn't be sure what had already happened on it.

In bed, there was a brief moment of hesitation, as if they both knew this was the moment of truth. If the chemistry was truly right, there would be no denying it. They would experience that explosion of emotion, physical pleasure and spiritual singleness as soon as their bodies touched.

From that first moment, as they began to explore each other's bodies with their hands and mouths, sophisticated in their movements beyond anything either had experienced before, they knew this was the real thing. Every lover's dream. Blake was tender with Claire and then rough, yet not once did he disappoint her, giving her what her body demanded, begged for. Excited as they were, they were both surprised that they didn't climax quickly. They wanted it to last and above all they wanted to please each other. Claire arrived first and soon felt Blake shudder as he spoke, saying for the first time, "I love you, Claire."

They had dinner in their room that night before making love again. The couple checked out of the hotel early so they could spend the day enjoying Manhattan. Having lived in the city for a year, Blake was familiar with many of the city's attractions. He took her to Central Park and some of the other well-known tourist attractions like Rockefeller Center. After lunch, they went to the Metropolitan Museum of Art. After dinner, he even took Claire for a drink at the bar where he used to work. Several of his former coworkers were there. They made a fuss over him, impressing Claire and embarrassing Blake.

Claire offered to share the costs, but Blake wouldn't hear of it. He worried, of course, that he was building a credit card bill that would take a long time to pay off, but he was happy to be with Claire and she was obviously pleased that he was treating her so well. Brad was not a cheapskate, but he was never as generous as Blake was. They didn't get back to Clarksville until after two o'clock Monday morning, exhausted and happy.

When August arrived, Zeke kept his promise and called Blake to see if he was still interested in painting houses. Zeke's offer was a godsend. Parker and Blake had been surprised to discover that while a lot of people needed home repairs and painting, not many wanted to pay for it. It didn't matter that their prices were reasonable. The reason homes had been allowed to deteriorate to begin with was that the owners couldn't afford to do the necessary repairs. Financially speaking, Zeke's offer saved their summer. Mike Wollman agreed to help out. Considering how hot it was that summer, Parker and Blake were happy for the help, even if it meant less money.

Throughout the summer, Claire and Blake got to know each other better. Blake's sister came for a visit, at Blake's insistence, so she could meet Claire and her family. Mr. and Mrs. Clark displayed a reserved warmth toward Blake after a short period of misgivings. They were bothered by the fact that Blake didn't seem to have a strong connection to his hometown, or its people, other than his sister, Judy. Certainly, it helped that Blake did a lot to take care of Mrs. Cotton, whose health was deteriorating. But, when Terrence Clark heard the story of Nicci's disappearance, he was uncomfortable with it. "I mean, who disappears into thin air in these times?" he asked when he brought it up to his daughter the next day. "Can we be absolutely certain she wasn't the victim of foul play?" Claire thought her father was being ridiculous. She felt he was still disappointed that she wasn't marrying Brad, another blueblood, and a doctor to boot.

Judy and Claire hit it off immediately. When she met the Clarks, she explained in more detail what had happened with Nicci. She assured them that Blake was in the clear and had never been suspected of any wrongdoing. The Clarks were reassured but spoke directly. "Our daughters, Deanna and Claire, are our treasures. I hope you understand our concerns," Mrs. Clark said.

When they got back to Blake's apartment, after spending the day with the Clarks, Blake introduced Judy to Mrs. Cotton. The old woman was skeptical at first, saying, "You don't look much alike for a brother and sister."

"I know. She's too pretty to be related to me," Blake said.

"Actually, people back home say I favor mother and Blake looks a bit like dad," Judy said.

Mrs. Cotton eyed them carefully. This was the first time Blake brought a woman to his place to spend the night. "Maybe there is a resemblance. My eyesight isn't what it used to be." The truth was that the siblings didn't look alike. Occasionally, when they were growing up, some thoughtless person would make a crack about the milkman or the mailman, but Mr. Stevens didn't take such remarks kindly and word got around.

Once inside Blake's apartment, Judy joked that they should ask Uncle John and Aunt Abigail to visit them in Clarksville. "He's a goddamn state senator. Don't you think that should have been enough to convince the Clarks, not to mention your landlord?"

Blake shrugged. "What do you think of Claire?" He walked into the kitchen and started to take two beers out of the refrigerator but thought better of it. He'd noticed that Judy drank three martinis at the Clark home. He opted for two cans of Coke instead and handed one to Judy.

"She's sweet. I like her."

"But?"

"Her parents make me wonder if they wish the British had won. They seem to be into royalty. Very heavy, my brother."

"Claire isn't like that, though."

"You sure?"

"Yeah, sis, I'm sure. She could have married Dr. Chambers."

"Maybe she didn't marry him because he's a dipshit. That doesn't mean she doesn't have feelings of unwarranted superiority."

"Tell me what you really think, by all means." Blake was getting annoyed now.

Judy smiled at her brother and walked over to where he was standing. "I think she's wonderful. And you can bet your ass that Claire Clark will never leave her very own Clarksville when you're not looking." Blake picked up his Coke can, shook it and sprayed his sister a little.

The next morning after a restless night on Blake's lumpy bed, Judy offered to make breakfast. "When did you learn to cook?" Blake asked.

"What I meant was I'd make coffee and pour milk in your cereal," Judy said. "If you have a banana, I'll put that in your cereal too, just like Mom did." Over breakfast they chatted for a few minutes about Judy's job, working as an administrator for the American Museum of Science and Energy. She loved her job and the commute to Oak Ridge wasn't overwhelming.

As they were clearing their plates and putting the milk away, Judy mentioned her ongoing project, namely going through the many boxes filled with papers her parents had left behind. "I swear, Blake, I can't decide which one of them was the bigger pack rat, mom or dad. I've been through a half-dozen boxes and you know what?"

Blake laughed. "No, tell me."

"Almost all of it is bills going back to the 70's and 80's, electric bills, water bills, phone bills, you name it."

"Why don't you just throw the boxes away, bring them to the recycle station and forget it?"

"I can't do that. I've thought about doing it, but I don't know. Maybe it's because I work at the museum. You'd be amazed by how many people show up with something related to the Manhattan Project that they were about to throw away.

Just last month, a man came by and showed us an ID badge his mother wore and a Coker bus ticket book. We were thrilled to add them to our collection."

"I'm thinking about visiting Colby Springs. I want Claire to see it. Maybe I can give you a hand."

"Yeah, that's going to happen."

"If you find any old baseball cards, they're mine."

Claire and Blake were sitting in a coffee house a block away from Claire's place when they decided to invite their friends to a barbecue on Labor Day. It was the last Saturday in August, the day Claire was to have married Brad. They had their first disagreement. It was over the barbecue's location. Blake wanted to use Mrs. Cotton's backyard. It would give him an excuse to spruce it up. The yard was still a mess, mostly weeds and loose trash that had blown into the yard over the last year or so. Mrs. Cotton was no longer able to pick up the trash that accumulated there. Blake had offered to clean it up for her, but Mrs. Cotton said no. "Kids walk along the tracks every day during the school year. They throw soda bottles and candy wrappers in my yard. I can't keep up with them."

Claire thought it was silly. "My townhouse doesn't have any yard space, but my parents have a huge backyard. Why not hold it there?"

"Well, will your parents be joining us?" Blake asked.

"I'm sure they would. Why?"

"It's their home. They would be the hosts, not you and I," he said. "I thought one of the reasons we wanted to do this was to let everyone see us as a couple now."

"I agree. But would we really be any less a couple if my parents are technically the hosts?"

"I would be your date in that situation. It's not the same as hosting a party together."

"But Blake, Mrs. Cotton's place, even if you clean it up, isn't exactly an attractive environment for us to present ourselves to the community." It was true. The old railway siding behind her house still had an old caboose on the tracks, rusted by years of neglect. It was parked right behind her house.

"Maybe we're not ready for a party, Claire."

"Fine, we don't have to have one."

"Let me ask you something. If I have a barbecue in Mrs. Cotton's backyard, will you come if I invite you?" he asked. "Would the setting be suitable enough for you to come by?"

"I guess you'll have to invite me and find out." Claire got up and walked out of the coffee shop, leaving Blake to ponder what had just happened.

The next day, Sunday morning, Blake drove to Claire's townhouse to take her to church. Blake had not attended any church services since Nicci's disappearance, but after they went out a couple of times, Claire had asked him if he'd like to attend church services with her. Naturally, he jumped at the chance. He rang her bell and waited. He was carrying flowers he'd picked from Mrs. Cotton's front yard. Claire took the flowers and asked him to come in. They didn't kiss. "I've been thinking, Blake. If it's really important to you, we can have the barbecue at Mrs. Cotton's. Will she let us do it?"

Now Blake kissed her. They hugged for an extra beat. "I've been thinking too, honey. You're right. I took a good look at Mrs. Cotton's yard and I guess it's a bigger mess than I thought. Do you think your parents would at least let us buy everything for the party?"

"My father will be more than happy to let us pay for everything. He's a very frugal man." The couple laughed, happy again. Each had offered to bend to resolve their disagreement. It deepened their affection for each other.

The party was a huge success. Although Blake invited Mr. and Mrs. Clark to the party, they declined, deciding to attend an afternoon concert in the park. Blake and Claire baked three pies using locally grown cherries and blueberries. They were a big hit with the guests. Parker and Penny quietly announced their engagement at the party. But the bigger surprise occurred later in the evening. The Clark's long back porch was beautifully designed with two archways, four square columns and a scalloped, decorative facia. It was on the porch, with everyone gathered around, that Dr. Remolina asked Victoria to marry him. Charles actually got down on one knee. He said, "Victoria, my sweet. I've been an impossible man to live with for most of my life. But when I met you everything changed. Out of our love, a new man was born. I want to spend my life trying to give you the happiness you've given me. My dear Victoria, will you marry me?"

Victoria was expecting a proposal, perhaps during the holidays. Charles surprised her. Tears filled her eyes. "Yes, yes, I will marry you, my love." The two-carat engagement ring he placed on Victoria's finger was pear shaped. It was obviously expensive and it was beautiful. Dr. Remolina had placed a cooler in the garage when they arrived. It was filled with champagne on ice. He asked Blake to help him carry it onto the back porch just before he asked Victoria for her hand.

Afterwards, the two newly engaged couples chatted with Blake and Claire about the day's events.

"Parker proposed to me at lunch, while our slices of pizza were warming in the oven at Rizzo's Pizzeria. We were standing at the counter."

"Right," Parker said. "I realized I didn't have enough cash to pay for the pizza so I asked her to marry me. I figured if she said yes, she wouldn't mind paying for lunch."

The day after Labor Day, Mrs. Cotton knocked on Blake's door at 9:00 am sharp. She was out of breath and sweating from climbing the stairs. When he opened the door, Blake was immediately concerned. But she waved him off. "What were you doing in my backyard?" she asked.

"Just looking it over. Is there a problem?"

"When you moved in here, I thought I made it clear that you were to stay out of my backyard. Do you think because you've done some work for me that you no longer have to abide by my rules?"

"I've really only been in your yard when I needed to get something out of the garage. That's where you keep your tools." The free-standing garage was also badly in need of sanding and repainting. He tried to laugh her out of her sour mood. "Is that where you've been hiding the money?"

"Are you being impertinent with me again, young man?"

Blake was shocked. He was sure Mrs. Cotton never said any such thing about her yard being off limits. Her tone was reminiscent of the early days of their acquaintance. It was as if they were starting over again. He wanted to tell her that she was wrong, that she never said any such thing, but something held him back. "I apologize," he said. "I must have forgotten the rule."

"I see. What other rules have you forgotten, Mr. Stevens? Is there a woman in your bed right now?"

"No, Mrs. Cotton. You're welcome to have a look."

The woman was still huffing, short of breath. "Don't need your permission, Mr. Stevens." They stood there facing each other, an awkward silence between them now.

"Would you like me to clean your yard?" Blake asked.

"Absolutely not. Just stay out of it, understand?" The old woman turned to go. She grabbed the railing and took extra care descending the steps, breathing hard the whole way.

Blake called Claire and told her what happened. "Oh no, Blake. Mrs. Cotton was always demanding, but she was never harsh like that. I'm worried about her." They agreed that Claire would stop by and look in on her later that afternoon. When she got there, Blake was sitting on the front porch waiting for her. He suggested that he stay there while Claire spoke with her former teacher.

When Mrs. Cotton opened the door, she was happy to see Claire. She invited her in and offered her tea. After chatting for ten minutes, Claire mentioned she was seeing Blake and Mrs. Cotton was pleased. "Did you speak with him earlier today?" Claire asked.

"I don't think so. No, wait, I asked him to clean up the backyard."

"Were you angry with him?" Claire asked.

"Not at all, why do you ask?"

Claire put her teacup down. "He seems to think you were cross with him."

Mrs. Cotton turned her head side to side as if she wanted to be sure no one else was close by who might overhear what she was saying. "When he moved in here, I had grave misgivings about him. A single man, already 32 years old and no real responsibilities. Who knows what people are capable of?" She stood and walked over to the kettle and poured more tea for both of them. "I'm happy to say, he turned out to be a wonderful young man."

"I think he is," Claire said. "Blake told me you seemed a bit out of breath this morning."

"Oh, yes, it seems to happen all the time lately." She pulled a cigarette from her half-filled pack.

"Maybe you should see a doctor. I'm sure there is something they can do to help you breathe easier."

"Do you think so, dear?"

"I do. Mrs. Cotton? It might be a good time to stop smoking too."

The old woman took a drag and inhaled deeply. She stifled a cough. "That would give me nothing to live for, Claire."

Claire held Mrs. Cotton's hand. She remembered a moment so many years ago, when Mrs. Cotton held her hand while she cried over losing a footrace in the school yard. Until that moment everyone agreed that Claire was the fastest runner in the class. A new girl, who moved to Clarksville from Nebraska, bet Claire she could beat her in a race. Claire had been only too happy to accept the challenge. The race wasn't even close. Claire lost.

Mrs. Cotton must have witnessed it from the window. She was fond of Claire and when the students came bursting into the room, Claire trailed well behind them. Mrs. Cotton met her in the hallway and took her hand. "Claire, there will always be someone faster, or better than you at something. It's a big world, young lady. However, I want you to remember something. Losing at something doesn't matter unless you stop trying. Defeat is never permanent unless you quit."

Looking at Mrs. Cotton now, she saw for the first time how fragile she was. "Would you mind if I scheduled an appointment for you with your doctor?"

"I suppose not. I don't feel very well lately."

15

As they did every year, students walked into Clarksville Regional High School for the first day of school, dragging their feet and feeling the weight of their backpacks as they picked up their textbooks. Some of them had laptops or tablets as well. When they weren't complaining about the teachers they got for German or algebra, they milled about, exchanging stories about the fabulous summers they had at the Jersey shore, or for the lucky few, some excursion overseas. Most of them had spent the majority of the summer working on one of the local farms. But as teenagers will do, they focused on the bright spots, wanting to impress their classmates.

Blake was pleased that Mark Mitchell had kept his word and given him a couple of honors classes. He knew these students would work as hard as he did. No one mentioned his heroic moment back in May and he was grateful for that. His Uncle John had made it his business to get Blake an appointment to meet the Governor of New Jersey to receive another award. Meanwhile, Connor Watts, the kid with the bayonet, was sent to a special boot camp in lieu of prison.

The next month was busy as both students and teachers got back into the routine. During the month of August, Blake had spent hours every morning thinking about ways he could make his classes more interesting and challenging. He was determined to combine video, lecture and group projects, including field trips, to make his course the most exciting in the department.

He was pleased with the early going and he now had the full support of Frank Holt and Mark Mitchell. He and Parker also teamed up to start a new student club designed specifically to attract students who they identified as shy and uninvolved in extracurricular activities. Blake explained it to Parker one day after a spirited tennis match. "We need to do something for the kids that don't seem to fit in," he said. It isn't hard to pick out these kids."

"Right, they act just the way you probably did in high school," Parker said.

As they identified prospects, they told them they were doing a study and gave each one a questionnaire that asked them to identify their interests and ambitions post-graduation. They hoped that by November to have identified several small groups of students with similar interests. They would then work with these students after school on group projects that focused on those interests. They started off slowly, but by mid-October, they had established a couple of solid groups. Some of the kids made new friends, which, to Blake's way of thinking, was one of the key goals of the project.

Throughout the fall season, Blake and Claire got closer to each other. They went to football games together. Clarksville's team wasn't nearly as good as the year before, so they suffered through some one-sided defeats together. After every game they returned to Hammer and Nails and enjoyed cheeseburgers. They double-dated too, a few times with Parker and Penny, and with Victoria and Charles. They were getting to know each other better. Blake and Claire had their fingers crossed that they wouldn't discover a fatal flaw that would doom the relationship. They both expressed surprise that they got along so well. "I never dreamed I could fall in love with a Yankee," Blake said one night as they were driving home from a movie.

"Oh, I forgot to mention something my father told me," Claire said. "Several Clarks served in the Union Army during the Civil War, but one, his name was Jerome Clark, ran off and fought for the south."

"Maybe that's why you and I get along so well," Blake said. "What happened to Jerome?"

"He died at Gettysburg."

"At the hands of the brave men from Tennessee's Fourteenth Regiment, I'm sure," Blake said. "At least four members of the Stevens clan fought in that war. Funny thing, though, my father told me that one of them fought for the North. When the war was over he tried to come home, but the people he knew all his life ran him out of town."

"You know, it isn't really surprising we get along so well," Claire said. "We both come from a rural area."

"Farms, small towns and churches."

"You've seen my small town. When am I going to see Colby Springs?" Claire asked.

"How about during the Christmas break?"

Claire was very excited. She sensed that although they had only been together for about seven months, Blake was getting ready to propose. She had worked hard to help him overcome any lingering fears of abandonment. Nicci's bizarre behavior had spooked him. They talked about it one night in bed after a particularly intense love making session at a Philadelphia area hotel.

Claire was resting her head on Blake's chest while he stroked her long, dark hair. "I'm truly in love with you," he said. "Is it possible that a love this strong could ever die without warning?"

"What do you mean?" Claire asked.

"One day you wake up and you know you're in love, all in, no reservations. Can you wake up on another day and discover it's over, nothing left?"

"You're thinking of Nicci."

Blake lifted Claire's head from his chest and kissed her forehead. "I didn't have the same feelings for her. I didn't even know a guy could love a woman the way I love you. But, yeah, I guess you're right, in a way. I am."

"You want to know if I would ever abandon you the way she did?"

"That would be extreme. What Nicci did was cruel. She didn't just fall out of love. She wanted to make sure she really hurt me."

"Have you considered the possibility that Nicci wasn't well, that she suffered from an undiagnosed mental disorder?"

Blake got out of bed and went to the desk. He picked up a nearly empty bottle of Chardonnay and poured what was left in his glass. He handed it to Claire and she sipped it. "There isn't anything I haven't thought of. Was she abducted? Not likely. Who empties an entire house as part of an abduction? Was it a scam from the beginning? Doubtful, I mean who puts in that much effort for a thing like that? What if she invested all that time and I broke up with her before she could pull the plug on me?" He folded his pillow and put it under his head. "Maybe she met somebody else. I can see that, but again, it would have been so much easier to just tell me it's over."

"There's no way to know for sure what she was thinking, or why she would do something so mean, Blake. We look for reasons when something like this happens, and…"

"We expect or insist on rational explanations," Blake said, finishing Claire's thought.

"Do you still think about her a lot?" Claire handed the glass to Blake. He finished what was left in one swallow.

"Not really. It's just that I know what it's like to have your heart broken. It's a little bit scary."

"Don't be afraid, Blake. I've never been with a man who completed me the way you do. I don't believe for a second that there is another man out there who could even remotely, do what you do for me, intellectually, emotionally, spiritually and," she smiled now, "in bed." She kissed him. "You're everything I ever wanted in a man, but I could never have imagined you. You're much better than any dream I've ever had."

They made love again, slowly and sweetly, the way only lovers who have no doubts can do.

Mrs. Cotton had gone to see Dr. Chambers a week after her conversation with Claire. The weather was still warm as the first couple of weeks of September usually were. Brad had called Claire to discuss the old woman's situation as soon as he saw Mrs. Cotton was on his calendar. "Anything you can tell me about her current condition would be very helpful, Claire."

"According to Blake, she is frequently short of breath. And she's become a bit forgetful." Claire told Brad about Mrs. Cotton's outburst concerning her back yard, how she had forgotten it only hours later. "I'm worried about her."

"Perhaps I should have called your friend instead of you."

Claire sighed. "I'm sure he would be happy to speak with you, Brad."

"My apologies. I admit I'm jealous, but I just cannot imagine how you find a bumpkin like Stevens attractive."

She knew Brad was trying to inveigle her into a conversation that might allow him to show her the error she was making by choosing Blake. She ignored him. "You'll let me know your thoughts on Mrs. Cotton?"

Of course, I will."

"Thank you."

"Yes, well, that's why I'm here. I assume it's fair to say you're well and thriving?"

"More or less, I suppose. How are you?"

"Well now, more or less doesn't sound like a ringing endorsement for our super-duper man. As for me, I'm on the lookout for villains with knives. Being a local hero is not to be underrated."

He was doing it again. Claire was losing her patience. "Brad, do you know how silly you sound? I'm sorry things didn't work out for us, but I hope you can see it's simply for the best that we move on with our lives." She was clutching the phone, wanting to hang up, but not wanting to be brusque with him. After all they were engaged to be married once.

"Do I sound silly, Claire? You can't imagine how silly I feel. You dropped me, a man who has loved you for years, as if we were teenagers waiting in line at the Dairy Queen. Another guy comes along in a sporty Camaro, offers to take you to McDonald's and off you go."

"It wasn't like that, Brad. And you know it."

"Perhaps, but that's how it felt. That's still how it feels. I never imagined you could be so casually brutal, Claire."

She said goodbye then. She couldn't help thinking about the way Blake felt when Nicci left. Obviously, Brad was going through something similar. Only she had never heard Blake say a truly unkind word about Nicci.

After Dr. Chambers examined Mrs. Cotton, he explained she was suffering from the onset of dementia. Thankfully, there were drugs available that could slow the process. Still, she would have to be watched carefully. Her COPD had also progressed and the combination of low oxygen saturation and dementia didn't bode well for the future.

16

Blake came home from work the day before Thanksgiving, happy for the extra-long weekend that the holiday provided. He was tired, but as soon as he got his satchel put away and took his coat off, he went downstairs to check on Mrs. Cotton, something he had been doing since September when Dr. Chambers diagnosed Mrs. Cotton's condition. He knocked on her door. Nothing, not a sound. He knocked again, louder and called her. Still nothing. So, he telephoned her. He could hear her phone ring. He had turned her landline phone's volume up to the maximum setting. After ten rings, he hung up. Maybe she went out.

Mrs. Cotton had given her car away to a needy family. She told Blake she wanted to do that while she still had a few marbles left in her head. Blake realized she might be out with a friend, but something told him that wasn't the case. They had been through this before, and not that long ago. He and Claire had all but begged her to give either Blake or Claire a spare key to her place, but she refused, saying, "Next thing you know you'll want me to change my will." She had been in one of her darker moods. The couple agreed to try again when she was more lucid, but they were reluctant, not wanting to offend her. Now Blake was left in a quandary again. Should he break her door down, or call 911? Remembering that the EMT squad could get the door open with minimal damage, he made the call.

Mrs. Cotton was lying on her hardwood floor. She had tripped on an area rug and fell, suffering a wrist fracture and a serious bump on her forehead. As the EMTs were putting her on a stretcher, the ambulance driver said to Blake, "It's a good thing you moved in here, buddy. She would have been a goner a while ago if you weren't here."

Blake smiled. He was feeling good about himself. He allowed it, maybe because it was Thanksgiving again and he was in a much better place than he had been for the last two Thanksgiving holidays.

An hour later, Mrs. Cotton was resting comfortably in the hospital. She was asleep and receiving pure oxygen and IV fluids. Claire met Blake at the hospital and waited for Brad to come into Mrs. Cotton's room. He arrived at seven-thirty, looking tired from a long day's work. He was a bit surprised to see the couple sitting at Mrs. Cotton's bedside.

"Hello, Claire. I see you and Mr. Stevens together everywhere it seems."

"How is she?" Claire asked, ignoring Brad's jab.

"She's dehydrated and her oxygen saturation levels are low. Do either of you know whether she's been using her oxygen concentrator regularly?"

"I haven't seen her use it," Blake said.

Dr. Chambers nodded. "We will want to keep her here for a few days. She has a mild concussion and, of course, the wrist fracture. But, frankly, I'm more concerned with her other issues. Has her next of kin been notified yet?"

Claire looked at Blake, who shook his head no. "Can one of you take care of that then?"

"I'll have to look for her sister's phone number," Blake said.

"No need, I have it here." He wrote the number down on a blank prescription and handed it to Claire. "I'll be in again later, when she's awake. Since neither of you are listed as next of kin, I assume you realize her privacy must be safeguarded."

Mrs. Cotton's eyes opened. She looked at everyone in the room, confused at first, but she recovered quickly. "I'm awake, you know. I've been listening to you. When can I get out of here? It seems my tenant prefers that I be here rather than in my home."

"Still looking for the money, Bella. Why don't you just tell me where you hid it?" Blake asked.

"It's in the bank, fool." She turned to Dr. Chambers. "I'm feeling much better, Bradley. May I go home now? I'm sure Mr. Stevens and your former fiancé can give me a lift."

Brad looked at Mrs. Cotton, then at Claire. She mouthed the word sorry. "Mrs. Cotton, I think it best if you stay here at least until Sunday." He explained her condition and asked her if there was anything she needed to make her more comfortable.

"My Bible, please."

"I'll bring it tomorrow," Blake said.

Blake and Claire left the hospital as soon as Mrs. Cotton fell asleep. It was around 8:30. They decided to get a bite to eat, settling on the Mexican restaurant where Jonna used to work. She was living with Zeke now and handling the paperwork for his construction business. Blake ran into her a few times because Zeke kept finding little jobs for Parker and him that could be squeezed in either after school or on weekends. The extra money helped. Jonna was always happy to see him. They chatted about her boys and Jonna made it clear that Zeke would always find work for him, grateful for the way Blake stood up for her against her ex-husband.

At dinner that night, Claire mentioned how excited she was about spending the Christmas holidays with him. "I don't know how to explain it, Blake, but I am so much happier this year than I was a year ago."

"Well, a few good things have happened this year." He reached for her hand and gave it a gentle squeeze.

"Funny, I thought I was happy with Brad, but now that you mention it, the first inkling I had that perhaps I was making a mistake occurred to me last Thanksgiving. He was rude," she said.

"In what way? Do you remember?" Blake asked.

"Actually, now that I think of it, he was already jealous of you."

"Me? I barely knew you. And you didn't care for me. You thought I was rude, as I recall."

"Life is full of surprises," Claire said, returning his squeeze.

Thanksgiving Day was festive at the Clark house. Dinner was served in the dining room, which was large enough to accommodate their guests, twenty-four well-fed people seated at two tables. Dinner was prepared by a staff hired for special occasions. There was fresh turkey and ham, complemented by stuffing, cranberry relish and locally grown vegetables. Dessert included apple and pumpkin pies. Before dinner, Terrance Clark entertained everyone, playing the piano he had bought recently. He had played throughout his school years, even earning extra money playing in a jazz quartet, while he attended the University of Pennsylvania. His older daughter, Deanna, stood next to Mrs. Clark and listened to him play. He was a bit rusty, but it was obvious he was a good musician.

Blake and Claire stood in the library enjoying cocktails and chatting with Victoria and Dr. Remolina. Deanna's husband, Nathan Brower, joined them. The couple had just set a wedding date. "We're going to tie the knot on New Year's Eve on Marco Island," Charles said.

"Not very original, I know," Victoria added, "but Charles loves Florida and he's usually too busy to get away."

"I'm happy you're getting married there. It will give me a chance to get some sun. I haven't been to Florida since college and spring break," Claire said.

"Have you been to Florida, Blake?" Charles asked.

"Just once. My parents took me to Disney World when I was ten."

"You'll love Marco Island. The gulf coast is marvelous. The water is calm and warm, even during the winter months," Nathan said. "I have a client who lets Deanna and I use her condo for a week every October." Nathan's law firm catered to the well-heeled in the Philadelphia suburbs.

Victoria put her hand gently on Blake's arm. "You'll come and be Claire's escort, won't you?"

Blake put his glass on a coaster that sat conveniently on a side table and poured more Bourbon. He offered Charles a refill which he gratefully accepted. Nathan declined. He took a deep breath, trying to think of what to say. He had assumed the wedding would be a local affair, perhaps, Philadelphia. When he heard the wedding would be on Marco Island, he knew immediately he would have a problem. There was no way he could afford to make the trip. Even with the extra money he made working for Zeke, airfare, hotel accommodations and meals would quickly add up. Over the last six months, he had overspent, treating Claire to dinners at upscale restaurants and splurging on a couple of special occasions, like their trip to New York. If he said he couldn't afford it, he would be acknowledging the truth. He had practically no savings. He had not recovered yet from what Nicci had done to his finances. He only had about $2,000 left in his savings account. He had, of course, managed to put some money into his 401K, but it didn't make sense to withdraw any of it, especially for someone else's wedding. He was trying to save for what he hoped would be his own wedding.

He was embarrassed by his financial circumstances. Certainly, he didn't want Claire to know he was practically broke. There would be a time to discuss finances with her, but he wasn't prepared to do that yet. Now, it seemed, he had no choice. Thanks mainly to an inheritance, Claire's family was well to do, if not wealthy. Her sister and brother in law were living in Villanova, part of Philadelphia's main line. The "main line" meant nothing to Blake, coming from Tennessee, until Claire casually mentioned it one day, laughing about it. She said, "My parents weren't thrilled that their daughter married a Jewish man, but when Nathan and Deanna moved to the main line, they got over it." Obviously, they had no worries about paying for a destination wedding.

Everyone looked at him, expecting he would say yes, he would come to the wedding. At moments like this, he always remembered what his father told him; when there is a problem, turn and face it. "Don't look the other way and don't pretend it doesn't exist. The first step in solving any problem is facing it, Blake," his father advised.

"I'm very happy for you both," Blake said. "I'm sure Marco Island is a wonderful place to get married, but, on a teacher's salary, I can't afford a trip like that right now. I'll be with you in spirit though." He raised his glass and toasted them.

Claire, Victoria and Charles stared at him in shock. Victoria spoke first. "You have to come. We'll cover your hotel costs, of course. We should have mentioned that."

"Why of course we will," Charles said. "And your flight will be taken care of too. We didn't expect you to incur such an expense simply because we've chosen a destination wedding."

"This is all very sudden. We have plenty of time to discuss it," Claire said, hoping to cut off further discussion. Obviously, Blake was uncomfortable, and he was well aware that Brad would be there as Charles' best man. Claire was grateful that Victoria didn't mention Brad.

Blake caught all of this immediately. The condescension, well-meaning though it may have been, was suffocating. He looked at Claire, whose face had gone pale. He noticed, too that Charles and Victoria made no offer of financial assistance to Claire, who would, after all, be facing the same expenses. He realized they weren't trying to offend or emasculate him. Regardless, he felt like the guy who showed up at a formal dinner party dressed in shorts and a ripped tee shirt. He raised his right hand and said, very calmly, "That won't be necessary. I can't let you do that. If I can come up with the money, I'll be there. If not, as I said a moment ago, I'll be there in spirit."

Mrs. Clark called from the kitchen that she could use some help. Dinner was ready. Claire, Deanna and Victoria walked to the kitchen while the men headed for the dining room. As she was leaving, Claire squeezed Blake's hand and kissed his cheek.

On the way into the dining room, Nathan tugged Blake's sleeve which made him stop and turn. He said, "That took a lot of guts. I'm impressed, man."

After dinner, the women went into the kitchen and the men headed to the library for after dinner drinks. Blake offered to help, but Mrs. Clark wouldn't hear of it. "The staff will handle the cleanup. We ladies will merely supervise," she said. Claire was glad to have a moment to talk to Victoria alone. She led her friend to the second floor, into her old bedroom and closed the door. They had spent many hours in that room, giggling and laughing when they were children. They sat on the bed together. "We've been best friends for a long time, Victoria and I love you, you know that."

"Uh-Oh. What did I do now?"

"Why would you mention your plans to have a destination wedding when you and I haven't even discussed it?"

Victoria stood. "Claire, I'm very sorry. I didn't know we needed your permission."

"You know that isn't what I meant. You put Blake on the spot, which I am pretty sure ruined his day. It wasn't necessary."

"Honestly, Claire, it never occurred to me that he was having financial difficulty, but while we're on the subject, are you sure he's right for you? I mean the man is lovely, but he's broke, for goodness sake. Doesn't that worry you?"

Claire stood up and faced Victoria. "No, I'm not concerned. "I can't believe you're saying these things. I have never been happier. He's very bright and he's sincere."

Victoria took Claire's hand and guided her back to her seat on the bed. "Honey, if you're happy with him, that's all that matters, really. It's just that Brad seemed like, well, a much safer choice. He is still devastated over losing you, by the way. He keeps hoping you'll come to your senses."

"It's over between Brad and I no matter what happens with Blake." Claire started biting a fingernail, an old habit she overcame ten years ago. Victoria gently touched Claire's hand and said, "Stop that."

"Thank you." Claire sat down on the bed again. "I doubt that Blake will be there now. I just wish you had spoken to me first," Claire said. "Not that I would try to change your mind. I want you and Charles to have exactly the kind of wedding you want. It's just that, had I known your plans, I would have approached the subject with Blake in a different manner."

"Did you know he was broke?"

"No, and frankly, I don't know if he is actually broke. We've never discussed it."

"Listen, you can work on him, Claire. I know you can. He'll come just to keep Brad away from you. Just ask him not to wear his boots or the cowboy hat to the wedding." Claire tried for a stern look, but she couldn't help it. "He hasn't worn his cowboy hat for months," Claire said. The women laughed, friends again.

On the way to her townhouse that night, Claire had a suggestion. By now she knew Blake well enough not to bring up the subject of Victoria's wedding plans. He needed time to work through it. But she wanted to reassure him, find a way to make him see that whether he attended the wedding or not, she loved him. "Mrs. Cotton is in the hospital. Would it be a terrible thing if I spent the night with you in your apartment?"

"Behind her back?" He was laughing, a good sign. "Somebody will tell her. I don't know how she does it, but that woman doesn't miss a thing."

"Do you think she would retroactively change my fourth-grade report card from an "S" to a "U" under conduct if she finds out?"

"Don't worry, honey. I'll vouch for you." They had a night of spirited love making. By morning they were both exhausted. They had agreed to get up early so Blake could take Claire home, before the town gossips were up and patrolling the neighborhood. He walked her to her door and kissed her. It was not yet six o'clock. "I changed your report card to an "I" for incredible," he whispered.

BOOK III

17

On Friday afternoon, the day after Thanksgiving, Claire left the church at 4:30, tired, but looking forward to seeing Blake that night. The night before was sweet and tender. She felt the bond between them was growing stronger. Although they hadn't been a couple for even a year, she was hopelessly in love with Blake. She had no doubt that she would say yes if he asked her to marry him.

She had dismissed Victoria's concerns. Yet, throughout the day, as she usually did with important matters, Claire considered Victoria's points, eager to discern their meaning and implications. It was true that Blake came from modest financial circumstances, but both of his parents had enjoyed professions and, of course, Blake was a college graduate. She hated it when Victoria suggested he was a hick. Claire was charmed by Blake's southern ways. For the sake of their friendship, she let it go, but she knew when the time was right, she would revisit the subject with her friend.

Being with Blake taught her that there were different kinds of sophistication. Certainly, some people, like Charles, Victoria, and Brad, were culturally sophisticated. Their love and appreciation for the arts, their knowledge of life's finer things, from good china to fine art, to wine, were admirable. But Blake was sophisticated in a different way. He understood the way people felt, easily grasping their needs and acting upon them. He was turning average students into good students and the way he stepped in to help Mrs. Cotton, who had no one to take care of her, was beyond heartwarming. After all, he didn't even know her.

As soon as she got home, she called Blake, looking forward to hearing his voice. She was surprised when he didn't answer. She decided to take a shower. He would probably call her back. She showered, took care of her hair and put on some makeup. She checked her phone. Nothing. She tried him again. Still no answer. She was a bit worried, but she thought maybe he was at the hospital visiting Mrs. Cotton. When her phone finally rang, she swept it up, anticipating Blake, but it was her sister, Deanna.

"Claire, are you home right now?"

"I am. What's going on Dee?"

"Have you spoken to Blake today?"

"Not yet. What's wrong?" She gripped the phone as if she could squeeze the news out that her sister obviously had for her.

"Oh, honey. Blake's been arrested by the Clarksville Police."

"Arrested? What on earth for?"

"Here, talk to Nathan. I'll let him tell you."

Nathan picked up the phone. "It's serious, Claire. I found him an attorney, the best criminal lawyer I know. She practices in both Philly and South Jersey."

"What are you saying?"

"Brace yourself, Claire. He was arrested for murder and bank robbery in Cherry Hill. He's going to be moved there tonight or tomorrow morning."

"Murder! Bank robbery? That's ridiculous. Is he in jail?" Claire asked, frantic now.

"I'm afraid so. We don't really know anything yet. I'll speak with his attorney as soon as she finishes meeting with Blake."

"This can't be true. He would never do such a thing."

"I know. We'll get to the bottom of this very quickly. I have to ask, Claire, when was the last time you saw him?"

"This morning, around six o'clock." Claire was feeling numb.

"Did you speak with him today at any time after that?"

"No." She was crying now. "Can I see him?"

"Not tonight," Nathan said. "Let's wait to see what his attorney says. Her name is Marie Ventrella Scott."

"Call me as soon as you hear something, Nathan, please."

"Of course. You want Deanna to come and stay with you?"

"No, she shouldn't drive all the way down here. I'll give Victoria a call."

Victoria raced to Claire's townhouse. In fact, she was delayed when a Clarksville traffic cop pulled her over for speeding. She managed to sweet talk him out of the ticket, breathlessly telling him she was on her way to see her friend, whose boyfriend had just been arrested for murder. The cop smiled. "Bank heist in Cherry Hill, right?"

Claire was sitting in her living room crying. She wiped her eyes as Victoria walked in. They embraced and Victoria headed for the liquor cabinet. "Gonna be a long night, Claire."

They sat and talked until midnight. Claire told Victoria what she knew. Nathan had called and brought her up to date. "Should I go to the jail tomorrow morning?"

"Do you think he could have done it?" Victoria asked.

"No, never. It isn't possible."

"I'm sure you're right, honey. What kind of evidence could they possibly have? I mean why would they arrest him unless they had reason to believe he did it?"

"There has to be some kind of mistake, a case of mistaken identity, don't you think?" Claire asked.

"I'm sure." Victoria was absolutely convinced that Blake was guilty. She hated herself for being a tiny bit relieved that her friend would be spared from making an enormous error if she married him. And it pained her too that Claire was in such agony. As much as she disagreed with Claire's choosing Blake over Brad, she cried right along with her. This was a tragedy. A man was dead and seemingly, Blake may have ruined his own life in the process. "If you want to see him, I think you should go, even if you have to drive to Cherry Hill. In fact, I'll drive you."

"Thank you, Victoria, I love him."

"I know. Things may not be as bad as they seem." Victoria hoped she was right, surprising herself.

18

Early on Saturday morning, Blake was placed in the back of a cruiser to make the trip to Cherry Hill. An hour after he arrived, he was put into a lineup. He was quickly identified by three of the five witnesses. The other two, including the security guard, said they couldn't be certain, but they couldn't rule him out either. Marie Ventrella Scott was there with him. Marie asked for a room where she could consult with her client. She reassured him that Nathan and Deanna were in touch with Claire. She promised to inform Mr. Mitchell, Clarksville Regional High School's principal, of what was going on. No doubt, he already knew, but Marie didn't say it. At Blake's request, she was also got in touch with Senator John Major, Blake's uncle, who offered to assist in whatever way he could.

She explained the legal process in New Jersey to Blake. Within a few days, he would appear before a judge to be arraigned. The charges would be explained to him. She was confident the judge would allow bail to be set, but she warned him it would probably be very high. The resulting bond could well be out of reach financially. Blake asked her to get in touch with his sister, Judy as soon as possible. She might be able to help. Before she left, Marie explained her fees. She said, "It seems clear, barring a miracle, that your case is going to trial; very likely in a Federal court, given the nature of the crime. You will need a very good lawyer. I would be happy to take the case, but even with a discount, it will cost you upwards of $150,000. And I'm not going to blow smoke here, Blake. Based on what we know right now, you could be found guilty."

Blake stared off into space, stone-faced, as if he wasn't listening to his attorney. But he heard every word. "I guess you'll need payment up front then."

"Yes, most of it, but let's not worry about that now."

By late morning, Blake was sitting in his cell trying to understand what had happened to him. Twenty-four hours earlier, he was grading papers while he listened to a country music station, feeling good about his relationship with Claire. He had no idea how this could happen to him, or anybody for that matter. After Nicci left him, he thought he couldn't possibly feel any lower than he did then. He was wrong, very wrong. This was much worse. Yet, he learned something from that experience. Never give in to circumstances. Find a way to fight. He vowed to do just that.

He ate lunch in his cell, a bologna and cheese sandwich that was so dry it stuck to the roof of his mouth. He was about to lay down on his cot when an officer, who looked a bit like Barney Fife, came in and told him he had a visitor. The officer handcuffed him and led him to a cubicle attached to a long, windowed wall. When he saw Claire, his spirits lifted briefly.

She was dressed in jeans and the white sweater he had given her back when they celebrated their three-month anniversary. She wore very little makeup, except for a bold, red lipstick. She looked great, but it was easy to see she'd been crying. He felt ashamed to have her see him in an orange jump suit. At least the guard had removed the handcuffs just before he sat down.

"Claire, I feel like I'm in some kind of nightmare and can't wake up."

She put her index finger through the small open space in the glass wall that made it possible for visitors and prisoners to hear each other. He touched the tip of her finger with his. They stayed that way for a moment. It was a kiss, expressed the only way they could under the circumstances. "Did you and Parker go to Cherry Hill yesterday? To play tennis, I mean."

"No, I never left my apartment."

"I heard there are photos. Do they look at all like you?" Claire felt terrible. She was interrogating Blake when she wanted to comfort him, but she had so many questions.

"That's the craziest thing about this. It looks just like me, but it can't be me. And the car looked exactly like mine too."

"There has to be an explanation. We just have to look for it."

"I'm glad you came, Claire, but I'm sorry you had to see me like this."

"I don't care. I had to see you. Nathan said you can probably get out of here on Monday."

Blake nodded, not saying anything. He didn't want to mention that the bond could be very expensive, possibly too much for him to make bail. "You should go now. You shouldn't be sitting in a jailhouse. I'll see you Monday, God willing. Pray for me."

"I will. I love you, Blake."

He nodded again, slowly this time. They let their fingers touch again.

On the drive home, Victoria asked Claire what she thought. "I don't know. He seemed distraught. The photos, the car, the eyewitnesses and the fact he has no proof that he was in his apartment all day. I'm worried about that."

Victoria chose her words carefully, never easy for her. "I wish there was a logical explanation for all of this, I do. But if this happened to someone else instead of Blake, logic would tell us he did it. When we talked about my wedding, he sounded like he was broke."

Claire looked out her window at the pine trees that dotted the highway. "I thought about that too. I want so much to believe him. I don't know what to think."

"When his patients are really sick, when they're facing a long road, Charles tells them to take one day at a time," Victoria said. "That's exactly what you have to do now."

On Monday morning Marie Ventrella Scott was there to meet Blake when he arrived at the Camden County Courthouse. Blake's first appearance in court, the arraignment, was straightforward. His rights were read to him. Then the judge explained the charges, which included murder in the first degree, bank robbery, possession of a deadly weapon and other related charges. Blake plead not guilty to all charges.

After reviewing Blake's history, the judge spoke. "I'm taking into consideration that Mr. Stevens has no prior arrests, he's gainfully employed and his uncle, Senator John Major, vouches for him. I'm setting bail at $1.2 million."

As soon as the proceedings ended, John and Abigail Major stepped forward. Senator Major introduced himself to Marie and addressed Blake. "I've known you your whole life, and I cannot believe you would ever do something so heinous," he said, pausing for a moment. He glanced at his wife, who was filling another tissue with tears. "Aunt Abigail and I will post the necessary bond so you can go home."

Blake shook his uncle's hand and hugged his aunt, thanking them profusely. He didn't claim his innocence, which bothered his Uncle John. Four hours later, Blake was released. Parker was waiting for him outside the jail. "Want to play a little tennis while we're here in Cherry Hill?"

Blake didn't think he could even smile, but Parker made him laugh, a little bit at least. "I just want to get home and take a shower, bro. Any news at school?"

"You've been suspended. Mitchell sent a confidential email to all teachers and staff.

"The least of my problems, don't you think?" Blake asked.

It wasn't as bad as it could have been. His Uncle John paid his bond and the school was required to continue paying him, pending the outcome of his case, provided that he went to a designated room in the county's school administration building every day during regular school hours. That worried him, because being cooped up all day, he wouldn't have the time he needed to try to figure out what had actually happened. Could someone like Brad have found an elaborate way to set him up? Could a friend of the late Derek Martinelli have something to do with this? He knew he was grasping at straws. Considering the photo with a guy wearing a Clarksville Regional High School cap, and the black Camaro, it was a sophisticated operation. And wasn't it possible that the photos were doctored? Was he a victim of identity theft? Common sense told him that was unlikely. Still, if someone did this to him, they certainly did a good and thorough job. But why? He felt he had to consider every possibility. For now, he could only hope and pray that Detective Wronko would decide it was a simple case of mistaken identity.

When they pulled up to Mrs. Cotton's house, he remembered she was in the hospital when the cops took him in. "Parker, is Mrs. Cotton still in the hospital?"

"She must be. Otherwise your stuff would be on the front lawn, don't you think?"

"I'm glad you can find so much humor in my situation. I'm probably going to spend the rest of my life in prison for something I didn't do."

"It's that last part that matters, Blakester. You didn't do it. We just have to figure out how to prove it."

Blake took a shower and got into clean clothes. It felt good. His stomach was growling now. The only thing he ate that day was a small bowl of Rice Krispies for breakfast before he went to court. He decided to go out and get something to eat. It was almost four o'clock. He wanted to call Claire but thought better of it. Certainly, they needed to talk, but he didn't want to do that in a public place.

He took a ride to the diner in Bridgeton where he and Claire went occasionally for breakfast on Saturday mornings. He looked out the diner's window while he ate a hot roast beef sandwich and mashed potatoes. The diner was on the corner of the town's biggest intersection. He watched cars go by. It was a cold day and people on the street walked quickly. He had always taken his freedom for granted, just like the people he was watching. That it might soon be taken from him so easily, shocked him. On his way back to Clarksville, Claire called him.

"Hi, honey. I heard you got out. Why didn't you call me?"

"I wanted to, but I had to get myself reoriented and I needed a little time to think," Blake said.

"About what, if I may ask?"

"About us, Claire. I love you, you know that. But circumstances have changed."

"Our feelings for each other haven't, certainly my feelings haven't changed. I love you, Blake Stevens."

"Our feelings haven't changed, but we're dealing with a very strange situation. My God, Claire, I know I didn't rob a bank and shoot someone. But my uncle had to put up $120,000 this morning to get me out of jail. I had to plead not guilty to something I had no idea even happened," Blake said. "And I've been suspended from my job."

"I know. This is a nightmare. But I want to be there for you and support you through whatever may come. That's what people in love do for each other. If the roles were reversed, I know you would be there for me."

Blake realized that Claire had not thought through the implications of the situation yet. Eventually, of course, she would, or friends and family would point out reality to her. "Claire, Clarksville is a small town and your family is a bedrock of the community. You have to distance yourself from me, and my situation until this is cleared up. Honey, my lawyer made it clear that, as it stands now, I'll probably be convicted if this goes to trial."

"I don't believe that. Someone will remember seeing you at McDonald's. The driver of the getaway car will be found. Something good is bound to happen."

"I can't help thinking I'm being set up, Claire. Whoever did this was very clever. They could be miles away now."

"Set you up? Oh my. I suppose that is possible, but who? And why?" Claire was beginning to worry now. She knew Blake wasn't thinking clearly. Who could think clearly in this situation? But the idea that someone could doctor a video from the bank's security camera seemed a bit farfetched. And Nathan had told her the photo of the getaway car came from a street camera, not the bank.

"I know. It sounds crazy. But the only other explanation would be that I did it and suffered amnesia. And that's just plain ridiculous," Blake said. "Anyway, I think it might be best if we didn't see each other for a while."

"I could not disagree with you more, Blake. You need me now and I need you. If we stop seeing each other, people will suspect I think you're guilty. That wouldn't be good for you, or for us."

Blake hadn't considered that possibility. "You're right, honey, but this is going to be hard on you, you know that."

"I don't care," Claire said. "I just know there's an explanation for all of this."

Claire noticed she had a text from Brad just as she pulled up to a red light. Mrs. Cotton was being discharged from the hospital. She ended the call with Blake, telling him about Mrs. Cotton. Then she called Victoria. "Do you have time to help me pick up Mrs. Cotton? She's ready to go home. You can help me get her settled."

Victoria laughed. "Sure, why not? You know she gave me the only D I ever got? The subject was math."

"I remember," Claire answered.

19

Mrs. Cotton was home, discharged from the hospital an hour after Blake's conversation with Claire. Brad Chambers told Claire he was releasing the poor woman, but not without misgivings. "Keep a watchful eye on her," he said.

The following day, Blake got home late. After he left the administration building, he'd gone to the school to see Mark Mitchell. The principal was sympathetic and did his best to be supportive. "You've had several misfortunes since moving to Clarksville, Blake. I hope this is the last of them." He assured Blake that the entire faculty and staff was behind him, but his tone was muted. He had his doubts. The evidence, at least what he'd heard from rumors, seemed overwhelming.

Blake opened the front door and headed for the steps to his apartment. Mrs. Cotton was waiting for him, a portable oxygen tank on wheels at her side. "What were you doing in my apartment this afternoon?"

Blake gave her a blank stare. Other than paying her a quick visit the night before, he hadn't seen or spoken to her.

"Well?"

"I just got home. I've been out since morning."

"Don't lie to me. I saw you. You thought I was asleep, but I wasn't." She was already short of breath. "You were in my purse, why?"

Blake was confused. Was she looking for a reason to get rid of him? "I wasn't here all-day Mrs. Cotton, honest." He stuck his hands in his pockets. "Do you want me to move out?"

"Everybody in this town thinks I should throw you out on your ear right now. The evidence against you is very convincing. You're either a damn fool, or the victim of a mystery worthy of Agatha Christie. Which is it?"

"Maybe both, Mrs. Cotton. I know I'm innocent," he said. "I'll move out if you want me to. Just give me a few days to see if I can find a place, okay?'

The old woman's face softened. "I spoke with Claire on the way home from the hospital. She believes in you. If she can stand by you, so can I. I taught for more than forty years, and I learned to be a good judge of character. I'm never wrong. Maybe this will be the first time. We'll see." Mrs. Cotton adjusted her nasal cannula. "In any event, who on earth do you think would rent to you in this town?"

"Good point. Thank you."

"Just don't come in again without knocking. And stay out of my purse." She took a few quick breaths and went on. "Claire must have left my door unlocked." She clutched her robe and, changing gears again, she tapped her temple with her index finger. "My doctor tells me I'm losing my marbles. I'm afraid I'm going to need your help. So, I guess you can stay." She turned to go. "Oh, and by the way, the rules around here haven't changed. Keep your car out of my garage."

"Right, sorry about that."

"That's not all. No woman, no matter how nice she may be, is allowed to enter your apartment without my permission, ever. Understood?" Mrs. Cotton held Blake's gaze just to remind him that nothing ever got by her; that, in spite of her deteriorating condition, somehow, she knew that Claire spent the night while she was hospitalized.

"Yes." Blake smiled, but he was worried about Mrs. Cotton. Unless he was suddenly having blackouts, he was sure he hadn't been in her apartment earlier that day.

For the next month, Blake waited for the grand jury date. Every day he checked in with the school administration's secretary and sat at a gray metal table in a small conference room during school hours. For the first couple of days, another teacher was also in the room. He had been suspended for suspicion of selling drugs to middle school students. He vehemently denied the charge and spent a good deal of time on his cell phone talking to his lawyer and two girlfriends he was struggling to keep secret from each other. He made conversation with Blake, but after the initial pleasantries, he became unpleasant. He knew Claire Clark and claimed to know the whole Clark family. He needled Blake about playing out of his league, telling him everyone knew he robbed the bank to support Claire's lifestyle. It was obvious to Blake that the man knew very little beyond what he read in the newspaper and whatever gossip was going around.

At the end of the second day, Blake asked if he could be moved to another room, but the secretary assured him it wouldn't be necessary. "I just heard that clown is going to change his plea to guilty."

From then on, Blake focused on books he borrowed from the Rutgers Law School library. After speaking with Nathan, Claire was able to find books that might be helpful to Blake. Marie also encouraged him to study. After work, Blake mostly kept to himself. At night, he stayed in his apartment.

He spoke with Claire on the phone every day, but he refused to let her be seen with him in public. He knew it could damage her reputation and the Clark family's standing in town. As much as Claire protested that it didn't matter, he knew better. He permitted her to visit once a week on Sunday afternoons, in Mrs. Cotton's parlor. They were both concerned about the declining state of her mental health. She seemed delusional at times. She never mentioned her belief that he had been in her apartment that day, a relief to him.

Christmas Eve was a somber event for the couple. They spent the evening with Mrs. Cotton. Claire prepared a simple dinner of meatloaf, baked potatoes and corn. Mrs. Cotton, who was in good form all day, had a gift for the couple, an antique candle lantern from the late nineteenth century. She said it would see them through dark times and lead them to sunlight.

The old woman was asleep in her chair by 9:30. Blake and Claire talked about Christmas Day. Claire's parents had made it clear that Blake was no longer welcome in their home. The Clarks were mystified by their daughter's refusal to see the obvious. It didn't help matters when a DNA sample matched Blake's DNA. A CSI team tested a piece of gum that had been discarded outside the bank. When it was a match for Blake, the investigators were pleased, certain they had eliminated any doubts about who committed the crime.

When Mr. Clark announced he would no longer welcome Blake into their home, he said, "My dear, sweet daughter, we did not raise you to be a foolish woman. Until now, you've always been so sensible," her father said. "The evidence dear, is clear now. There is no longer any room for doubt, if there ever was,"

Mrs. Clark added. "You must cut this man off. In the long run, you'll be doing him a kindness. Perhaps when he sees he has lost your support, he will come to his senses and confess," she said. "I'm sure he can avoid the death penalty if he comes forward now." Claire was torn by her parents' attitude, but steadfast in her belief that there had to be another explanation, one that would clear Blake.

While Mrs. Cotton snored, Claire made a suggestion to Blake. "I want us to spend the day together tomorrow. It's our first Christmas. We can go to Philadelphia and spend the night," Claire said.

Blake stared at the Christmas tree branches. "No, you should be with your parents." He turned to Claire. "When this is over and I'm cleared, your parents might still hold it against me if I kept you from spending Christmas Day with them. I know it's a big day for your family."

"Not this year."

"No Claire, every year is special." He reached over and kissed her. "I got you something for Christmas. It's just a little old thing, but it comes from the heart." Claire carefully undid the red wrapping and opened a tiny box to find a gold locket, inscribed with the words faith, hope and love. She put it around her neck and kissed Blake, softly. She cried a little but regained her composure quickly. She handed him a larger box. He opened it and saw a leather-bound journal with his initials embossed on the cover.

"It's perfect, Claire. I know you've been telling me I should keep a journal. Now I have to." They kissed again. A few minutes later, Mrs. Cotton began to stir. They got up and Claire helped her get ready for bed.

The Clark family spent a quiet Christmas Day together, just the immediate family. They exchanged gifts and had a prime rib roast, surrounded by Brussel sprouts and red potatoes, prepared by Claire and Deanna. It was Deanna who insisted that the sisters prepare the meal. Keeping Claire busy was a priority.

On Christmas night, they had a surprise visitor. Brad stopped by to wish them a Merry Christmas. He brought an expensive bottle of brandy for Mr. Clark and a fine bottle of sherry for Mrs. Clark. When Claire saw him, she looked at her father, hoping he would ask Brad to leave.

Ignoring his daughter's look, Mr. Clark said, "So good to see you, Brad." He shook the doctor's hand. "I trust you had a joyful Christmas." Then he turned to Claire and said, "Claire, please escort the good doctor to the dining room. We were just about to have dessert. This brandy will certainly go well with whatever you ladies have prepared."

Claire escorted Brad to the dining room, where he shook hands with Nathan and hugged Deanna before taking a seat. "I have something for you too, Claire." From the pocket of his charcoal gray blazer, he pulled out a card. Claire accepted it but didn't open it. She placed it on the table.

"Aren't you going to open it, dear?" Mrs. Clark asked.

"No mother, I'm not. In fact, I hope everyone will excuse me. I'm not feeling well." The next morning the card was still sitting on the dining room table. Claire wasn't curious. She put it in the trash.

20

The Cherry Hill homicide squad was very thorough in collecting possible evidence from in and around the Palmyra Bank. Detective Terry Wronko was very pleased that a CSI saw the gum and decided to collect it. There was no question now that Blake Stevens had been to the bank that morning. That his DNA matched the sample extracted from the gum, eliminated the detective's doubts. Never mind he didn't seem to be the type who would commit a serious crime. Wronko had seen too much over the years to take a suspect's demeanor, no matter how innocent looking, at face value.

Marie Ventrella Scott took the news stoically. She called Blake and suggested they meet in her Philadelphia office. "Blake, this is very bad news, I'm afraid."

"Yes, ma'am I know that. What do we do now?"

Marie flipped open a note pad. She made a few notes. "I think it might be time to consider a plea bargain. The chances of acquittal were already small. DNA is very hard to dispute. I can't guarantee that the DA will go for it, but I feel we have to try."

"I don't know much about DNA, but considering where they found the gum and when they did the test and all, isn't it possible they're wrong? How do we know where the gum was collected?"

"You think Detective Wronko would actually set you up? Let me disabuse you of that notion right now. I've worked with a lot of cops. Wronko is a straight shooter, not a doubt in my mind about it."

"If you say so, ma'am. But they have to be wrong."

The attorney's face softened a bit. "It's possible and we would certainly challenge the finding at trial. It will add to your costs, though, because we would need the finest DNA expert to do the necessary work and testify."

"Whatever it takes. I'm not going to plead guilty to something I didn't do. I would dishonor my family and my name."

In spite of her effort to hold it in, Marie let out a sigh. "Okay, we can always revisit this option as the trial date gets closer. We do have a few things in your favor. None of the people who know you, here or in Tennessee, believe you would ever do the things you've been accused of. Aside from a few speeding tickets when you were younger, your record is impeccable. And, the prosecution has not been able to come up with an ironclad motive."

"That's because I didn't do it. I had no motive."

Marie smiled. She put her pen down. "Blake, I didn't say the prosecutor hasn't established any motive. There's a distinct possibility that they will say you were motivated by your need to find the money to attend the wedding of Victoria Gibson and Dr. Charles Remolina." She glanced down at her notes.

"Marco Island, right? I understand there are several witnesses to a conversation you had about the wedding.'

"That's crazy," Blake said. "Really, Marie, if I wanted to raise money for a quick trip to Florida, I could have borrowed it from my sister, my friend Parker, or my Uncle John, if it was that important."

"Did you ask any of them for a loan?"

"Of course not. Like I said, it just wasn't that important."

Marie stood up and walked to the window. She wasn't getting through to her client. "Listen carefully, Blake. Pretend for a moment you're on the witness stand, however unlikely that may be. The prosecutor is questioning you, okay?"

"Okay."

"Mr. Stevens, are you in love with Claire Clark?" Blake looked at Marie. "Answer the question like we're in a courtroom," she said.

"Yes, I am."

"Are you aware that Ms. Clark was engaged to Dr. Bradley Chambers prior to her relationship with you?"

"Yes."

"Are you also aware that Dr. Chambers would be the best man at the wedding of Dr. Remolina and Victoria Gibson? That Ms. Clark was the maid of honor?"

"Yes, I was aware of that."

Marie moved closer to Blake. "And is it still your testimony that going to that wedding on Marco Island wasn't -how did you put it-that important?"

Blake stood up and stepped behind his chair. He put his hands on its soft leather back. "I get your point Marie, I do. But isn't it a big leap to suggest I would rob a bank and shoot someone because I didn't trust my girlfriend to be alone with her ex?"

Marie nodded. "If that was all they had I would readily agree with you, Blake. But given what they have, the photos, the eye witnesses, and the Camaro, they won't need a strong motive to convict you. That's why we have to consider a plea."

"No."

Marie sat down again and motioned for Blake to do the same. "You were engaged to a woman in Tennessee?" She raised her eyebrows and waited for an answer. Blake nodded. "You didn't tell me that, why?"

"I didn't think it was relevant to the case, I guess." Blake stood up again and started pacing. He knew what was coming next. "I guess you know what happened then," he said.

"Yes, but I want you to tell me. Don't leave anything out."

Blake told her the story including how Nicci took off with the money in their joint account.

"That put a significant dent in your finances, didn't it?" Marie asked.

"Yes, I'm afraid so."

Marie nodded. "Again, Blake, the prosecution will almost certainly suggest that you robbed the bank because you were broke. They'll suggest you were desperate to make sure you had enough of money on hand, to get to the wedding and entertain Claire properly. That you weren't about to give her well-to-do former fiancé a chance to upstage you."

"I see what you mean," Blake said.

"Please think about a plea bargain. The best deals are the ones that get made early, Blake."

21

The wedding of Dr. Charles Remolina and Victoria Gibson was going to be a classy, black tie affair to be held at the Marriott Hotel on Marco Island. Claire didn't want to attend the wedding, not without Blake. But she couldn't refuse Victoria, her best friend since childhood. Blake encouraged her to go. "You'll always regret it if you don't go," he said. "Listen, if my lawyer is right, if I'm convicted, we will never see each other again, anyway. In time, you'll move on with your life. Victoria will always be your best friend."

Claire was touched by Blake's generosity. She could see his hopes were already dimming. He had lost weight, and although he continued his running, he stopped his weight training routine. He hadn't picked up a tennis racket since his arrest in spite of Parker's urging.

Not wanting to add to Blake's worries, Claire was determined to keep her trip as short as possible. Victoria wanted her to come to Florida the day after Christmas and stay a full week. She refused. She would arrive on Friday, the 29th and return on

New Year's Day in the afternoon. She was well aware that Brad planned to be in Florida for the full week.

Less than an hour after she arrived, she ran into Brad in the hotel lobby. He was sitting in one of the chairs that faced the elevators, dressed in madras shorts and a yellow short-sleeve button down shirt. She had the feeling that he had parked there just waiting for her. He smiled broadly when their eyes met. He stood and approached her. "Good to see you Claire. Forgive me for saying so, but you look like you could use a drink."

"Yes, I could." Brad steered her to the bar situated on the beachfront and asked her what she wanted to drink. To his credit, he didn't simply order what had been their usual drink, gin and tonic. She picked up the menu and looked it over. "I'll have a margarita, please." It was Blake's favorite drink. Anything to make her feel close to him.

Brad noticed the change of course but didn't comment. He ordered the same thing. "You've been having a hard time." It wasn't a question. Claire just nodded. "I'm sorry, truly I am. I want you to know that I won't press you while we're here. If you want to talk about it, I'm here. If not, no worries. It must be torture for you."

Claire was surprised. She was sure Brad would take every opportunity to point out that he had been right, that Claire made what he would call a cardinal error when she got involved with a stranger like Blake. She was dreading the moment when she would have to shut him down. "It has been, as you say, torture." She wondered if Victoria had coached Brad. It seemed she must have. Certainly, she had confided her fears about dealing with Brad's overbearing manner.

"As much as I love Victoria, I can't wait for her wedding to be over. I feel so alone and I can't imagine what Blake must be going through."

"Considering what he's facing, I don't imagine there is anyone in this world that can comfort him right now. You, on the other hand, face a daunting task the next few months." He took a sip of his margarita, glancing at Claire to gauge her reaction.

She looked out at the Gulf of Mexico. She turned to face him. "What do you think I should do?"

The question surprised Brad. He was careful. "Maybe you should use the few days, while you're here, to give yourself time to gain some perspective." He turned to look at the water. "If this isn't a beautiful and relaxing place, I don't know what is."

"Perspective, yes. A wonderful man is probably going to prison. I'll pick up the pieces and he will waste away."

Brad saw an opening, but still he was cautious. "Do you believe him? Very important question, I think."

Claire turned to face the water again. She put her drink on the bar and asked the waiter to hold it while she walked along the beach. "Mind if I join you?" Brad asked.

She nodded and started walking. Brad wanted to hold her hand but didn't dare. He just walked alongside her, not speaking. He wanted to see if she would answer his question. Claire stopped to pick up a tiny white shell. She looked it over as if it held all the answers. "You asked if I believe him. I do. I don't know why, but I do. The DNA evidence frightens me, but when I look into Blake's eyes, I see an innocent man."

"For your sake, I hope you're right, Claire." He took her hand now. "You are an intelligent and thoughtful woman. Yet, I hope at least a tiny part of you is preparing for the worst should it come to that."

Claire pulled her hand away, casually brushing a bit of sand from her other hand. She released a sad laugh. "That's the worst part of this, really. The moment I allow for the possibility of his guilt, I know all will be lost. I could never do that to him. Or to me, for that matter."

"I'm worried about you Claire. Please take my advice." He gestured toward the gulf. "As I said a moment ago, this is the perfect setting for some contemplation of your future."

The following afternoon, the prospective bride and groom got together with the wedding party and ran through a quick rehearsal. During the rehearsal, Brad teased Claire a little bit, suggesting she could have been the matron of honor had she married him. In the spirit of the moment, Claire bantered with him a little, saying, "Lucky for you you're not stuck with an old married woman."

Brad laughed. "There is nothing lucky about that for me, dearest." Claire walked away. She didn't see Victoria gently punch Brad's arm for his misstep.

That night, the men and women went their separate ways. Brad had a suite ready for a bachelor party which was little more than a quiet evening of hors d'oeuvres, good Scotch and a few gag gifts.

Victoria, on the other hand, wanted a bachelorette party that involved a party bus to take the women across Alligator Alley to Miami's South Beach. She wanted a naughty theme, but knowing that Claire was struggling so hard, she settled for some bar hopping and finally a karaoke bar where Claire surprised everyone. She had already had too much to drink, but now she acted out in a manner not seen since college. She flirted with a guy at the bar, then got up and sang Madonna's *Like a Virgin*, which had the entire bar cheering.

The group got back to Marco Island just before 3:00 a.m. Victoria spent her last night as a single woman taking care of Claire, who by that time was paying the price for too many margaritas. Surprisingly, Victoria wasn't drunk. She had just enough drinks to tell Claire that she and Brad were scheming to get them back together once Blake headed for prison. "He's changed, Claire. He's been taken to the woodshed and he realizes he has to do better if he's going to make you happy."

Claire wasn't listening to her friend. Her mind was elsewhere. "I haven't had that much to drink since prom night," Claire said, still feeling inebriated. "I think about him a lot, you know."

"Blake? Of course you do." Victoria said.

Claire was feeling so vulnerable. She had been ever since Blake was arrested. A heartbreak she had managed to keep at bay for years, had recently surfaced. "My son, I think about him all the time. I know nothing about him. Was he adopted by a good family?" Aside from her sister and her parents, Victoria was the only one who knew Claire was a mother. "Where does he live? Is he happy?" Claire was crying now, working up to a good crying jag.

"Your father made sure he was adopted by a very good family. You know that," Victoria said.

"Do my parents ever even wonder about him? Maybe they know where he is."

Victoria got the tissue box and put it next to Claire. "I can't have a maid of honor with puffy eyes, Claire. Really, now. Pull yourself together."

"He's going to knock on my door someday, Victoria. I know it. What kind of man will he be? Will he be happy? Happy to see me?"

"When he finds out he has the Clark family's blood, he'll be thrilled," Victoria said. Claire laughed, exactly what Victoria was hoping she would do.

By 5:30 a.m., Claire was exhausted, but feeling better. She took a shower, longing for a good cup of coffee to help her get back to normal. She came out of the bathroom wearing a light bathrobe, with a towel around her head and another cold, wet one around her neck. She looked at her friend who was buttering a bagel. "Brad has been very kind, Victoria. Is it him, or is it some kind of weird strategy to get me back?"

"Trust me, it's real. If Blake doesn't get through this mess, would you consider taking Brad back?"

"I can't think about something like that right now," Claire said. She removed the towel from her forehead but left the other one around her neck. "Blake has to make it through, he has to."

"I'm afraid he's toast, Claire. But you go ahead and be loyal to him now." Victoria poured coffee for Claire. "It's the right thing to do. I truly admire you for what you're doing. When this is over, Brad will be waiting for you."

"I hate you Victoria, you know that?"

"Yes, but I'm the bride. I'll be lovable again by noon."

22

The wedding went exceedingly well. Dr. Remolina kept expenses down by limiting the number of guests to a close circle of family and friends. But for those who made the trip, it was well worth it. The bride, wearing a simple, traditional white gown, was beautiful. Her parents were delighted that their daughter was now married, especially to a well-known and highly respected physician.

The couple exchanged vows at sunset on the hotel's top floor balcony, overlooking the Gulf of Mexico. The minister was an elderly man who made a nice living performing marriage ceremonies in southwest Florida. The couple chose to recite vows they had written for each other. Neither of them was especially eloquent, but they covered the basics, promising to stay together for life. It may have been Claire's imagination, but she was sure Victoria's voice dropped almost to a whisper when she said "poorer." Richer was much easier to hear.

The reception, held after the ceremony, was one that attendees would not soon forget. The party moved down to an elegantly decorated patio that led to the beach. Dr. Remolina insisted on the finest hors d'oeuvres, including Beluga caviar and foie gras, shrimp and oysters. The main course included sea bass, lobster tails, and prime beefsteaks, served with top shelf wine and liquor. For dessert, the hotel pastry chef prepared key lime pie and petit fours. A nine-piece band serenaded the couple and their guests throughout the reception. Champagne, one hundred and fifty dollars a bottle, was served throughout the event. It continued to flow when the revelers paused to welcome the New Year.

Naturally, the bride and groom had the traditional first dance. They also made the first cut of the three-tier wedding cake, prepared by the hotel's pastry chef. They lovingly fed each other a piece of cake.

Brad had been looking forward to the opportunity to dance with Claire. He would get to hold her in his arms again. He sensed she was more vulnerable than she knew. He counted on his touch, the right words and the hideous situation she was in, to open her eyes to what he was offering her. When the bandleader announced that the members of the wedding party could join the bride and groom on the dance floor, he looked for her. Claire had moved at least fifteen feet away, hoping that, somehow, she could avoid the moment. But Brad walked over to her and took her hand. Others were watching, some of them wondering what she would do. Brad took her hand and gently pulled her onto the dance floor.

While they danced, Brad whispered in her ear, "I can't tell you what I'm feeling at this moment, Claire. My insides are shaking, as if I were having an epileptic seizure."

Claire pulled her head away and looked at him, trying not to laugh, not sure whether he was serious. "Was that supposed to be romantic?"

Brad's face flushed. "I suppose I could have chosen a better analogy, but I do hope you get my point." Claire didn't respond. "You know, Claire, we could be living a fairytale life, like Charles and Victoria. I still dream of the possibilities for us. I just want you to know I'm prepared to wait for you."

The dance was ending. Claire stepped back and said, "I'm so sorry if you are suffering. I guess we're both miserable at the moment." Brad wisely kept his distance after that. He had planned on asking her to dance several times, but he could see now that it wouldn't have the desired effect. He consoled himself with the thought that he had delivered his message. Blake Stevens would be tried, convicted and sent to prison soon enough. He just had to be patient.

The next morning, just before noon, he insisted on giving Claire a ride to the airport in Ft. Myers, nearly an hour away. Claire refused at first, saying she had arranged a shuttle. But then Victoria called her. When she heard that Claire turned down Brad's offer for a ride, she said, "Throw him a bone, Claire. He's been really sweet." Claire relented.

On the ride to the airport, Brad took a moment to reiterate his feelings. "You know I love you, but I do wish you well," he said. Then he added, "If your friend Blake isn't successful in overcoming his troubles, I'll be there for you."

"I know," was all Claire could manage.

Then Brad surprised her. He had carefully thought out what he was about to say. "Of course, if Blake is proven to be innocent, I want you to know that I'll be very happy for you and him. Perhaps you'll marry him. If you do, I have only one request. I want to be your family doctor. In fact, I insist" He felt he had struck just the right tone.

Claire laughed. "Thank you for taking care of me this weekend. It has been a difficult time for me. Thank you for being a gentleman, not that I thought you wouldn't be." When they got to the airport, Brad parked in short term rather than dropping her off at the departure lane. He walked her to the terminal. "See you in Clarksville," he said, unable to produce a smile.

Claire looked at him. It made her sad to see him so unhappy. She reached over and kissed him lightly on the cheek. "Thanks again," she said.

Blake did his best not to think about Claire being in Florida with Brad for the wedding. He had a much bigger problem on his hands, but that didn't lessen his concern. He loved Claire, loved everything about her. His attorney had been right. That Claire would be spending at least three days in Brad's company was indeed a problem. A jury would easily recognize that. He saw clearly now that, under the circumstances, had he not been arrested, one way or the other, he would have come up with the money to attend the wedding.

Every time he reviewed the fateful day that threatened to ruin his life, he chafed at his extremely bad luck. A phone call from Claire, Parker, or even his sister, at the right time would have been so helpful. Had Mrs. Cotton not been hospitalized, she could have vouched for him, that he was home all day. If he had gone to Cherry Hill with Parker to play tennis, he would have been in the clear. This was more than bad luck. It felt more like a plot against him, but by whom?

Judy called him the day before Claire was scheduled to leave for Florida and asked him to come home to Tennessee. He explained the condition of his bail. He would need permission to leave the state. She urged him to ask. After he thought about it, he knew she was right. Sitting all alone in his apartment while Claire was on Marco Island, would be torture. He asked his attorney about it.

"I'll talk to the judge, but I'm not hopeful," she said. But, she was wrong. The judge approved the request. It would be the first time he would be in Colby Springs since he left for New York almost two years ago. He didn't bother to tell Claire he was going. He was sure it would only give her something else to worry about. Anyway, he would be home by the time she returned from the wedding.

Judy picked him up at the Knoxville Airport on the 30th. The plan was for Blake to spend the holiday in Colby Springs and fly home on New Year's Day. "Well, you don't look so bad," Judy said.

"I think I weigh what I did when I was a freshman in high school."

"I would offer to cook for you, fatten you up a little, but you would probably lose more weight with my cooking."

"Yeah, I'd weigh what I did in the 6th grade if I had to let you feed me." They laughed.

"You know, I asked you to come home for a couple of reasons," Judy said. "For one thing, it was time for you to do it. With Claire in your life, that bitch, Nicci, isn't even visible in your rearview mirror, so it was time."

"And?"

"Well, Claire is at the wedding in Florida with her ex, right? Given what's going on in your life right now, you needed a distraction, dear brother, badly." They drove on for a while, headed down Interstate 40 toward home. Blake was actually looking forward to seeing Colby Springs. He knew why. For just a few days he could feel safe, as if he was going far back in time to a place where things made sense. His sister was right about Nicci. Considering what he was going through now, that situation felt like a mere inconvenience.

"I thought maybe you wanted me to come home so I could help you go through Mom's papers."

"Ha! Believe it or not, I'm down to one last box. I saved it for you." She poked her brother gently in the ribs.

Blake and Judy spent the afternoon riding around town. It was a beautiful day, no clouds, 62 degrees and a mild breeze. They drove by their childhood home. Then Judy drove slowly past the house that Blake and Nicci purchased. He had put the house on the market just before he left for New York. Luckily, it was in his name only. Nicci had suggested that she be added to the deed after they were married. She said she was afraid her credit might not be good enough to get approved. It took almost a year to find a buyer. A local real estate agent, not known for his ethics, bought the house for the amount on the mortgage. That cost Blake his down payment, another ten thousand dollars.

They drove to the Colby Springs tiny downtown area. Judy parked her yellow Mustang in front of Marsha Lacy's Meat and Three, a southern version of a diner. Blake enjoyed the turnip greens, white beans and country ham that made the place so popular. That, and the sweet tea were like a tonic for what was ailing him. A lot of locals came in. A few of them were old friends or acquaintances. None of them seemed to be aware of Blake's current troubles. Instead, people had comments about Nicci.

"I knew that mean girl couldn't keep you away from us forever," a woman Blake went to high school with said.

A teacher he used to work with, Owen White, came in with his family. When he saw Blake, he did a double take. "Hey, is that you brother? I'm as short-sighted as the bulls on my daddy's farm, but, I'd know you anywhere, Blake Stevens."

The two men chatted a while. At one point, Owen looked around, as if he was about to tell Blake a secret. He was still standing in front of Blake's table. "Hey buddy, I'm glad you came home for a spell. That no good gal, Nicci? Heard she up and moved back to France."

Blake nodded. "I hope she stays there this time." He looked at Judy and said, "Thank you."

"For what?"

"Getting me here. I feel human again."

"Have you been working out?"

"Some."

Judy nodded. She understood.

The following morning, they went to a Waffle House a couple of towns over for breakfast. "What do you want to do today?" Judy asked.

"Nashville?"

"On New Year's Eve? Too much traffic. And it looks like rain. I hate to drive in the rain." They went back to Judy's townhouse. It was a nice place. There were still a couple of units for sale in the complex, with a starting price of $240,000.

"How did you manage to buy this place?" Blake asked. "Mom and Dad leave you all the money?"

"Ha, all what money, Blake? Most of it went to the Colby Springs Baptist Church, remember?" Mr. Stevens had been a deacon at the church and served on its executive committee.

"How could I forget? 'Y'all will have to make your own way, just the way your mother and I did,'" he said, imitating his father's voice.

"I bought this house cash. You remember the house I lived in when I was married. Sold for over half a million."

"So, you bought this with your half?"

Judy put her reading glasses on and started looking through her mail. "Uh-huh."

"It's nice. You might have to mortgage it to pay for my defense. I'd promise to pay you back, but my lawyer keeps telling me I'm going to lose."

Judy turned to face her brother. "We'll do whatever it takes. She walked over to a kitchen cabinet and took out a bottle of Jack Daniels. She offered him some. "Early for that, isn't it?" He asked.

"Not for me, my brother." She filled a rock glass three-quarters full, no ice. She took a healthy swallow and put the glass down. "I have an assignment for you. Pick up that white box sitting on the floor and put it on the dining room table."

"You told me you quit drinking," Blake said. He placed the carton on the padded table.

"I lied a little. I cut back, though."

"While you're going through these, I think I'll check emails," Blake said.

"Excuse me? Do you know how many boxes of this stuff I waded through? We're down to one box and you are going to help me go through it."

"Tell me, Judy, what did you find in all those other over-stuffed boxes?" Blake asked.

"Not much, I admit, but there were a few pictures, our baptism certificates, and mom and dad's marriage certificate, things like that."

"Well," Blake said as he lifted the top from the box, "what's left is probably just gas and electric bills she paid in 1977. Why don't we just put it in the dumpster and go to Riley's Tavern?"

"You want a beer? I have plenty in the fridge."

"Later."

"Let's get to work." She took another swallow of her Jack.

Blake looked at his older sister, a smile on his face. "You always were bossy." He sighed and added, "Okay, let's get this over with."

23

They quickly worked out a system. Judy explained that it was very important that they take the time to read every page of every document. "I found my birth certificate stapled to a receipt for the crib they bought for me. Mom's mind just wasn't organized in a way I could understand."

She suggested that Blake hand her any envelopes he found. She would go through those while Blake sorted out the various utility bills, auto repair receipts and insurance statements their mother saved. After 30 minutes of fruitless effort, Blake was ready to quit. He picked up the still half-filled box and said, "Mama never allowed us to waste time, remember? She always said, 'Every single second is precious. Don't waste time.'"

Judy didn't answer him. She was reading something, riveted. Blake put the box back on the table. He had never seen such a look on his sister's face. "What's that?" He asked.

She sat down on one of the dining room chairs. She looked at Blake and handed him the documents. There was a letter their mother had written ten years ago, a month after their daddy died. Blake looked at the document next, confused by what he saw. It was an adoption certificate indicating that Mr. Ernest Stevens and Mrs. Patricia Stevens were adopting baby boy B, born on February 14, 1985. The baby's name was Lee Davis, born to Stacy Davis, age 17.

"What does this mean?" Blake asked. "I mean who in the holy hell is Lee Davis?"

Judy stood up and went to her brother. "I think it's you. I think you were adopted."

Blake looked at the document again. He sat down. He felt as though he couldn't breathe. Suddenly, his whole life felt like a lie someone had told him over and over again to keep him in the dark. "Read the letter," Judy said.

Blake looked at Judy. "You better read it to me, stepsister."

She pulled back and slapped his face, harder than she intended. "Don't you ever say that to me again." They hugged until she pulled away from him and began to read.

My Dear Blake,

I am not at all certain where to start. If you're reading this, it means I neglected to, or couldn't bring myself to destroy this letter. Maybe we should have told you all about this, but I have no regrets. You turned out to be a fine son and an outstanding man, just as we hoped and prayed you would. I couldn't give birth again after your sister, Judith came along. But your daddy and I desperately wanted another child, a boy. You and your twin brother were born to a 17-year-old girl from

Johnson City. Her name was Stacy Davis. She was unmarried, scared and poor. She had you at the Johnson City Memorial Hospital, where daddy and I worked at the time. As a nurse, I knew about the birth, but your birth mother's kin never visited. I don't suppose many people in her life even knew she was expecting. I told your father about you. He came to the nursery and saw you. Daddy fell in love with you right away, just like I did, son. I'm sure you remember his stories, how he ran the hospital, how he was in good with government people. He took care of everything.

We couldn't afford to take both boys and to be completely honest, even though I was a nurse, I was deathly afraid of taking care of two infants. Anyway, since you and your brother were identical twins, we couldn't tell you apart, so we just took baby B and named you Blake. I don't know a thing about your twin other than his name was Jeb Davis. Apparently, you were each named after a Confederate General. Your name was Lee. A couple from Knoxville adopted Jeb. Sorry, that is all I know about him.

If you're reading this, I'm sure you are wondering why we never told you about being adopted. As much as I wanted another child, I was afraid to adopt. I have seen a few adopted children seek out their birth parents and wind up confused and hurt by the experience. I knew I would be crushed if I had to share you with another mother. Forgive me if I sound selfish, but that is just a weakness the Lord gave me to work on, I guess. After the adoption, we waited two years to move to Colby Springs, my hometown. We told everybody that I had gotten pregnant and had you. No one questioned it. People took us at our word. In any event, your daddy made sure to destroy the hospital records in Johnson City before we left town. I suppose somewhere in the Johnson City government office, there is a record if you really want to pursue it, son.

Know that I love you and only want you to be happy and secure. You are a Stevens in every way that matters.

Love,
Mama

P.S. Your sister Judith was too young to ask questions. She doesn't know anything about this.

Judy and Blake sat there stunned by the news. "It's funny, isn't it? I mean people used to argue about whether I favored mama or daddy," Blake said. "I couldn't look like either one of them, could I?"

Judy didn't answer. She was deep in thought. There was something about the revelation that she could feel but couldn't quite grasp. She got up and went into the kitchen. She picked up the bottle of Jack Daniels and filled another glass halfway. She picked up her glass and carried the two drinks into the dining room. Mechanically, as if under a spell, she placed coasters on the table and then put the glasses down.

"Have a drink with me, my brother," She said. They clinked their glasses together and drank. Suddenly, Judy let out a whoop. She slapped her brother's shoulder. "Blake, that explains it. It explains everything. It has to!"

"Explains what?" But he was catching up with his sister quickly. "Holy shit!"

"Right, that is why you were seen in the bank when you couldn't have been there. The DNA match, maybe even that damn Camaro, everything."

Blake stood up and swallowed his drink, feeling the whiskey burn as it went down. He sat down and stood up again. "But how? How could my twin brother know anything about me? Or where I live, what I do?"

"Beats me, but all we have to do is tell the cops and let them do the spadework. I think you may be in the clear, Blake."

They sat quietly for a while, savoring the first moment of relief in weeks. Blake picked up the letter and read it again. He was shocked. He wanted to be hurt. He felt like he should be angry. And, perhaps, he would be under other circumstances. Considering what he was facing, though, he couldn't help being elated. He stood up and walked over to his sister. He bent down and kissed his sister's cheek. "Happy New Year, Sis. And thanks."

Blake landed in Philadelphia just two hours after Claire arrived. It was raining and the roads were slick. The temperature was dropping. He was so excited, he couldn't remember where he parked his car. It took him twenty minutes of searching to finally come up with the right floor and row number. As he was crossing the Commodore Barry Bridge into New Jersey, he called Claire. She was very happy to hear his voice. He asked how the wedding went. She talked about the ceremony and the reception.

She mentioned the Gulf of Mexico and beautiful weather, trying not to rub it in. "It was so lovely. I miss it already," She said. "Please don't be angry with me, but I drank too much and sang at a karaoke bar during the bachelorette party."

He laughed. "I'm happy for you." He told her about his trip back home. "My sister was lonely. I guess she wanted company for the New Year holiday." He was bursting with good news, but he wanted to see Claire's face when he told her what he discovered in Colby Springs. They chatted a while about how cold it was in Philadelphia, with snow expected later that evening. Blake asked Claire if he could stop by her apartment on the way home, which surprised Claire. He had not been there even once since his arraignment. She was puzzled. "Is anything wrong?" she asked.

"No, I just want to see you. I won't stay long," he said.

"Okay, but don't get here too fast. I need to take a shower after that airplane ride." It was almost three o'clock.

Blake decided to stop by his apartment and take a shower too. He tossed his bag on the floor and shaved in the shower to save time. The hot water felt so good. For some reason, the water at his sister's place, never got hot enough to suit him. He put on a dress shirt, jeans and a blazer. He remembered he brought something back for Mrs. Cotton, a vase made by the Tennessee Pewter company.

He was about to knock on her door when she opened it. "What do you have there?" she asked.

"Just a little something for you from Tennessee."

"Doesn't look like a pardon. How was your trip?" She shooed him into her apartment. "I boiled water as soon as I heard you come in. Let's have some tea."

"I don't really have time Mrs. Cotton. I'm going to see Claire."

"She can wait. I want to talk to you." Mrs. Cotton said. She didn't really have anything in mind. She was lonely and she missed her tenant. She poured the hot water into the mugs and handed him the tea bags. While the tea steeped, she opened her gift. She was very pleased. "Very thoughtful, especially under the circumstances."

"Circumstances may have changed."

"Oh, do tell, young man."

Blake explained what he and Judy discovered in Colby Springs. He was clearly excited about the possibility that his nightmare might be over. Mrs. Cotton, who was enjoying a few lucid hours, was delighted by the news. She clapped her hands together. "I just knew you couldn't possibly do such a thing," she said. But she was worried nevertheless. "Have you informed your attorney yet?" she asked.

"No, you're the first one I told. He gulped his tea, hoping he might be able to keep his visit short. He wanted to check his watch, but he knew that would hurt Mrs. Cotton's feelings.

"There may be a few more hoops to jump through before you can put this completely behind you," she said.

"I guess, but my lawyer should be able to handle that for me."

"I certainly hope that's true. Tell me, Blake, do you know if your twin brother is alive?"

It was the first time Blake thought of that possibility. "He has to be, Mrs. Cotton. It's the only explanation for the bank photos and the DNA evidence."

"The Cherry Hill Police may not see it that way, Blake. It could be your brother, of course, but from their point of view, it could just easily be you, I'm afraid." She took a sip of tea and wiped her lips with her napkin. "Blake, you may well have to prove he's alive to satisfy the authorities."

"I didn't think of that," Blake said.

Mrs. Cotton motioned for Blake to help her stand. "Listen, don't let me keep you. I'm sure Claire is waiting for you. Thanks for the vase. It's lovely. And don't worry my boy, I'm sure things are looking up for you."

On the way to Claire's apartment, Blake realized that Mrs. Cotton had brought him back down to earth. He was still hopeful, of course, but now he realized that it might not be as simple as he imagined. He pulled into one of the visitor spaces in Claire's complex. She was indeed waiting for him. She opened the door before he could ring the bell. She had a bit of sunburn from being in the Florida sun. They kissed deeply and embraced for a long moment, neither wanting to let go.

"I have some news," he said. Claire just stood looking at him, searching his face for a clue of what he might say. He led her to the couch.

They kissed again. "Please don't keep me in suspense, Blake. What is it?"

"I have an identical twin. I think, somehow, a brother I never knew I had until this weekend, must have robbed that bank and killed that man."

Claire was shocked. "Blake, if this is a joke, it is not the least bit funny."

He pulled the adoption certificate and his mother's letter out of his jacket pocket. He handed them to Claire. "Here, read this."

Claire read everything carefully, her eyes getting bigger with each paragraph. Tears began to flow down her cheeks. She reached for Blake and hugged him. "I just knew it, Blake! This is wonderful news, honey." They kissed and then the inevitable happened. Away from each other too long, they simply couldn't stop. They never even bothered to go to the bedroom. They wrestled with each other's clothing and let their bodies collide. Their lovemaking was ferocious, ending quickly.

Later, after they showered, Claire became very quiet. She reached for a tissue and wiped away a few tears. Blake was about to reassure her. He was sure they were almost home free, but something in her countenance was different. "What is it, Claire?"

"Oh Blake, there's something I haven't told you. You'll hate me when I tell you."

Blake didn't respond immediately. He finished buttoning his shirt and fastened his belt. "But you are going to tell me, right?" Again, he wanted to reassure her, but after his experience with Nicci, he hesitated for a moment.

"I had a child when I was eighteen. I gave my son up for adoption."

Blake was stunned. Go slow now, he told himself. He wondered why Claire never told him about this, but he felt she must have had her reasons. Eventually, he would learn what they were. "Do you know re your son is?"

"No, but lately, I can't stop thinking about him. What if he turns out like your brother instead of like you?"

"Anything's possible, honey, anything. We know that. Do you know who adopted him?"

"No, my father's lawyer told me he was adopted by a business executive. He told me her husband is a college professor, just like my father."

Blake smiled. "Isn't it likely then that he'll grow up to be a good man?"

"I hope so." Claire stood and rested her head on Blake's shoulder.

"Was your twin brother adopted by a good family?" she asked.

"I don't know. Maybe you can find your son and see for yourself how he turned out."

Claire shook her head. "I don't think so. It doesn't really work that way. It was a closed adoption."

"Have I met your son's father?" Blake asked. "I mean, is he local?"

"One time, I think. Do you remember the day we stopped at that farm and bought pumpkins to take to class for the kids? I introduced you to the man that sold them, Joshua Tallica."

"Not really. Wait, was he the heavyset, tall guy with the Temple University ballcap?"

Claire nodded.

"Does he know about the baby?"

Claire started to cry again. "No. Nobody outside my family and Victoria know about my son. And now, you know." She wiped her eyes again. "Do you hate me?"

"I'm proud of you. That had to be an excruciating experience for you. But you went on with your life. You're a good woman, Claire. I love you."

They stood and hugged for a while, sensing that their bond was made stronger by Claire's revelation and Blake's reaction to it. When they sat down again, Blake said, "We need to talk more about your son, that is, if you want to."

"I don't know that there is anything to talk about. I hope you won't ask me a lot of questions. I try not to think about it, but that doesn't always work. Anyway, shouldn't we discuss what comes next for you?"

"We need to do that. For now, I don't want to tell anyone about this. Let's see what my lawyer thinks." After his brief conversation with Mrs. Cotton, he realized his attorney and probably law enforcement, would have to do a lot of work to unravel the mystery. Hopefully, they would resolve it quickly. A lot of things could go wrong. If they couldn't find Jeb, might they decide it wasn't worth the additional expense involved and go ahead with a trial?

Claire agreed. They would sit tight until Blake had a chance to consult with Marie. Knowing she wouldn't be working on New Year's Day, Blake decided to wait until the next morning before he called her. Thanks to the Christmas break, he didn't have to report to the school administration office until January 5th, which would give him some time to work with Marie. There were several leads he was sure she would want to pursue. Could they find Blake and Jeb's birth mother, Stacy Davis? Might she know who adopted Jeb and what his name was? It was also possible, if not likely, that the Hall of Records in Johnson City, Tennessee would have the information they were looking for.

Breaking another rule, Blake and Claire decided to go out to dinner until they remembered that none of the local restaurants were open that night. Then Blake remembered that there was a Cracker Barrel in Pennsville, about 45 minutes away. They took the ride and found that the restaurant was nearly empty. About twenty minutes later, Terrence and Elizabeth Clark walked in with another couple. Without thinking, Claire called out to her mother. At first the woman was excited to see her daughter, but as soon as she saw Blake, she blanched. The other couple noticed the exchange.

To make things easier on everyone, Claire got up and walked over to her parents. The other couple knew Claire, of course, but they were surprised by the cool reception she received from her parents. No one said a word about Blake. Happy New Year greetings were exchanged and Claire promised to call home later that evening.

She returned to the table. Blake asked, "If I'm exonerated, do you think it will change anything with your parents?"

"I hope so. This situation is making them look bad but put yourself in their place. Would you be happy if your daughter was seeing a bank robber who murdered someone?"

"I suppose you meant to say someone who was accused of these crimes, right?"

"Of course, sorry." She patted his hand. Blake asked for the check.

The next morning, Blake got into his car at 8:00 a.m. and started driving to Philadelphia. He was sure Marie would want to see the documents he had uncovered. It was slow going because, as expected, it had snowed during the night and the roads were slippery. He called his lawyer's office, and learned she was working in Cherry Hill that morning but had a very tight schedule. He assured the receptionist he had uncovered a major development and needed to speak with Marie as soon as possible.

As he was looking for her building number, Marie called him back. "This has to be quick, Blake. I'm swamped today."

"I have an identical twin brother. I just found out over the weekend. I was in Tennessee visiting my sister."

"And how do we know this?"

"I have documents. I have an adoption certificate and a letter from my mother, explaining everything."

Marie removed the Tootsie Roll Pop she was stirring her black coffee with. She sucked the coffee off of it. "Well, I'll have to see those documents, of course. Can you bring them in, or scan them and email them to me?"

Blake pulled up to her building. He was looking at the large faded, brass plate with the name of her law firm on it. "Just got here. Can I come up?"

Marie laughed. "Sure, but walk don't run. It's icy out there. Don't break your neck."

Excited about sharing his find, Blake assumed Marie would stop whatever she was doing to pour over the documents, but that didn't happen. Her assistant was waiting for him at the elevator. "I understand you have something for Ms. Scott?"

He handed the documents over to the young woman. "Can I see her?"

"She's headed into a conference. She'll call you after she's had time to review them."

"Will that be today? I mean should I hang around the area and wait for her?"

"I really can't say. In any case, I don't think she'll be able to meet with you today. If you would like to step over to my desk, I can see when she might have an opening."

"Listen, my entire life is on the line here. I need to see her," Blake said.

The woman, very pretty and dressed in a dark blue pants suit adorned with a pearl necklace, was glancing down at her calendar. Slowly, she lifted her head, clearly annoyed. "Oh, I see. You want me to put you at the head of the line, in front of Ms. Scott's other clients whose lives are also, as you say, on the line, is that it?"

Blake felt like a fool. "Sorry, Ma'am. I guess I'm just a wee bit excited."

The woman, already impressed with Blake's good looks, was now charmed by his manners. "I'll be sure she gets this."

Blake left the office and decided to stop somewhere for breakfast. He wasn't comfortable being in Cherry Hill, but since he was there, he decided to take a ride over to the tennis club and watch a few matches. Out of the corner of his eye, he spotted a red Mini Cooper parked in front of the coffee shop across the street from the tennis club. That has to be Parker's car, he thought. He pulled into the space next to the Mini Cooper. He walked in and surprised his friend, who was sitting in a booth with his fiancé, Penny.

"You back for another bank job?" Parker asked as soon as Blake approached their table.

"If I could do just one thing over again, you know what that would be?" Blake asked.

"No, tell me."

"I'd find a better friend to play tennis with."

"I wouldn't blame you," Penny said. The couple were both dressed for tennis.

Parker and Blake smiled. "Seriously, Blakester, how's it going? You're not dressed for tennis, so what brings you up here?"

"My lawyer has an office here and I had to drop off something." He looked around the room, but the coffee shop wasn't very busy. "I went back to Tennessee for New Year's and I discovered something very promising. That's all I can tell you now. My lawyer would be pissed if she knew I told you anything."

Parker held up his hand. "Cool! You think whatever it is could clear you?"

Blake nodded. "I'll tell you everything as soon as my lawyer says it's okay."

"It can wait. Listen, I'm about to give Penny a tennis lesson. I have an extra pair of shorts and sneaks. How about if you do the lesson? That way, we won't be fighting on the way home."

Blake thought about it for a moment. "Sure, let's do it. Why aren't you two spending the break at Penny's place? You could be at Disney World right now."

She smiled. "I'm moving to Clarksville. Now that we're engaged, your dopey friend asked me to move in with him."

"Just in time for winter? Must be a test girl. How do you like the snow? Think Parker is worth it?"

"You guys deserve each other," Penny said. Blake and Parker laughed. It felt good.

Blake gave Penny a good lesson on the basics, focusing on her forehand and serve. Penny did pretty well, too. It turned out she had been an all state softball player in high school. She was a good athlete.

It was almost 11:00 a.m. when they walked to their cars. Blake decided he might as well go home. As he was starting his car, his phone rang. It was Marie's assistant. "Are you still in the area, Mr. Stevens?"

"Yes, what's up?"

"Ms. Scott had a cancellation. She would like to see you. Can you come to the office now?"

Blake's ride to the office was interrupted when a Cherry Hill police officer pulled him over for speeding. He was doing 45 in a 25 mile per hour zone. The cop was a middle aged, short man, who looked like he barely passed the minimum height requirements. Blake noticed his name badge, GL Poland. The officer took Blake's information and looked it over in his cruiser. When he came back to Blake's car, he was obviously annoyed. He said, "Get out of the car." Blake grimaced as he felt the cold wind hit him. He was still a bit sweaty from tennis. Poland then proceeded to put Blake through a sobriety test, hoping he could find a reason to arrest him. Then he checked Blake's car for other infractions, demanding that he open the trunk for inspection. When he found nothing that might incriminate Blake, he handed him his speeding ticket and said, "Get out of here, punk." Obviously, the officer had discovered who Blake was.

Marie greeted him warmly and told him to have a seat at the small conference table in her office. "These documents could be enormously helpful to us. Tell me, do you have any proof that your brother is alive?"

"No, I was hoping the people in homicide would do that."

"I'm sure they will. Assuming they find him, they will also be asking him about his whereabouts on Friday, November

24th. No doubt, he'll have an alibi for that day. Placing him at the scene, may be difficult, but certainly not impossible."

"So, this isn't over?" Blake asked.

"Oh my, no. Did you think it was?"

"Yeah, I guess I did."

"We have a lot of work to do, but I'm confident the prosecution will delay the grand jury at least until they can find this guy. I assume you never met him?"

"Met him? No. I didn't even know he existed until this past weekend."

"Right, and your sister, she never heard of him either, correct?"

"You read the letter?"

"Of course. I'm just thinking out loud here. The prosecution will ask these and other questions. Please don't be offended, Blake. This is the first bit of good news we've had, but we can't afford to get ahead of ourselves."

24

Detective Terry Wronko was getting ready to meet with the assistant prosecutor who was handling the Blake Stevens case. In his 27 years working in the criminal justice system, he had never seen a case like this one. They had Stevens nailed. They doubted his case would ever go to trial. Since the death penalty in New Jersey was abolished in 2007, this dirtball would probably take a plea and hope for the slim possibility of parole which wasn't likely, certainly not for years.

Then, he heard that Stevens apparently had an identical twin brother. He laughed. The likelihood that a brother, one Blake Stevens didn't even know about, had committed the crime, struck him as farfetched. But he did the necessary due diligence and soon learned that there was such a person born in Johnson City, Tennessee on the same day as Blake. His name was Jeb Carr. He was raised in Knoxville by his adoptive parents, McClain and Lucinda Carr. Mr. Carr was a delivery driver for a furniture store and Mrs. Carr worked as an assistant manager for a restaurant in downtown Knoxville. Jeb

Carr had a record, having been in prison twice. He served 18 months for robbing three convenience stores and did a second stretch for forgery, something he was apparently good at. That fact gave Detective Wronko pause.

When Richard Murray, the assistant prosecutor, arrived, he didn't bother with small talk. The men had known each other for years. Both men played golf. They saw each other frequently on the golf course during the spring and summer months. Murray was the taller of the two men and the better golfer.

"Good to see you, Terry. Haven't seen you since Labor Day weekend."

"Don't remind me, Rich. I shot a 96 that day. Almost threw my clubs in the woods."

Murray smiled. "What do we have on this Stevens case?"

"A good bit of trouble is what we have." He handed Murray the file and gave him a quick rundown on the status. "I gotta admit, it makes the case against Stevens a little weaker."

Murray scanned the pages and scratched his chin. "A little weaker? Ventrella Scott will sing an aria praising the sanctity of reasonable doubt. Have you been able to find the son of a bitch?"

Wronko shook his head. "The last known address we have is in Granbury, Texas."

"Where the hell is that?"

"It's a suburb of the Dallas Fort Worth area, about 70 miles outside the city."

"I assume you've had it checked out?"

Wronko smiled. "Listen Rich, we've combed the Dallas - Fort Worth area. Apparently, Jeb Carr hasn't been seen in Granbury since the end of October, three months ago. We checked out his parents in Knoxville. They haven't seen him since he visited in early November. According to his stepmother, he was living in Dallas."

"You tried the..."

"Birth mother? Yeah. She's a real beauty," Wronko said. "She lives in Knoxville, too. Told Knoxville's homicide boys she doesn't remember having any children and certainly doesn't want to hear from them if she did."

"Drugs?"

"Drugs, too many Moon Pies, who knows? I wasn't there."

"Yeah, but did the Knoxville boys think she was telling the truth?"

"You mean do those hicks have a clue about how to interrogate a witness?"

"Easy, Terry. I did my undergrad at Vanderbilt. I learned right off not to confuse slow talking with slow thinking."

Wronko smiled. "I know that. Just pulling your chain. They pressed her pretty hard. The guy I talked to thought she really didn't remember having any kids."

"Now what?"

"Well, one question we're trying to answer is whether Carr is even still alive. At the same time, we're looking at traffic tapes that haven't been erased to see if we can place him in the Philadelphia area around the time of the robbery."

"That's a long shot, isn't it?" Murray asked.

"Yeah, but we're also checking for stolen Camaros going back as far as August."

"Keep me posted. I have to go over this with my boss. He won't be happy. You can be sure Ventrella Scott is going to demand we drop the charges pending further investigation."

The two men shook hands. "Call me crazy, but until the DNA evidence surfaced, I never really liked Stevens for this, Rich. He isn't the type. And the photographs almost look like the perp posed for them. That doesn't make sense."

"Well, keep working with the Knoxville crew and see if you can scare up any travel money so you can take a look for yourself," Murray said. "Knoxville has enough of its own cases to keep them busy."

Anticipating a motion to dismiss the charges based on the new information that Blake uncovered, Richard Murray went to work. As Marie predicted, Detective Wronko interviewed Blake again. Wronko wanted to know how Blake learned he had an identical twin. Over the phone, he questioned Blake's sister, Judy as well. Working with the FBI, they soon learned Jeb Carr's Social Security number and ran it to see if they could uncover anything useful. The last job he held was at a donut shop in Granbury. He quit that on October 31st, Halloween. He didn't own any credit cards. After a thorough investigation, the authorities couldn't find any evidence that Carr had died, but they couldn't confirm he was alive either. After his last job, he simply disappeared.

When Marie Ventrella Scott called Richard Murray, they agreed to go to the judge together and stipulate what was to happen. The state would drop the charges pending further investigation. However, Murray asked the judge to advise Blake that if he left the state while the investigation was ongoing, the prosecution might interpret that as evidence of guilt if Stevens failed to notify his attorney of his whereabouts.

Everyone readily agreed. The grand jury trial was removed from the docket and Blake's arrest warrant was dismissed. Blake was very happy to hear the news. He immediately applied for reinstatement as a teacher at Clarksville Regional High School. But the school board, which met in special session to discuss the matter, was not prepared to reinstate Blake unless he was completely cleared as a suspect in the case.

Claire wanted to throw a party for him to celebrate his change of status, but he wouldn't hear of it. His lawyer had done an excellent job of tamping down his euphoria. "Until I'm cleared and Jeb Carr is tried and convicted, I don't think we should celebrate anything," he said. He agreed to a quiet dinner with Parker and Penny in a nice restaurant in Philadelphia. Parker used the occasion to announce they had set a date for the wedding. They would be married in June.

As spring approached, Mrs. Cotton's COPD acted up again. She was now using supplemental oxygen 24 hours a day. Blake was working in her yard late one afternoon when he heard her calling through an open window. "Somebody, help me. I can't breathe." He ran into her apartment and immediately saw she was in distress. Whether it was a lack of oxygen, dementia advancing, or both, she didn't recognize Blake. She was struggling to catch her breath, while at the same time trying to swat Blake away. She didn't recognize him. She picked up an old, thick, yardstick, like the one she had playfully threatened her fourth graders with many years ago, to keep Blake at bay.

"You stay away from me. The police are on their way." Blake backed off and went into the hallway, making sure to stay close to the door so Mrs. Cotton couldn't slam it shut. He called 911. By the time they arrived, Mrs. Cotton was barely conscious and they rushed her to the hospital. Blake rode in the ambulance with her. He called Mrs. Cotton's sister to let her know what was happening. The woman was suffering from bronchitis and not able to help. Then he called Claire and gave her the news. She agreed to come to the hospital as soon as she finished grading some tests.

It was almost two hours before Dr. Chambers arrived. By then, Mrs. Cotton was resting comfortably, getting a steady flow of oxygen. Just five minutes before the doctor arrived, Jonna Martinelli walked into the room, wearing a nurse's aide uniform. She smiled when she saw Blake and Claire.

"I don't know if you heard, but I went to school to be a nurse's aide," she said. "Zeke sent me. He wants me to go to nursing school too."

"I'm so happy to hear that," Claire said. The two women looked at Blake.

"Is that what you want to do?" he asked.

Jonna filled Mrs. Cotton's empty water pitcher with fresh water. The old woman was sound asleep. "It beats being a waitress."

"If being a nurse is what you really want, I'm sure you'll do well," Blake said.

"Thanks Blake. I think I finally found my true calling."

"You'll be a wonderful nurse," Claire said.

"Thank you. I just hope I can get through anatomy and physiology," Jonna said. "Anyway, I think I'm going to like being a nurse. Seems like I've spent my whole life doing for others, so why not be a nurse?"

Dr. Chambers, wearing his white lab coat over a striped blue shirt and muted brown tie, was standing in the doorway now. He walked into the room, surveying the people there.

"Speaking of doing for others," Jonna said, jerking her thumb toward Brad. She turned to leave but remembered something. "Oh, Blake, I almost forgot. Zeke is looking for you. He has a job if you're interested." She turned and walked out. She didn't even glance at Brad as she left.

Brad was holding his electronic medical chart, studying Mrs. Cotton's records. He was silently cursing himself for not referring her to another doctor. His stomach still churned whenever he saw Claire together with Blake Stevens. When he heard the news that Blake might be in the clear after all, his spirits sank. He called Claire to say how happy he was that things might work out, but his heart wasn't in it and Claire noticed. The second time he called, Claire didn't bother to pick up.

"No need to wake the patient just yet, I'll stop by later and examine her." He wrote something in the chart and then, just as he was about to leave, he shook his head and said, "Won't be long now. That girl will be back serving enchiladas at the Mexican restaurant, where she belongs."

Blake stood and walked over to Brad. He leaned toward him and whispered, "I'm sure you'll do whatever you can to help Jonna this time. I wouldn't want your reputation to suffer."

Brad's face reddened. "I will take that under advisement, coming from a man with such a sterling reputation of his own."

Later that night, after Dr. Chambers had the chance to examine his patient thoroughly, he called Claire and told her the news wasn't good. Mrs. Cotton was deteriorating rapidly and the family should begin the process of finding a nursing home for her. "She can remain at home a while longer, Claire, but her oxygen saturation levels are declining even with supplemental oxygen, I'm afraid. It's a bit unusual to have a patient with COPD get so much worse so quickly. I've referred her case to a pulmonologist. She needs the care of a specialist now."

"Are you telling me you're not her doctor anymore?"

"I will certainly take care of anything that might be better handled by an internist, but Dr. Carson will take the lead in treating her lung disease."

"Fine, I'll get in touch with her sister," Claire said. "Is there anything else I should know?"

"Yes, I still love you. I beseech you not to do anything hasty. Perhaps I'm not right for you, although I can't accept that. I'm certain that Stevens is someone who will always find trouble." Brad knew he should shut up, but he simply could not. He was miserable. "You'll recall, he wasn't in town 24 hours when he was stabbed," he said.

"Brad, I've tried to be patient with you. I am well aware that Blake and I still have much to learn about each other, but if he and I should part company, I doubt it would change a thing as far as you and I are concerned."

"I don't believe that," Brad said. "How can you be with a man who would take up with Jonna Martinelli? You know everything you need to know about that poor girl's morals."

Claire held her breath for a moment. She was angry now. "How would you know anything about Jonna's morals, Brad?

Judging by the way she acts whenever she's around you, I really wonder about that. Care to respond?"

In that moment, Brad knew he had stepped into a trap of his own design. He wondered, of course, whether Jonna had told Blake about his brief affair with her, the pregnancy and the abortion. Given what Stevens said to him at the hospital that day, he was sure Jonna told him. Did Blake tell Claire? Probably, but what difference would it make now? Claire was obviously in love with Blake. Still, Brad believed that if Blake Stevens was no longer around, he could win Claire back. He had little doubt that given enough time, Stevens would do something that would open Claire's eyes once and for all. He merely had to bide his time. "Your insinuations don't warrant a response, Claire. May I assume you'd like to be kept up to date on Mrs. Cotton's condition?"

"Please do. Thank you, doctor."

25

Blake called Zeke to ask him about the job Jonna mentioned. "I got about four months of work as a subcontractor starting next week hanging drywall for a new subdivision. You'd do the mudding and taping too. Interested?" Zeke asked.

Blake was interested, but the school year had about six weeks remaining. "I'd have to ask for a leave of absence. Let me check on that and get back to you." Summer wasn't that far off and he would be without a paycheck from the school soon. He s definitely interested.

"I know you can hang drywall. Ever do mudding and taping?"

"I can hang it, but I'm not too keen on the mudding and taping stuff," Blake said.

"Hell, I don't blame you. Tell you what. You hang it and when it's ready you can paint it. Think your buddy, Parker, will want to work for us too?"

"I'll ask him," Blake said, "but he can't start until school is out." Zeke was fine with that. The men agreed that Blake would start work in one week, which was fine with him, since he was tired of sitting in a cubicle with nothing to do every day.

He was easily granted a leave of absence with the stipulation that he would apply for reinstatement as soon as the murder-robbery case was solved. He knew that cutting ties to the school would be difficult, but after he made the call and wrote the letter, he was still surprised by exactly how difficult it was to let go. He loved teaching and thoroughly enjoyed his students.

Initially, hanging drywall wore him out physically, but he soon rebuilt his stamina. He and Claire saw each other frequently, but he could sense she wasn't quite as eager to be with him as she had been before his arrest. He wondered if it was simply the sign of a relationship that was maturing; reaching the point where every night together no longer feels like New Year's Eve. But he knew better. One night, on the way back to her apartment after a movie, he decided to confront her.

"Claire, I have the feeling you don't feel the way you once did about us."

"What do you mean? I think we're doing fine."

"I agree. We're getting along and we see each other a lot, but we're not making love as often as we used to. We haven't been out with any of our friends since the dinner we had when my arrest was dropped." He pulled his Camaro into a space in front of Claire's place.

Claire looked away, staring now out the car window. "I don't think I want to talk about this right now."

"Okay, when would be a good time?" He tapped her shoulder to get her to turn back to him.

"Blake, my parents are putting so much pressure on me. They feel that even if you are completely exonerated, I should end our relationship."

"Honey, I understand that. I think they had their hearts set on you marrying someone else. I guess they never did like me much. I still hope in time, they'll see how much I love you and accept me the way they accepted Nathan."

"I know. I feel the same way, but they are really struggling with your, I don't know, background, I guess."

Blake caught on immediately, but he decided not to put it into words. He knew it wouldn't help and it might make matters worse. There was nothing he could do to fix a problem like that. Mr. and Mrs. Clark were obviously concerned about the gene pool, specifically his genes and how they might affect any children he and Claire might have. After all, it was likely that his twin brother was a bank robber and a murderer. The Clark family had to consider its bloodline.

"Maybe you're right. We should talk about this another time."

"Thank you." She leaned over and kissed him. "I wish we could spend the night together." Claire's policy of setting what she felt was the proper example for students rarely wavered.

Blake was in no mood to go down that path with her. "I'm tired and I have a lot of sheetrock to hang tomorrow."

"Will I see you tomorrow night?"

"I'll call you."

Claire was struggling with more than her parents' misgivings. For a long time, Claire had been successful in putting her own past into a quiet corner of her mind, minimizing her worries and misgivings about her teenaged pregnancy. Now, she was struggling with thoughts about her son and his well-being. She felt guilty too that she had never told Joshua he was the father of a baby boy, one who was now eleven years old. The day after her conversation with Blake, she drove over to see her parents. It was an unseasonably cool evening. Her mother was at a historical society meeting but her father was home. He quickly grasped that something was on his daughter's mind.

"Why don't we sit in the kitchen. I'll make us some tea," he said.

"Daddy, do you and mother ever think about my son, your grandchild?"

Mr. Clark put the kettle on the stove and turned up the heat. Claire's question surprised him. From time to time he worried that she would ask about her son, but not lately. "Not often, Claire. I went through a great deal of trouble to make certain he was placed in a wonderful home."

"Lately, it seems, he's all I think about."

"That's natural. You're going through a trying time. And trying times tend to rekindle other difficult moments in our lives."

"Did we do the right thing?" Claire got up, got two cups and saucers and put them on the kitchen table.

"That's not an easy question to answer. Time goes by and inevitably, we forget, or perhaps bury, the details of the circumstances at the time the decision was made. We probably replace some of that knowledge with wishful thinking," he said. "We project a better outcome if only we had chosen a different path. But, Claire, we cannot know that." He took some milk from the refrigerator and put it on the table. He fished two tea bags from a canister and placed one in each cup. "We did the right thing, I assure you."

Claire felt tears building. Anticipating her, Mr. Clark reached for a tissue and handed it to his daughter. "But how do we know he's all right, that he's thriving? What if he's suffering somehow?"

"My dear Claire, perhaps it will help you to know that on occasion I've kept in touch through our attorney. Your son is doing just fine; splendid actually. I promise you."

Claire was shocked. "You have, and you never told me this? How could you?"

"Your mother doesn't even know. What good would it do to keep you informed? It hasn't done me a bit of good, other than to know my grandson is well. But suppose he wasn't doing well? Is there anything you or I could do about it?"

"I suppose not. I'm glad to know his life is good." She placed a teaspoon next to each teacup. "I feel so guilty for not telling Joshua he was the father of my child. We deprived him of a basic right, Daddy."

Mr. Clark poured the boiling water into the cups. "This may surprise you, dear, but you needn't feel guilty. On that score, I live with enough guilt for both of us. I had to switch to the later church service so I could avoid seeing him every Sunday. He's a good and decent man."

"Is it too late to tell him now? Doesn't he have a right to know?"

Mr. Clark added some honey to his cup and a splash of milk. "Someday, you might want to do that, but I wonder if that would be helpful to him and his family right now. His wife knows nothing of this, of course, nor do his three little girls. And suppose he decided to go to court to open the adoption records? If he was successful, can you be certain that such an intrusion into your son's life would be beneficial to him, or his adoptive parents?"

"I didn't think of it that way," Claire said. She sipped her tea. "Thank you." She reached over and kissed her father's cheek, something she hadn't done in a long time.

"We all have secrets, dear. Some are best kept that way, at least until the time is right."

The summer passed slowly by. The weather turned hot and muggy and stayed that way. Zeke managed to get another subcontract, making it possible for Blake to work steadily into the fall hanging drywall and painting. He kept his mind occupied, thinking about his students, now and then, wondering how well they had performed on their final exams. When school started up again, he thought about which classes he might have had.

But the one thing that truly occupied his thoughts was the lack of progress the authorities were making on tracking down Jeb Carr. Too, he was disappointed that progress in resolving his case seemed at a standstill. He had been sure he would be back at school by the fall. It was clear to Blake now that he was stuck in some form of purgatory. His life could not move forward again until the murder and robbery at the Cherry Hill branch of the Palmyra Bank was solved. He spoke with his attorney one Friday afternoon. She apologized, but she said her trial calendar was so busy she didn't have time to check the status of the investigation. She told Blake she was confident Detective Wronko would be in touch if there was anything to report. "If it will make you feel better, maybe you should call him," she said.

Terry Wronko, who now had doubts about Blake's guilt, took his call. "Hey, Blake, I'm right in the middle of something. Don't have much time to spare."

"Yes sir, sorry to bother you. Just wondering if you might have learned anything new recently."

He could hear Wronko clicking the keys of his computer keyboard. "Well, we got an email from a Sergeant Creter of the Tennessee State Police. They're tracking down several stolen Camaros similar to yours. The only other thing I have is from the police chief in Granbury, Texas. He has a picture of your brother standing with a woman in front of some pecan trees. We know the guy in the photo is Carr. We don't know who the woman is."

"Do you know when the photo was taken?"

Detective Wronko took a closer look at the email. "Good point. The chief didn't mention it. I'll ask him."

Blake could feel his anger building. From his perspective, the thing he needed most was verification that Jeb Carr was alive, at least as of the day after Thanksgiving when the robbery occurred. Placing his biological brother at the scene was also important. The way he saw it, his chances of being cleared would improve a great deal if the authorities could confirm that Carr was alive. That it hadn't occurred to Detective Wronko to ask such a basic question was hard to understand. If the photo was taken sometime after Thanksgiving, he'd be halfway home. "You will get back to me when you find out, I hope. Seems kind of important," he said. His Southern upbringing, polite to a fault, was not always helpful.

Wronko intuited Blake's low-key frustration. He laughed. "You sound like my brother-in-law, always polite even if you're pissed off."

Blake didn't appreciate the condescension. "Detective? This may be funny to y'all, but my life has been turned upside down by this mess. Is anybody actually working my case?"

"Can't say it's at the top of our list, Blake, but yeah, we're on it."

That's when Blake realized he had to take action on his own. It was his only real hope of getting his life back. He packed a bag that afternoon and called Zeke to let him know he had to go out of town for a while. Then he called Claire and told her he had some family business to take care of in Tennessee. He asked her to look in on Mrs. Cotton, too. She asked a few questions, particularly how long he would be gone.

"I don't really know. I'll call you when I can."

Claire said, "I don't like the sound of that. Can you come over tonight and talk about it?"

"No, I've already left. I'll call you in a few days."

26

One week after he was born, Jeb Carr was destined for St. Leo's Orphanage in Bristol, TN. Karen Carr, a woman who had suffered a miscarriage the day before, happened to be talking to a nurse in the labor and delivery unit. The nurse mentioned baby boy A and how word around the hospital was that strings had been pulled to allow some bigshot to adopt Baby Boy B. "We all know who it is, but everything's been hush-hush if you get my drift," she said. "You didn't hear it from me, but Ernest Stevens, our hospital's administrator and his wife Patricia are adopting the other baby."

When Karen Carr heard that baby boy A was available, she beseeched her husband McClain to adopt him. "McClain, this is a gift from God. We were hoping for a boy, weren't we? It's what you been saying, right?"

Mr. Carr was reluctant. He was secretly relieved that Karen had a miscarriage. Another mouth to feed wasn't welcome news. "We already got the two girls, Karen."

Mrs. Carr started to cry, loudly. "Please, McClain I won't ever ask for anything again, I promise." Seeing his wife was inconsolable, he agreed to adopt. Karen Carr was delighted. She insisted they name the boy McClain, "just like his daddy," she said. A man with strong southern roots, McClain instead chose Jeb.

Mr. Carr drove a truck, mostly local runs. His passions were poker and Bourbon. Although he loved his family, he could be harsh at times. Jeb learned early he was a distant third, behind the two girls. When he was 7, his father, drunk and angry about being laid off, told him he was adopted. It wasn't said in a kindly, reassuring manner. Young as he was, Jeb understood. Mr. Carr had a way of letting him know the Carr family didn't need another mouth to feed. As he grew older, he learned in bits and pieces that he had a twin brother who, according to Mrs. Carr, lived in a small town near Knoxville. Jeb, a bright kid, was clearly more intelligent than his parents, which rankled his father. By the time Jeb was 13, they were regularly getting into arguments about how certain things should be done. Often enough, the end result was Jeb getting a beating. By the time he was a junior in high school, the father and son rarely talked.

When Blake made all state, second team as a senior, Mr. Carr took pleasure in pointing that out to his son. There was a photo along with the story. The resemblance was unmistakable. Mr. Carr pointed to the photo one morning at breakfast. "Looks like we got us the wrong one, Karen."

By then, Jeb had a man's body. He picked up the sports page and shoved it in his father's face, saying, "You got that backwards old man. I'm the one who got screwed." The men engaged in a fist fight, not their first, while Mrs. Carr screamed for them to stop. This time, though, Jeb got the better of his father. Afterward, McClain locked him out of the house and told him never to return. It was left to Mrs. Carr to fetch her son's clothing and personal effects and take them to him. Mr. Carr relented long enough to allow Jeb to return home to finish high school. College was, of course, out of the question. Having paid for one daughter's dental assistant training and the other's cosmetology schooling, there was nothing left for Jeb.

Eventually, Jeb's years of being hurt morphed into hatred, which he directed as much toward Blake for his good fortune as he did toward his parents. He joined the army and was booted in the middle of his advanced training program because of his involvement in drug dealing. He dabbled in crystal meth for a while, but after trying it himself a couple of times, he stopped. He was bright enough to see where that was leading. He took a few odd jobs, trying to find himself, but he had trouble staying focused long enough to learn the jobs. He drifted back into selling drugs and was making decent money. But, one night on a whim, he stuck up a convenience store. He got away with just over a hundred dollars and a trash bag full of cigarette cartons. He did it again a week later and again he got away with it. On his third try though, he was caught midway through the robbery. He was tried and convicted for all three robberies and served eighteen months. In prison, he learned the art of forgery from a cellmate. "You can make you some good money making up driver's licenses and signing other people's checks if you know how to do it right," his cellmate told him.

When he was released from prison, he made a good living producing forged documents for illegal aliens and other criminals, something his cellmate never mentioned. Occasionally, he would forge a signature on checks and make a few bucks, but he longed for a big score. When he was convicted for forgery, he served a full five-year term.

Tired of prison, and on the wrong side of 30, he decided it was time for a fresh start. He met a young woman who was turned on by his past yet saw through his rough exterior. He was bright. If she could get him to make the right moves, they could both get what they wanted out of life.

27

Blake was going to find his identical twin brother and bring him to justice. If that's what it took to clear his name, he was ready. He was now certain that his career as a teacher and more importantly, his life with Claire, depended on it. I have to get this matter resolved, he thought. Otherwise, sooner or later, Claire's family and, most likely, her friends, will convince her that he wasn't right for her.

He knew just where to start; Jeb Carr's last known whereabouts. Using some of the cash he'd earned working for Zeke, he decided to fly to Dallas to meet with the police chief in Granbury. As soon as the plane hit cruising altitude, he pulled out a notebook and wrote down the questions he wanted to ask the chief. When and where was the picture taken? Who took it and who was the woman in the photo? Assuming it was taken recently, wasn't it at least possible the woman knew where Jeb was?

He was still angry. Detective Wronko seemed like a decent sort, but he was casual about the case when to Blake's mind, it demanded a sense of urgency. What Blake didn't realize was that the homicide squad was swamped. The bank robbery aspect of the case was being handled by another division. Regardless, that didn't help Blake's situation.

His flight to Dallas arrived on time. He rented a Ford Fiesta, the least expensive car he could find, for the 70-mile ride from the airport. Granbury, Texas was a town of about 8,000 residents. Using GPS, he had no trouble finding the police station. The chief's name was Darren Harms.

Blake was so eager to see the chief that he didn't even bother to make an appointment. He imagined he would walk into a small office and ask for Chief Harms. When he arrived, he was surprised to find what looked like a sophisticated operation. The white, two-story building was much larger than he expected. It housed other government offices as well, including the city manager's office. He went through a security checkpoint and stopped at the reception desk. Since he didn't have an appointment, the woman behind the desk, who was eating a BLT sandwich, asked why he wanted to see the chief.

"My name is Blake Stevens. I'm doing some investigative work on a crime committed in New Jersey," he said, feeling lame.

"That's interesting. What brings you to Granbury, Texas?"

"The man who committed the crime may have lived here."

"You don't look like a private investigator. Are you a reporter?"

"No, I'm just the guy who was accused of the crime."

The woman immediately sat upright. This was a new one. Maybe she had seen it before, on television perhaps, but apparently this guy was the real thing. She did her best to look relaxed. "The nature of the crime?"

"A bank robbery and murder. When can I see the chief?"

The receptionist, an attractive Hispanic woman, was nervous now. She reminded herself that the man in front of her had cleared security, but these things weren't absolutely foolproof. She took a small bite of her sandwich and chewed slowly. She wiped her mouth and said, "Let me see if one of our officers is available." She picked up her phone and punched an extension. She spoke briefly to someone, nodded and hung up. "Take a seat over there," she said, pointing toward a bench seated next to the wall. "Sergeant Porzio will be here shortly."

Sergeant Porzio walked out from behind a partition and signaled for Blake to follow him. He was a short, portly man with a full head of curly, gray hair. He was in uniform, his sergeant stripes prominently displayed. "What can I do for ya?"

Blake explained what he was doing in Texas, describing the crime, his arrest and the emergence of new information. He mentioned the photo of Jeb and his interest in seeing it. Porzio kept nodding, but he didn't say a word until Blake finished. He tapped his computer keyboard as Blake told his story. Sergeant Porzio smiled. "That's a hell of a story, man. If I understand you right, you want to see the picture we got of this Jeb Carr fellow."

"That's right, sir, but I have some very important questions about it too."

Porzio smiled again. "Yeah, I'll bet you do. Shoot."

"You have the picture?"

"Your brother is currently wanted for check kiting and that's just for starters." Porzio turned his computer monitor around to show the photo to Blake. His first reaction was surprise. The guy in the picture staring back at him was a dead ringer. But then he looked at the woman in the photo. He was so shocked, he couldn't breathe. It was none other than Nicci. Her head was resting on Jeb's shoulder. Wearing a sheer blouse, with a mischievous smile on her face, she left little to the imagination. He leaned forward to take a closer look, not wanting to believe what he was seeing.

Porzio noticed his discomfort. "See something interesting, Mr. Stevens?"

"Where did you get this picture?" he asked.

"We found it on the kitchen counter of Carr's last known address. Why?"

"Here in Granbury?"

"That's right."

Blake was sweating now. The implications of the photo were overwhelming. He felt sick to his stomach. "Any idea of where, or when the picture was taken?" He gripped the chair to steady himself.

"Well, it's a copy of the print we found. We know it was taken with a digital camera, so it's not an old photo, exactly. You see the lower right-hand corner? There's a piece missing. Most likely they tore the date off. This dude is slick as an icy road, man." Porzio swatted at a fly he was eying. "Considering that we found it taped to the refrigerator door, it's almost as if it was left there so it would be found."

Blake nodded. Did Nicci, and Jeb want him to see them together? "I'm not from here, so I'm wondering if you can tell from the background where it was taken."

"As you can see, it's just some trees," Porzio said. "Could be anywhere. We're not even sure it's Texas. Not much to go on there."

Blake asked for a copy of the photo. Porzio printed one for him. Then he asked for Carr's last known address, but Porzio hesitated. "Officer Porzio, you probably know the charges against me were dropped, but until this matter is resolved, I'm in a real bind, sir."

Porzio tapped a few more keys. "Can't help you, pal." He looked around to make sure no one was watching. He moved the monitor a bit in Blake's direction. Then he winked at Blake. "I gotta take a leak. Be right back." Blake waited until Porzio was out of sight, then he leaned over and found what he needed. He saw an address in Granbury, a house leased under the name of McClain Carr, Jeb's stepfather. He quickly wrote it down. When Porzio returned, he asked Blake if he had any other questions. Blake said no.

28

Nicci Brevard was born in Romainville, a suburb of Paris, France, the only child of an American woman from Fort Worth, Texas and a French architect. She grew up in Romainville until the middle of her 17th year. That's when her parents finally divorced. Their marriage had been a contentious affair from the start. When her father announced he wanted to marry his latest lover, the marriage was over. Mrs. Brevard reclaimed her maiden name as part of the divorce.

Her mother returned to Fort Worth with her daughter. Nicci was glad her parents were finally ending the charade. But she was especially relieved to be leaving France. For the last six months she had been sexually abused, almost daily, by the bakery store owner where she worked after school. That she looked older than her years and acted seductively didn't justify what was happening to her. She was petrified when it happened the first time. After the second time it happened, she told the bakery owner, "I'm going to tell your wife."

He laughed. "Go ahead. "C'est la manière française."

When six months later Nicci finally found the courage to confront the man's wife, the woman laughed. She spoke some English. "You think you're the first one? She handed Nicci a hundred Euros and added, "You brought this on yourself. You're a petite pute, Nicci. Leave now, before he sees you." Confused, but afraid to burden her struggling parents, she never told a soul about the abuse. Nevertheless, she was hurt. As she grew into adulthood, she tended to look for ways to do the hurting rather than be hurt.

Nicci was, of course, bilingual. When she moved to Texas with her mother, she quickly learned that her French background, including the ability to speak French, made her exotic to the people she met. She played it for all it was worth, especially with boys. After high school, she attended college for one year, but soon grew bored with it. She decided to try working for a while. She worked as a receptionist in a doctor's office until the doctor's wife noticed she was flirting with her husband, who seemed receptive to the come on. The doctor's wife called her a slut and fired her in front of the doctor, who didn't dare to complain.

She decided to work for a bakery again. The owner was delighted when she learned that Nicci had some skills in French pastry. Her business improved dramatically as a result. "Nicci, you're a gem. You practically saved my bakery. I don't know what I would do without you."

Nicci was pleased by the praise for her work, but not satisfied. She soon began to find ways to steal cash from the register. She was careful at first, but when the owner didn't notice anything amiss, she got bolder. Naturally, she went too far. Again, she was fired.

That's when she went to work for one of the banks in Ft. Worth. It was also how she met Jeb Carr. He was a frequent visitor, always depositing checks and returning a few days later to draw out the cash once the checks cleared. Nicci realized what he was doing, of course, but she never reported it. She thought he was handsome and she was turned on by his boldness. The way he smiled seemed to her an acknowledgment that she knew what he was doing and liked it. She smiled in return. They understood each other perfectly. One day he asked her out to lunch. Within a week they were living together in his tiny apartment. Not long after that, her mother died suddenly, struck by a brain aneurysm. Nicci and Jeb quickly moved into her mother's rented house in Granbury. She transferred to the bank's Granbury branch. Together, appealing to each other's worst instincts and fueled by their anger at the world, they decided to even at least one score and make a bundle while they were at it.

29

Blake drove to the address he had picked up from Sergeant Porzio's computer. He pulled up to the front of the ranch style house and ran into his first bit of luck. Next door to Jeb's house he saw a tall, middle aged woman with a protruding belly watering her lawn. He got out of his car and walked over to her. "Howdy," she said.

"Hello, my name is Blake. I'm looking for my twin brother, Jeb. Do you know if he's home?"

"Goodness, if you ain't the spittin' image of your brother." The woman was staring at his face. "I'm Paige Jamison."

"Nice to meet you ma'am. Is he home?"

"Mr. Jeb hasn't been here for a while now. He moved away. Didn't he tell you?"

"He mentioned he might move, but I thought he meant he was moving after the first of the year. Where did he say he was going? Was it New Mexico, Santa Fe maybe? I think that was it." Blake was nervous, but he was enjoying playing the role of amateur sleuth.

"They mostly kept to themselves. The woman he was living with, I don't think they were actually married, not that I care about that. She said something. Let me think for a minute."

"Take your time," Blake said.

"Oh, come on Paige, what did she say?" The woman put her finger to her temple, trying to remember. "Oh, wait! I got it. She said something funny. For the better part of three days, I saw a bunch of cars and trucks coming and going in front of their house, ya know? People went in empty handed and came out with furniture."

"Interesting. What did she say?"

"I asked her if she was moving and she said she was. Where to? I asked her. She said, 'We're moving to another planet.'" The woman laughed again. "With all this hot weather here, I'd like to move to another planet, I'll tell you that."

He thanked the woman for the information and turned to go.

"Don't you think that was a hoot? Another planet."

"Hilarious," he said with his back to the woman, but he was grateful. He knew where to find Jeb and Nicci now. He had to get back to New Jersey first. He just made the three o'clock flight to Philadelphia.

When Blake got home, he dropped his bags on the hallway floor and knocked on Mrs. Cotton's door. His flight to Philadelphia arrived early, just after seven o'clock. He had spent the entire ride home feeling that she was having a problem that needed attention. He didn't know why he had such a feeling, but he couldn't shake it. Was it driven by guilt? He knocked a second time, a bit louder. The door swung open and there was Claire wearing a dress, looking like she was ready to go out to dinner. "You're home. I'm so glad. I stopped in to see Mrs. Cotton and she looked terrible. I felt it would be best if a doctor saw her. I called Brad and he agreed to come over."

She led Blake to Mrs. Cotton's bedroom. She was wearing her oxygen cannula and listening to Brad as he explained again that she must use her supplemental oxygen at all times now. Brad too was dressed like a man going out to dinner at a nice place. He rolled his eyes when he saw Blake, but Blake couldn't tell whether it was directed at him or the futility of getting Mrs. Cotton to comply with his orders.

Blake decided it was the latter. He asked Brad, "What can I do to keep Mrs. Cotton on the straight and narrow?"

"Stick around. That might be a good place to start," Mrs. Cotton said. "You're never around when I need you."

Blake looked at Claire. "She told me she tried to call you and you wouldn't take her call. Then she managed to get to the hall and tried calling to you just when I was coming through the front door. I told her you weren't home."

"Lucky you stopped by to see her," Brad said. Then he turned to Blake. "In the future, I hope you will let someone know if you're going to be gone for more than an hour or two. When Claire found her, Mrs. Cotton's oxygen saturation levels were dangerously low."

"Claire knew I was gone. That's why she came over here, Brad." He looked at Claire. "I was probably in the air when Mrs. Cotton started calling me."

Brad picked up his bag and walked to the door. "Claire, I'll call you later to check in on our patient." She walked to the door with Brad and spoke quietly with him. Blake didn't follow them, nor did he make any effort to hear what they said. He was tired and he had work to do. He couldn't spend energy worrying about what Brad and Claire might be up to. Until he found his brother, there was no point in worrying about the future. There was no future, not with Claire, unless he solved the crime he didn't commit.

When Claire returned to the bedroom, Blake said, "Are you sticking around for a while? I need to get a few things done upstairs. I'll come back as soon as I'm finished."

"Of course. I plan to stay here all night. Dr. Chambers wanted to put her in the hospital again, but Mrs. Cotton refused to go. Maybe we can take turns?"

"Sure, I'll be back in less than an hour." But it took Blake longer than he expected. First, he got a call from Parker, something about was going on at the school. Blake lost track of the time and they talked for almost 20 minutes. Then, as he was unpacking he picked up the picture of Nicci and Jeb. They looked so happy together. Was it his imagination that Nicci had never looked that happy when they were together? He folded the photo and slipped it into his pocket.

It was almost ten o'clock when he finally went down to Mrs. Cotton's apartment. Claire was sleeping on the couch. He touched her arm and she sat up. "I thought you weren't coming," she said.

"Sorry, I had more to do than I thought. Mind if I ask you something?"

"Not at all, but I think I know what you're going to say. Please sit down." She patted the cushion next to her.

Blake sat. He took a deep breath. "I suppose I could ask you, what do you think I'm about to say, but I don't want to play games. Were you and Brad going out to dinner tonight?"

"He asked me to dinner, but I turned him down."

"I see."

"Do you? It's been such a confusing time. I feel a bit foolish telling you this, but I thought you and I might be engaged by last Christmas, until this nightmare occurred. I do love you, Blake. We just need to be patient with each other until this thing is resolved."

"Are you sure you wouldn't be better off with him? I mean, he can offer you things I'll never be able to give you."

"That may be true, but there are many things you offer that Brad isn't capable of giving a woman."

They kissed and held each other for a moment, both aware that it was neither the time or place to do anything more than that. "When I was in Texas, I learned some things. I think there is more than one mystery about to be solved here." He took the photo out of his pocket and showed it to Claire. "Allow me to introduce you to Nicci and my twin brother, Jeb."

Claire stared at the photo in disbelief. If she didn't know better, she could be looking at a picture of Blake and Nicci. The woman was better looking than Claire imagined. "What did you find out in Texas?" She felt her eyes tearing up and she didn't know why.

"I met a woman, their neighbor. She repeated something Nicci once said to me. The neighbor saw they were moving. She asked where they were going and Nicci said they were moving to another planet."

"I don't understand."

"You remember I told you Nicci was born in France? When I asked her what it was like living near Paris, she said it was like living on another planet."

"So, you think they're in France?"

"Whenever somebody asked her that question, that was her answer, so yeah, I think she's in France, or headed there."

"You have to tell Detective Wronko tomorrow morning."

"Of course, but if I couldn't get him to go to Texas, what are the chances he'll go to Paris?"

"He doesn't have to go to Paris. The FBI or the Justice Department can have them extradited," Claire said.

"I thought about that. But they have to find them first. I don't think those two are going to suddenly start living normal, everyday lives."

"You're thinking of going to France, then?"

"I have to. I can't afford to just sit tight. As long as I'm a suspect, I'll never get my job back and your parents will never accept me," Blake said. "I'm worried about something else too. The family of the man who was shot and killed will demand justice. What if the prosecutor decides to go ahead with the case he has against me?"

"He would lose. You didn't do it."

"They have eyewitnesses, the photos, the black Camaro, and they will argue I did it for the money to keep up with you and your friends. You can be sure the Remolina wedding and even your previous relationship with Brad will be trotted out as evidence of motive. The Clark name will suffer and neither one of us wants that."

"Please don't worry about me or my family name. If it comes to that, I will testify on your behalf that there was never any financial pressure on you, not by me. I'll tell them I love you. That I know you could never do such a thing."

"Claire, you are sweeter than Tennessee honey, but even if I'm found not guilty, the attorney's fees will bankrupt me, or maybe I should say my sister, Judy." He paused a moment. "And, being found not guilty isn't the same as actually being innocent."

"I wish you would be patient a bit longer. Why not give the authorities a chance to find your brother?"

"And leave our relationship on hold? Relationships either move forward or they die, Claire. Don't you know that?"

"Our love for each other will never die, Blake." She dabbed the tears in her eyes before they could start flowing. "When are you leaving?"

"I want to talk to Detective Wronko and my lawyer tomorrow. I plan to leave the day after that."

"What makes you think you can find them?"

"Call me crazy, but I know Nicci, probably better now than when we were together. I'll bet she's in her home town."

"Which is?" Claire asked.

"Romainville."

Early the next morning, Blake told Zeke he wouldn't be at work for about a week maybe ten days. Zeke was angry. "I got a shitload of sheetrock waiting for you. You're putting me way behind schedule. What the hell, Blake."

Blake apologized and explained he was working on his case, that he was close to finding the guy who did the robbery. He would have to leave town.

"You do what you gotta do, but I'm gonna do what I gotta do too. Can't promise there's a job when you get back."

Next, he called Detective Wronko, who was not happy to hear from him.

"Listen, Blake, we just spoke two days ago. There's nothing new here. Unless you have something significant to tell me, you have to stop calling, understood?"

"I believe I know where Jeb Carr is and who he's traveling with. That's worth a minute of your time, I hope."

Wronko was dying for a cigarette or maybe a double shot of Scotch, and it was only half-past eight in the morning. He picked up a pencil and said, "Shoot."

"I think Carr is in Romainville, France with my former fiancé, Nicci Brevard."

"Where the hell is that?"

"It's a suburb of Paris, less than ten miles from the city."

"Uh-huh, what makes you think Carr is there?" Wronko asked.

"That's where Nicci is from."

The detective gave in to the urge. He lit a cigarette. "What makes you think your brother hooked up with your ex?"

"She's the woman in the picture you mentioned."

"No kidding? Wow." He paused a moment, thinking. "Now, as I recall, I didn't show you the photo. How'd you happen to see it?"

"I went to Granbury, Texas. Saw it at their police station. It's Nicci."

"I assume you got permission to leave the state?"

"No sir, not exactly, but I'm back."

"Jesus, Mary and Joseph, do you have anything else that might indicate they're in what's it called," he checked his notes, "Romainville?"

Blake told him about his conversation with Carr's neighbor and how Nicci told her they were moving to another planet, the same thing she always said when asked about living in France.

"I see. Well, Blake, has it occurred to you that maybe this Nicci gal said that specifically to throw people off the track? I mean why wouldn't she say the same thing if they were moving to Mexico or Brazil?"

"No, I didn't think of that," Blake admitted. "Would it hurt for the FBI to check it out?"

"I'll put a request in, but it could take a while for them to actually chase it down. They'll make some phone calls, but so far Carr seems to be pretty sharp. I can tell you he's off the grid. No credit cards, no bank accounts, no cell phone and no email. We checked. And if this Brevard woman is with him, I doubt we'll find anything on her either. If Carr and Ms. Brevard are in France, it's not likely they're living under their given names."

"What would it take to get the FBI, or somebody in government, to go over there?"

Wronko took a deep drag and blew the smoke out, hard. "Look, if your information is right and the French authorities identify them, we'll have their asses extradited back to the US.

If they don't find them in Lettuceville, your lead will be considered a dead end. Like I said earlier, they could be in Brazil."

"Lettuceville?"

Wronko laughed. "Yeah, Romaine, my favorite lettuce. One more thing, Blake. I appreciate your help, but you have to take my word for it, we're doing everything we can."

"Detective, please understand. You wouldn't be looking for them in France if it wasn't for me. Thanks to my legwork, we now know who the woman is and where they're heading," Blake said. "And another thing, detective, I know what Nicci is capable of."

"Well, you did a good job, but it doesn't change the fact that I have more work than I can handle."

"I understand, and I won't call or visit you if you'll agree to keep me posted on a weekly basis."

"These things don't move that fast. I'll call you when there's news. Promise."

30

Blake knew he was on his own. He was sure Detective Wronko had no intention of calling him. By seven o'clock that night, he was packed. He had his passport and 300 Euros he picked up at a currency exchange in Cherry Hill. His flight to Paris would take off early the next morning. He decided not to call his attorney. He knew what she would say. It didn't matter. He had to look for Jeb and Nicci. Certainly, he would recognize them. One way or another, he had to be sure they were captured. He wanted his life back. He had enough of purgatory.

But he was wrong about Detective Wronko. Just before 8:00 pm, he got a call from the detective. He was sitting in Mrs. Cotton's kitchen waiting for coffee to brew. "I told you I would keep you posted," he said. "Looks like Carr and Ms. Brevard haven't left the country yet, after all. We think they're leaving for Paris tomorrow morning from Baltimore."

"Wow, how do you know that?"

"You remember Jeb Carr's adoptive parents? Well, Jeb's old man got in touch with the Tennessee State Police. He got a Visa bill for stuff he didn't purchase," Wronko said. "Looks like the last time he visited his dear old ma and pa, Carr helped himself to one of their credit cards. The old man was pissed. He gave the trooper an earful about what a dog his son was. I guess he never liked him very much."

Blake stood up and started pacing. "So, they're headed to Romainville?"

Wronko took a drag on his cigarette. "Not so fast. They bought a ticket to Dubai that leaves two days after they get to France," he said, exhaling smoke from his lungs. "They're leaving from Baltimore, or so they think."

"Wait, why would they be going to Dubai? That doesn't make sense."

"Care to take a guess?" Wronko was pleased with himself. He was finally close to solving this case. He would have Carr and Brevard arrested in Baltimore. If he could place Carr in New Jersey when the crime took place, it was very likely that Blake would finally be off the hook. He could feel it in his bones.

"Does it have something to do with extradition?"

"Bingo! The United Arab Emirates won't extradite. The US doesn't have an extradition treaty with them. That doesn't mean we won't get them eventually, but it's not guaranteed and it would take a lot longer."

Wronko explained that the FBI and the Maryland State Police would be at the airport to meet them just before they boarded the plane. "We'll have them in custody in just a matter of hours."

While Blake was in his apartment talking to Detective Wronko, Claire was sitting in Mrs. Cotton's bedroom watching over Mrs. Cotton. As a favor to Dr. Chambers, a pulmonologist, had made a house call to see her that afternoon. "I've never seen a patient with COPD go downhill that fast," the doctor said. "I recommend hospice care. She won't last long."

Blake walked downstairs and gave Claire the news. She was thrilled. "Soon, we'll have all this behind us," she said.

"How's Bella doing? She looks like she's laboring."

"The doctor says it won't be long now. He recommends hospice. It's to be expected, I suppose. I wish there was something we could do for her."

Blake nodded. "You're here right now. I'm sure that's enough. Are you hungry? Why don't I run out and get us something?"

"Okay."

As Blake walked through the kitchen into the foyer, he noticed a stack of mail that had yet to be opened. He picked it up and brought it back to the bedroom. "If you're looking for something to do, maybe you can go through this stuff. You're the executor of her estate now." It was true. On the day after her last hospital discharge, Mrs. Cotton called her lawyer and had him make some changes to her will. She instructed the attorney not to reveal the nature of the changes, with one exception. She named Claire Clark her executor. Claire had objected at first, but quickly realized that there were no good alternatives available. Mrs. Cotton's sister was in no condition to act in such a capacity.

"Probably a good idea," Claire said. She reached over to pick up a waste basket and set to work. Blake came back to the apartment in a good mood. He had picked up a bottle of Merlot to go with a veggie pizza, Claire's favorite. In spite of Mrs. Cotton's condition, he couldn't help celebrating a little. His nightmare would soon be over.

He called her from the kitchen. "Are you as hungry as I am? Got your favorite pizza, honey." He was feeling more confident now than he had in a long time. He searched for a corkscrew, doubting he would find one.

Claire walked into the kitchen, a sheaf of papers in her hand. "I don't understand this."

"What's that?"

"Mrs. Cotton's Visa bill."

"What did she buy?"

"Airline tickets, a lot of them. Two are for Paris, leaving tonight at eleven o'clock from Philadelphia. There are two more, flights from Paris to Dubai. Isn't that where Detective Wronko told you they were going tomorrow night from Baltimore?"

Blake didn't answer. He picked up his phone and called Detective Wronko, but Wronko was on the phone. Instead, Detective Vince Mastria answered. He assured Blake he was up to date on the case. When Blake told him about the flights from Philadelphia, he let out a low whistle. "I'll get back to you," he said.

Blake grabbed his keys and headed for the door. "Where are you going?" Claire asked.

"The airport. They're not getting away with this."

"I'm coming with you."

In spite of his agitated state, Blake laughed. "This isn't a movie, honey. Anyway, we can't leave Mrs. Cotton alone."

Claire put her hand to her mouth, briefly ashamed that she forgot about Mrs. Cotton. "Of course, be careful," she said. She hesitated a moment. "Wouldn't it be wiser to wait until you hear from the detective?"

"If he calls while I'm on the way there, fine, but I can't take that chance. I'll do whatever I have to. They're not boarding that plane."

As soon as Terry Wronko got off the phone, Detective Mastria told him about the tickets purchased on a credit card held by Blake Stevens' landlord. The men agreed it didn't make sense. How could Jeb Carr get access to the old woman's credit card? There was no evidence that Carr was even aware of the woman's existence.

"I can understand if Stevens used the landlord's credit card," Mastria said, "but it's a real stretch to figure the twin brother for it."

"So, what are you saying, Vinny?"

"Suppose it's the other way around, that Stevens is setting up Carr? The other day you mentioned that Stevens identified the girl in the photo as his ex-girlfriend. Anybody bother to substantiate that?"

"Not yet."

"What if nobody in that hick town where Stevens is from can ID the girl?"

"We can sort that out later. Right now, we need to get somebody to Philadelphia International. You can bet your ass that Stevens is already on his way there."

"FBI?" Mastria asked.

"Yeah, Homeland Security, too and call our homicide contact on the Philly force. I don't want to get her nose out of joint."

When Blake got to the airport's International terminal, it was already 9:30. By now, Blake assumed that Carr and Brevard were at the gate. How was he going to get through security? He was well aware that attempting to breach security protocol could get him into enormous trouble, regardless of his reason for doing it. Still, he had to try something. He got as close to the security checkpoint as he could and caught the attention of one of the officers, who was busy checking boarding passes. As he was explaining the situation, he saw a woman he thought was Nicci. Her hair was now cut very short and she was wearing large sunglasses, an odd choice at that hour. She was approaching the baggage x-ray line. He called out, "Nicci Brevard!"

She flinched but kept walking. Then he saw his mirror image walking up behind her. He pointed to Jeb and said to the TSA officer. "That man, he's my twin brother and he's wanted for murder."

The officer looked at Jeb, then at Blake and shrugged. "How do I know you're not wanted for murder instead of him?"

Blake, operating purely on instinct now, shoved the guard and took off after the couple. He couldn't afford to wait another minute. Out of the corner of his eye, Jeb saw him coming. He grabbed a computer bag off the conveyor belt and swung it at Blake, hitting him a glancing blow on the jaw. Blake was not deterred. He grabbed for Jeb, but his brother managed to pull away. By now, a couple of armed TSA officers joined the fray. One of them reached for his weapon.

That's when Jeb, just as big and strong as his brother, managed to wrestle it away from the officer. He turned and started to run. Blake ran after him with a TSA officer right behind him and Nicci not far behind, screaming obscenities at Blake. Just as Blake got close enough to tackle him, Jeb turned and fired the gun, wildly, barely missing Blake, but hitting Nicci's left hip. There was no time to think. As if he was the last player who could tackle a receiver before he scored a touchdown, Blake tackled Jeb, knocking him down. The gun dropped out of his hand, traveling only about two feet on the carpeted floor. Jeb squirmed away from Blake's grasp, trying to pick up the gun. That's when another officer fired, hitting Jeb's temple at point blank range.

Nicci was screaming in pain and trying to stand, but a female TSA officer held her down.

Passengers waiting for their flights were screaming and running for cover. Pandemonium broke out and more security forces arrived on the scene. It took a while, but the authorities managed to secure the area and restore order. It was at that point that Detective Wronko and two agents from the FBI arrived on the scene. Jeb Carr was dead and Nicci Brevard was seriously wounded. Blake was taken into custody and hustled off to a room in a private area of the airport.

The FBI agents were waiting for Blake in an interrogation room. Terry Wronko joined them. "Nice going, Stevens. You interfered with an ongoing investigation. Instead of making two arrests, we have a body cooling in the morgue and your ex-fiancé is headed for surgery."

Blake looked at the detective, deliberately waiting before he responded. "I've been arrested. I spent a weekend in jail for something I didn't do. Y'all haven't been as helpful as a man in my situation would hope for. I'll say it one more time. I didn't rob that bank and I didn't shoot anybody." He paused for a moment to gather his thoughts. His heart was still racing. "Now you may have been ready to capture them, but if you were in my shoes, considering it's my life on the line, would you just sit by with your fingers crossed?"

"You think you helped yourself? You believe you solved the case? Jesus Mary and Joseph, you are naïve." Wronko reached for his cigarettes but knew better than to light up in a non-smoking facility. "We could have taken both Carr and Brevard alive, had a chance to interrogate them. Sooner or later we would have nailed them for the Cherry Hill job. Now, we may never know. If Ms. Brevard doesn't survive and it doesn't look promising, that's not good for you. Assuming the Feds let you slide on this airport matter, you may still be prosecuted on the bank thing if we can't place the late Mr. Carr at the scene on the day of the crime."

"That's ridiculous," Blake said, but he was worried now.

"You remember the guy who was killed in the robbery, right? Hot shot with a lot of powerful people behind him, family and business leaders, both. I told you this before. They want justice. It just might be that you will do."

One of the FBI agents, a woman named Eve Walker, cleared her throat. "Does Mr. Stevens' connection to the murder-robbery include any DNA evidence?"

"Yes, it does," Wronko said. "We found gum outside the bank with his DNA on it.

Agent Walker smiled. "Well, I assume you haven't had a chance to compare the two DNA samples. These men are, or were, identical twins, right?"

"That's right," Wronko said. "We didn't get a sample of Carr's DNA because during the investigation, we didn't know he existed," Wronko said.

Agent Walker played with the band aid that covered her pinky. She had lost a nail during the fracas. She was young, only recently having become an FBI agent. "Well let's make sure we get a DNA sample from Carr. That might clear things up."

"I don't understand," Blake said. "We're identical twins. Aren't we a perfect match in just about every way?"

"DNA testing has advanced to the point where it's possible to distinguish one identical twin from another." She looked over at Detective Wronko and the other FBI agent in the room. "It's sophisticated and most crime labs don't routinely look at things like that," Walker said.

"That's right," the other agent said.

"Were you aware of that, Detective?" Blake asked.

"Not really, but it doesn't matter. Like I said, we didn't know you were a twin at the time we were working the case."

"Neither did I," Blake said.

Ten days later, the State of New Jersey officially dropped all charges against Blake Stevens. The gum that Jeb Carr had discarded on the sidewalk in front of the bank, confirmed that he was indeed the man who robbed the Palmyra Bank and shot a customer in the process.

Nicci Brevard's condition improved. She would survive. At first, she refused to talk to the authorities, other than insisting that she and Jeb had never been to New Jersey, that the authorities had it right from the beginning. Blake Stevens was their man. Two days later, Detective Wronko, accompanied by Agent Walker and a representative of the Philadelphia Police Force, visited a more alert Nicci again. Blake begged Detective Wronko to let him come to the meeting, but Wronko, knowing that it might hinder their ability to tie up loose ends, refused. "I'll ask all the questions I know you have, Blake."

They stood around her bed and broke the news. Nicci Brevard had her hair combed and a touch of lipstick on her face. She was still in pain, and she was annoyed that these people wanted to speak with her again, but she was determined to stick to her story.

Agent Walker spoke in a friendly, soft tone "Ms. Brevard, you are facing very serious charges. If you cooperate with us, we can help you."

"What exactly am I being charged with?"

Detective Wronko started to speak, but Agent Walker held up her hand. "Ms. Brevard, you will be charged with bank robbery and murder. We believe we will eventually be able to tie you to a car theft and then there's the fact that you absconded with furniture, jewelry and funds at least half of which rightly belonged to Mr. Blake Stevens."

"I don't know anything about a bank robbery or stolen car," Nicci said.

Exasperated, Wronko spoke. "DNA evidence has cleared Mr. Stevens. Your friend, Carr committed those crimes in Cherry Hill, New Jersey. We think you were the driver."

"Thinking and proving are very different things." But Nicci was shaken by the news. Her demeanor changed as the news sunk in. "What kind of deal are you offering?"

"We'll talk to the DA. For starters, I think I can persuade Mr. Stevens not to press charges on the theft of his household possessions. The rest depends on how cooperative you are."

"Those things were mine too," Nicci said. She tugged on her lower lip. "In any case, I want something in writing first."

Agent Walker shook her head. "Ms. Brevard, you are exhausting my patience. I will have your case moved to a Federal jurisdiction if you don't start cooperating immediately. We have unlimited resources. We will not stop until we have you securely tucked into one of our maximum-security prisons. Tell us what you know and we will take it from there."

Nicci pulled her bedsheet up higher, close to her chin. "Can I have something for pain first?" she asked.

"Later. This won't take long," Wronko said.

"Jeb and I met in Dallas. He knew about his brother, but Blake didn't know he was a twin. It was Jeb's idea for me to move to Colby Springs, that stupid hick town, in Tennessee."

"So, you worked Blake Stevens from the beginning to wipe him out?" Wronko asked. "Why?"

"It was Jeb. I was in love with him. He was just so angry that Blake got such a good deal in life and he got screwed. Blake had it all; he grew up in a really nice house and he was raised by a nice family. He got to go to college, too. Jeb's parents treated him like dirt. It was because of them that he wound up in prison. They never gave him a thing. His old man beat him all the time. I just figured that if Jeb felt like he could get even somehow, he would be different."

"Was he?" Agent Walker asked.

"For a while, he was, but then, when I got back to Dallas, after we sold the furniture and all, Jeb said we were leaving money on the table. We could rob a few banks and make it look like Blake did it."

"Didn't it bother you that you might be ruining a man's life? A man who loved you?" Wronko asked.

"Please, Blake is a fool. First thing I did when I got there was to see what bank he used," She reached for a tissue and wiped a tear from her eye. "Not that there were a lot of banks to choose from in Colby Springs. I applied for a job where he banked and got it, no sweat. Then I just waited for him."

"Do you feel any remorse over what you did to Mr. Stevens?" Wronko asked.

Nicci ignored him and looked at Agent Walker. "I've been getting screwed my whole life. I don't feel anything, but I did love Jeb. He was different, I guess. Jeb was my everything. I'd do anything for him."

Agent Walker asked, "Did you rob more than one bank?"

"No, just the one. I got spooked when he shot that guy. And we didn't get away with as much money as we thought we would."

"How did you get your hands on Bella Cotton's credit card?" Wronko asked.

Nicci smiled. "It wasn't hard, detective. It just took some planning. Getting caught doesn't mean you're stupid. We were unlucky, that's all, unlucky." She paused for a moment, thinking about what she wanted to say next. "We spent a whole month getting ready for the bank job. If it wasn't for that stupid customer it would've been perfect."

"Carr shot and killed that customer, Ms. Brevard," Wronko said.

"He didn't mean to. Things just sort of got out of hand. I'm sorry the man died, really."

"Mrs. Cotton's credit card?"

"Like I said, we didn't have any trouble finding Blake or where he lived. I asked around a little and heard he went to New York for a while. I knew he'd want to teach somewhere. It took me a while, but I kept searching high schools on the Internet. I knew he had that bigshot uncle in New Jersey, so that's where I looked. It didn't take long and the rest was easy," she said.

"You had tickets to Paris and Dubai from Baltimore. Why take a chance on being seen in Clarksville?" Wronko asked.

Nicci smiled. "Jeb was smart. He wanted a backup plan, just in case. You have to admit, he was pretty slick. Anyway, we just waited until Blake wasn't around. Jeb figured that old lady wouldn't know the difference between him and Blake. He just went to her house one day and took her card."

Detective Wronko shook his head. It didn't matter how long he worked in law enforcement. He was still capable of being surprised by human behavior. Nicci Brevard was actually justifying monstrous acts in the name of love. Now, she would probably spend the rest of her life in prison, plenty of time to think about her choices.

31

Claire was ecstatic about the news that Blake was finally free. She pretended to be annoyed that he risked his life, but she was proud of him for being so fearless. After Blake was cleared of all charges, things happened very quickly. Sadly, Mrs. Cotton succumbed to her disease a week after Blake was cleared. She died at home surrounded by Claire, Blake, Victoria and Parker. She lived long enough to know that her faith in Blake was justified. One of the last things she said was that she hoped he would return to teaching as soon as possible. Mrs. Cotton was buried next to her husband in the old Clarksville cemetery. So many of the town's people came to the funeral service that a lot of businesses had to shut down that morning.

Blake quickly reapplied for his old teaching job. The school board approved his application and Principal Mark Mitchell was only too happy to have him back. Parker was delighted to hand over the tennis coaching job to his friend. He married Penny, but the couple had a change of heart. They decided to stay in Clarksville and start a family instead of moving to Florida.

Blake and Claire were asked to attend the reading of Mrs. Cotton's will. James Simons, her attorney, held the reading of the will in Mrs. Cotton's living room. Always a frugal woman, Mrs. Cotton had saved a good deal of money over the years. Mr. Simons explained that she left the bulk of her estate to the New Jersey Teacher's Association scholarship fund that helped underprivileged students cover college tuition costs. But she also left something for Blake. He picked up the document, cleared his throat and started reading her wishes aloud. "I leave my home and all of its contents to Mr. Blake Stevens. Mr. Stevens has not only shown great courage in dealing with troublemakers, he went to a great deal of trouble to take care of me and my home. He worked hard to make my home livable again, so he might as well have it. In taking ownership, he is free to do with it as he wishes."

After Mrs. Cotton's death, Blake had expected he'd need a new place to live. Now, he was the owner of a two-family home filled with very desirable antique furniture. A few days later, he asked Claire to help him clear out Mrs. Cotton's papers, clothing and old school books. He was going to move into the first-floor apartment and rent out his old place. It would provide a good source of extra income. That's when he got another surprise. As the couple went through the bureau drawers in her bedrooms, dining room and kitchen, they discovered many small, white envelopes filled with cash. Some had as little as twenty-five dollars. Some of the envelopes were filled with rent money he paid her. One envelope was marked, indicating it held the two thousand dollars Blake had given her the day he moved into his apartment. All told, Mrs. Cotton had more than $16,000 in cash sitting around her house. Blake laughed, remembering his ongoing discussions with Mrs. Cotton about where she was hiding her money.

Claire thought Blake would wait until Christmas to formally propose, but he surprised her one night, near the end of October, soon after he inherited Mrs. Cotton's house. He told her he wanted to celebrate his recent good fortune and his freedom. He invited Parker and Penny, and Charles and Victoria to join them for dinner at Butcher and Singer, an upscale restaurant on Walnut Street in Philadelphia.

Over cocktails, he took her hand in his and said, "Claire, you've seen me through a long nightmare. You gave me hope when I needed it most. You're my best friend and I feel like I'm one of the few lucky men in this world to be completely in love with a woman who is perfect for me. Will you marry me?"

Claire was surprised by the suddenness of Blake's proposal, but ready. "Yes, I'll marry you Blake. I'm so excited." Blake slipped the engagement ring on Claire's finger and signaled the server who was standing nearby with champagne.

Everything would have been perfect were it not for Claire's lingering feelings of guilt about her son. Her conversation with her father had been helpful, but she was still wrestling with whether to tell Josh he had a son. It was Mrs. Clark who finally helped her find a way to cope with her worries.

A few days before Halloween, she was at her parents' home helping her mother prepare for their annual Halloween cocktail party, which was more a celebration of founding father,

Samuel Clark's birthday. She decided to have a conversation with her mother about her adopted son.

Mrs. Clark smiled when she brought up the topic. "Your father warned me that you might bring this up," she said. She walked into her bedroom and came out with a photo of her grandson. "His name is Kyle. He was nine when this was taken. He looks like his father, doesn't he?" she asked.

Claire was dumfounded. "You keep in touch with my son and you don't tell me? How dare you." She was angry and crying.

"Please calm down, Claire. We have no contact with your son, none. Our attorney sent this to me after I begged him. Your father has no idea about that. He's never even seen the picture."

"But why would you keep it from me? How could you not realize how much it would mean to me just to see his picture? Tell me, please, everything you and Dad know about him."

"We really don't know a thing beyond what your father told you. This is the only photo I have." She handed it to Claire. "As I said, your father has never seen it. He would be quite angry with me if he knew I asked our attorney for it." Mrs. Clark folded the last of the napkins. "We probably should have told you what we know, but you never asked. And we never speak of the matter, do we?" She put an autumn themed centerpiece on the dining room table, a bowl filled with pine cones and a few gourds, surrounding an orange colored candle. "That was a painful time for all of us. I guess we didn't want to upset you."

Claire knew her parents would never lie about something so important. Had she asked sooner, they would have told her what they knew. "Mother, do you think we should tell Josh about Kyle? Dad doesn't think it's a good idea."

"Neither do I, Claire. I believe we should let nature take its course," she said. Mrs. Clark was setting the table now with Halloween themed ceramic plates for the party.

"What do you mean let nature take its course?" Claire asked.

"Oh my, I just think it's quite likely that Kyle will eventually seek out his birth parents when he's an adult. That would be the proper time for you to introduce him to his father, don't you think?"

"Why? You think it will be easier on Josh if he doesn't find out he has a son until he's older and his girls have been raised?"

"Don't you? As an older man, good Christian that he is, I'm sure Josh would be more gracious about the situation. It will be easier on him, his wife, I'm sure, and his girls. He might even see the wisdom of your decision to give Kyle up for adoption."

Claire could see the wisdom in her mother's words. She simply had to be patient and let nature take its course, just as her mother said. Things had worked out with Blake. In time, they would work out with Kyle.

Although they were engaged, Blake felt it was important to speak with the Claire's parents about the marriage. He knew Mr. Clark, in particular, had misgivings about his past, his humble background and perhaps most of all, his genes. Although he knew there was nothing Mr. Clark could do or say that would change things, he wanted to clear the air.

On the evening of the cocktail party, Blake asked Mr. Clark if he might speak with him and Mrs. Clark privately. There were at least forty guests in attendance. Mr. Clark found his wife and led her, along with Blake, to his office. He didn't sit down. He simply turned to Blake and waited.

Blake looked him in the eye. "Sir, Mrs. Clark, I just want you to know how much I love Claire. I'll take care of her and any children we may have. I want you to know that."

"Terrance Clark glanced at his wife and said, "Are you asking for our blessing?"

"I guess I am, yes."

Terrence smiled. "I appreciate your gesture of respect. It's an old-fashioned notion. But, I can't tell you we were wholeheartedly in favor of your relationship with Claire. I'm sure Claire has explained our reservations to you. I must say, however, that you have conducted yourself like a gentleman in every way. That has to count for something."

"Thank you." Blake stood there, waiting for an answer. He needed Terrence Clark to say the words.

Mr. Clark looked at his wife, smiled and turned back to Blake. "You have our blessing, Blake. Welcome to our family."

Claire hadn't briefed her parents yet on the actual wedding plans, so Mr. Clark took advantage of the moment. "Do you plan to marry next summer, or perhaps in the fall of next year?" He was hoping for a delay, which might give Claire time to reconsider.

But Mrs. Clark could see that her daughter was deliriously happy with Blake. Looking into Blake's eyes, she realized that Blake had immediately grasped the implications of her husband's suggestion.

"Claire and I plan to be married on Thanksgiving Day."

"Oh, my," Mrs. Clark said. "That's wonderful, Blake." She knew her daughter's marriage was a fait accompli and she was happy for her. At that moment Claire walked in.

Her father turned to greet her. "I've just given Blake our blessing of your marriage, Claire. It seems you two have decided to marry in a matter of a few short weeks."

Claire looked at Blake and said, "Yes, Daddy. We'd like to be married here in your home if you will let us."

"If you aren't comfortable with that, we can make other arrangements," Blake said.

Mr. Clark held up his hand. "That won't be necessary, Blake. We'd be delighted to hold our daughter's wedding in our historic home." Mrs. Clark clutched her husband's hand, which pleased him.

One week later, busy planning their wedding, they attended another one, a quiet ceremony held in the old Presbyterian church downtown. Jonna and Zeke were married. Afterward, the couple held a small reception at the Mexican restaurant where Jonna used to work. It was during the reception that Claire and Jonna happened to have a quiet moment in the ladies' room.

"You and Blake are getting married soon, I guess. He's a great guy," Jonna said. "Better than the good doctor, that's for sure."

"Why don't you like Brad, if I may ask?"

"Blake didn't tell you? Typical of him. Like I said, he's a classy guy."

Claire waited for Jonna to answer her question. When she didn't Claire said, "Please, I'd really like to know."

Jonna checked herself in the mirror one more time. "How do I look?"

"You look beautiful. I'm so happy for you and Zeke. He's a good guy too."

Jonna smiled. "Dr. Chambers? Let's just say he's a man who's grateful for Roe V. Wade. For some people, social status trumps everything, I guess."

Claire blushed. "I see."

"You dodged a bullet there, Claire."

Claire woke up early on a cloudy and cool Thanksgiving morning. She shivered in expectation of the busy day ahead. She wouldn't be attending the Clarksville Regional High School's annual Thanksgiving Day football game against Salem that morning. There was simply too much to do. When she heard later that Clarksville Regional won 7-0, she was pleased, laughing at herself, because, exercising her bride's prerogative, she decided the victory was a promising sign for her own future. She showered and got dressed before she called Victoria, who arrived an hour later to help her prepare for the most important day of her life. She had never felt so happy and secure. She and Blake had both been tested by unimaginable circumstances. Their love survived and it grew. The future was indeed bright.

By noon, the sun was out and the weather turned warmer. Blake had his tuxedo laid out on his bed. He stood at the foot of the bed and thought about his long journey. He'd been knocked around some by life. He marveled at the way life's troubles had a way, behind the scenes, of clearing the path for a better future. He understood now that not giving in to bad luck, seeing things through, even when common sense might suggest giving up, could actually lead someone to a happy ending.

Yet, he knew, in spite of the incredibly bad luck he'd endured, overcoming one misfortune in no way immunized him from future problems. Now, though, there was a difference. Whenever life's inevitable storms cropped up, he would have Claire at his side. He couldn't ask for and didn't need more than that. He and Claire would be happy together.

His doorbell rang. It was Parker, dressed in his tuxedo and holding a six pack. The two men each had a beer. "You nervous?" Parker asked.

"Were you when you married Penny?"

"I still am."

"Here's the rings, dummy. Don't lose them," Blake said.

"You really aren't nervous, are you?"

"Best day of my life, Parker. Nothing to be nervous about."

At four o'clock that afternoon, surrounded by close friends and family, Claire Clark and Blake Stevens took their vows. Thanksgiving dinner awaited.

ACKNOWLEDGEMENTS

I want to thank my many faithful readers for continuing to read my work and offer constant encouragement. Friends like Brenda Albright, Bob Duncan, Peggy Elliott, Dennis Gillespie, Deanne Girouard, Linda Kilpatrick, author James LePore, Frank Riley, Kevin Wronko and others offered helpful insight to several drafts of *Deceived* that helped to improve my work. I want to say a special note of thanks to Jean McCarthy, who read this book, carefully edited it and challenged me to keep working until the story was as good as I could make it. I want to thank my wife Nancy, to whom this book is dedicated, for her unwavering encouragement and support as well as her patience in reading, correcting and re-reading *Deceived* numerous times.

ABOUT THE AUTHOR

Len Serafino is the author of the novels, *Back to Newark, Keep Breathing*, and *The IOU*. His first book, published by Adams Media, was *Sales Talk*. In 2017, he co-authored with Robbie McCammon, *Baseline to Baseline -Maximize Your Tennis*. He also writes flash fiction and short stories, available on his Web site, www.lenserafino.com.

A native of Newark, New Jersey, Len lives with his wife Nancy in Nolensville, Tennessee.

Made in the USA
Columbia, SC
03 August 2018